THE TOXIC FRIEND

J. A. BAKER

Boldwood

First published in 2018. This edition first published in Great Britain in 2023 by Boldwood Books Ltd.

Cover Design by Head Design

Cover Photography: Shutterstock

A CIP catalogue record for this book is available from the British Library.

Paperback ISBN 978-1-80549-171-2

Large Print ISBN 978-1-80549-170-5

Hardback ISBN 978-1-80549-168-2

Ebook ISBN 978-1-80549-172-9

Kindle ISBN 978-1-80549-173-6

Audio CD ISBN 978-1-80549-164-4

MP3 CD ISBN 978-1-80549-165-1

Digital audio download ISBN 978-1-80549-167-5

Boldwood Books Ltd
23 Bowerdean Street
London SW6 3TN
www.boldwoodbooks.com

To all my friends out there who help keep me sane and grounded. Thank you for not being like any of the weird characters in my books.

If you want to understand today, you have to search yesterday.

— PEARL BUCK

Family quarrels are bitter things. They don't go according to any rules. They're not like aches or wounds; they're more like splits in the skin that won't heal because there's not enough material.

— F. SCOTT FITZGERALD

WHITBY

THE PRESENT

1

The people in the crowd jostle for space, a huddle of hot bodies crushed together, pushing, shoving, manners and decency all but forgotten. Their heads bob about as they stand on tiptoe, everybody teetering and falling as they peer across the road in the vein hope of getting a better view of the deceased. Dead bodies. That's what it's all about. It's the thought of death and blood and gore that draws the crowds, especially round these parts. This is a rarity: a tragedy like this happening in their neck of the woods. The closest they usually come to crime is the odd bit of shoplifting, or the occasional argument in the pub on a Friday night when the alcohol is flowing freely, but this... this is something completely out of their comfort zone. A crime of this ilk is in a different league. There have been murders here in the past, many years back, but it's hardly commonplace; this is a rare occurrence that shocks and horrifies the locals. This place is a friendly area famous for its tourists and landmarks, not for its dead.

It was a young neighbour who told the locals; the same woman who alerted the authorities, calling for an ambulance, yelling that they had to hurry up. She was the one who listened to the screams, the one who burst in and found the victims. She was the one who heard them die.

Voices filter out from the mass of curious bodies that sway from side to side as they push forward towards the crime scene, their murmurs and chatter piercing the chill of the mid-morning spring air.

'Two people involved apparently.'

'I heard it was three.'

'Police won't release any details but we all know who lives there, don't we?'

'It was poor Gillian who sounded the alarm. In a right state she is, by all accounts. She was out the back, sweeping up leaves, and heard screaming.'

The mumbling and gossip hang over their heads and swarm about, words and sounds buzzing around in an invisible haze only to be swallowed up by a collective gasp as the front door opens and a police officer steps out. His face is impassive as he scans the hordes of onlookers before marching past, bending down and dipping into a nearby unmarked car. The disappointment of the waiting crowd at not seeing anything of any significance is so tangible, you can almost taste it.

They crave information. Any snippet will do. Any morsel of gossip to satiate their all-consuming need to know about the crimes that took place behind that door. Their expressions say it all. Each and every one of them is desperate, driven on by panic and curiosity. Despite the shock, they all sense it: the splinter of excitement that is coursing through their veins, the rush of adrenalin at being so close to where the violence took place. When it comes down to it, we are all voyeurs, each and every one of us; we're all attracted to death and cruelty like moths to a flame. It makes us feel just that bit more appreciative at being alive, at not being one of the victims.

A young woman wearing a strappy T-shirt and tight, faded jeans pushes her way forwards, her head thrust out, a snaking vein of annoyance protruding from the side of her throat as she raises her arm and shouts over to the officer standing guard outside the large, terraced property.

'Oi! What's going on in there?'

Behind her, the muttering and grumbling grows, anger now driving their voices at being kept in the dark, raw fear fuelling their shouts at the thought of it happening to one of them. She feels herself grow hot and continues her tirade, her voice a screech above the hubbub of the pulsing crowd behind her.

'Most of us here have lived in this place all our lives. We have a right to know if there's a madman running loose!'

Clapping erupts from the multitude of angry bodies as she pushes even further forward, her face puckered into a mean, angry grimace, her eyes narrowed in concentration. She has a right to speak up. They all do. They deserve to be kept in the loop, to be informed about what's going on.

'We've been standing here for fucking ages and you've told us nothing! We're not leaving till we know what's happened, are we?'

She turns and nods at the rest of the onlookers. More clapping and jeering spills out and spreads around them like raging wildfire as she stares at the sea of faces looking at her. A broad smile splits her acne-covered features as the roar from the ever-growing multitude of watchers explodes into the cold, still air. She nods at them in recognition. They're all here for the same reason – to make sure their neighbourhood is safe. She can help that happen. She can take charge here, be their new leader, a self-elected spokesperson for their close-knit neighbourhood.

Bristling with new-found confidence, she surges forward once more, making sure the police officer standing outside the property can see her. This is her territory. She belongs here. She waves her arm around to catch his attention. She's going to do something about this whole sorry mess, make sure they're all kept abreast of proceedings. This is her home after all, her town. She has spent her entire life here. She has every right to know exactly what is going on – what went on in that house, and the police have no fucking right keeping it from her. Who do they think they are, anyway? Jumped up, overpaid nobodies, that's what they are. A load of pompous arses who spend their time milling around doing not much of anything while taking home big, fat salaries out of the public purse. All these people here, paying their wages, contributing to their mortgages while they swan in and out of the crime scene, their lips sealed, telling the local people nothing. Zero. No information at all so far. It's a fucking disgrace is what it is. The whole thing boils her piss.

The police officer stares ahead, his body rigid, his features unmoving despite the insults being hurled his way.

'Fucking pig! Get on with your fucking job instead of standing there like a useless dickhead!'

The door to the house opens a fraction, a teasing crack of darkness. A collective breath is held before it's pushed further ajar, revealing a shadowy hallway within. Silence descends as all eyes hold fast to the goings on at number forty-three. They wait and watch. Nothing happens.

'Come on! What the fuck's going on in there?' a voice from the back hollers.

More waiting, a shift in tension, movement from within the house. There's a deep sigh as an androgynous individual in a white, billowing outfit complete with hairnet and mask, appears out of the darkness and carefully backs out of the door. The ghostly figure leans forward, its body bent over an unseen object that's concealed in the greyness of the house. There's a moment of silence, a pregnant pause of anticipation before the figure moves again, its hands holding on tight to a gurney. The white-clad individual drags it out of the doorway with a clatter and wheels it over the step. The gurney rumbles onto the path and remains still for a few seconds before another person emerges at the other end, wearing identical forensic clothing, their features hidden from view behind full-face masks. A series of gasps and cries tinged with mild excitement pierce the air as a body bag, strapped to the gurney, is wheeled into a nearby vehicle. All eyes follow the concealed mound of flesh as it is pushed towards the van and unceremoniously hauled inside.

T-shirt woman stands, mouth gaping open, as another trolley with yet another body bag tightly secured to it is pushed out of the open doorway, and also wheeled towards the van. She stares at the vehicle, visualising the still, pale bodies inside it, wondering how they died, trying to imagine the scars and the cold flesh, picturing the dark, pooling blood. A crackle of expectancy hangs over everybody. The silence doesn't last long. A guttural voice punctures the momentary lull.

'What the fuck is going on?'

A rotund man wearing dark-blue overalls steps out of the crowd, a gathering that has merged into one huge, pulsating organism. Unrest ripples through the pack of ogling faces as they watch him push his way to the front. His solid midriff presses against the police tape, stopping it from flapping in the strong, north-easterly breeze. It sticks to his belly, flesh enveloping the narrow strip of plastic as he lunges forward, the yellow and black warning sign no barrier to his large frame.

'If you wouldn't mind moving back, sir,' a uniformed officer says as he holds his hand up to indicate his disapproval of the man's proximity to the cordoned-off area. The policeman stares down at the protruding gut before diverting his gaze elsewhere.

'So it's a crime scene, is it then?' the man asks, a deep frown slicing through his forehead as he stares up at the policeman next to him. 'Somebody killed them, did they? Or one of them killed the other one then topped themselves? Typical, isn't it? Selfish bastards. Too cowardly to do the time. Bring back hanging, that's what I say.'

'I'm afraid I can't tell you anything, sir. Now if you wouldn't mind stepping back?'

The portly man moves away before turning to the people and bellowing at them, 'Lock all your doors tonight! Keep your kids inside, everyone. There's a fucking murderer on the loose.'

The crowd moves, their collective energy slowly morphing into a sinister entity that radiates negativity, pure hatred. They need answers and they won't rest until they get them. They are all fearful, terrified of the unknown. Terrified of the killer amongst them.

Suddenly, everybody stops; the noise dropping to a barely audible hum. Heads turn. The distant roar of an engine catches their attention. They swing round to see a local news van screech to a halt at the end of the road. A handful of reporters and cameramen tumble out of it and within a matter of seconds, the crowd disperses as people wander over towards them, their pace growing faster the closer they get, the idea of being involved in any sort of interview too attractive an option to ignore. They want to have their say, to let everyone know how fearful they are about this situation, to tell the police that they need to find the person who did this. Their voices deserve to be heard and what better way than in front of a TV camera? They are a jumble of limbs as they push forward, desperate to speak, anger swelling within them, faces angled towards the microphones and cameras. This is their chance to put their points of view forward. This is their chance to shine.

On the periphery of the original crowd stands an individual

who shrinks away as the gawping people part and filter off, most heading over to where the reporters are setting up their equipment. Thrusting hands deep into pockets, the lone person waits a while, wondering what is being said behind the closed curtains of number forty-three, wondering if the police in there have any idea what actually happened: what was said, who was present, what really took place in that awful house. It's doubtful. Nobody could know. Nobody would ever guess the events that led up to this moment in time. Nobody.

A gust of wind whips in from the sea, an invisible hand pushing the lone person forward. The figure blinks hard against the roar of the elements, dips their head and shuffles away towards the main road, then stops and takes one last glance at the crime scene before smiling broadly and heading off towards the beach until it is no more than a speck in the distance.

A group of dog walkers mill about on the sand, throwing sticks into the frothing sea, calling to their animals to fetch. Their bodies mask the lone figure, concealing their movements until, after a short while, the walkers disperse, leaving an empty stretch of beach: a long expanse of soggy, mud-brown sand. The place is empty. There is nobody there. The lone figure has gone.

2

TRISH

She has no idea how her life has come to this. It wasn't how she had planned it all those years ago when she was fresh-faced and painfully naïve, but then it never is, is it? That's just how life goes. It starts off easy enough; you amble through, get a few bounces along the way and suddenly, before you know it, life has you by the throat and is shaking you about like a ragdoll until you are dizzy and sick with it all. That's when she knew it was easier to let it all wash over her, to go along with whatever shit was thrown her way. Far easier than trying to rail against it. It was like swimming against the tide, constantly trying to do the right thing by other people and keep the peace, so she just gave in, accepted her lot and rolled with the punches.

She smiles sadly, her chin trembling as she slumps down into the chair; probably not the best analogy to use, given the life she has had, but that's just how it is. Nothing she can say or do will change what has gone before. One long stream of misery and hardship interspersed with the weekly bout of violence. That's how she would sum up her life if asked – she is punch drunk on despair. She's dealt with it however, 'made the best of it' as the saying goes. And it hasn't been all bad. She bites at the inside of her mouth and drums her fingers on the edge of the chair, the thick oak echoing out a dull, solid beat. It hasn't been all good, either. She's still here though. She grew a second skin many years back; took the beatings and painted a smile on her face. No choice, really. She learnt how to not feel anything. It was the best way, the only way. She stopped feeling when he came home inebriated, she stopped feeling when the blows came her way. Actually, she just stopped feeling. It was a necessity, the only way she could continue to exist, because if she allowed herself to feel, then it would have become unbearable. She switched off to it all, shut down her emotions, refusing to question her choices, refusing to reflect on what she should or shouldn't have done. Because if she had started to think and reflect on that, mulling over what has gone before and what she could have done to prevent it, then she would have come to one conclusion: that her entire life has been a complete waste; every decision she has made that has led her down this path and got her to this point; it is all her own doing. That's the hardest thing to deal with. Worse than any beating she has ever endured. Worse than sitting in the dark because their electricity had been cut off after drinking the week's wages. Worse than all of those dark times in her life is the fact that she knew what he was like when she met him but went right ahead and accepted his offer of a drink anyway, ignoring the inner voice warning her to stay away, to steer clear of a man who drank like a demon and spoke with his fists. She forged ahead and accepted it all, blind to the dangers. Silent in the face of fear.

Her eyes move along the mantelpiece to the family picture that's sitting there, teasing her with what could have been and torturing her with the missing face. *Her face.* She's thought of the kid frequently over the years but was certain that the child was better off without her. She wouldn't have been able to give her the life it deserved; she knew that, but it didn't stop her thinking about her absence. Sometimes she would wake on a morning with an ache so deep and cavernous, it felt as if her insides had been scooped out. She learnt how to ignore that as well. She became a self-taught woman, even convincing herself that the child was whiny and needy – too much like hard work – telling herself over and over that having a little one around would have impinged on her day-to-day existence. That's how she coped with it. That's how she managed to get on with the rest of her life: by being half dead, refusing to allow sentimental nonsense to muddy her thinking. She did what had to be done, knowing that regrets solved nothing. Regrets simply reminded her of things she could no longer change.

The drink helped. Oh God, did it help. It blotted out chunks of the nasty stuff, built a wall in her head to keep out the thoughts that would sometimes sneak in and bite at her, niggle at her, worm their way into her veins; constantly reminding her what a useless mother she was, what a thoughtless, dark human being she had turned into. Regardless of how tough she became, those thoughts were never far from her consciousness. They bubbled away so close to the surface, there were days when she felt as if she would be sucked under by them and sink to the bottom, drowning in her own pit of despair. Far easier to numb everything with vodka and gin and tell herself she did the right thing than to sit around maudlin and miserable. Nobody wanted to be around miserable people. When she got like that, Russ hated her. When she got like that, she hated herself.

She kept the next child that came along. She deserved it. She'd already given one away and made damn sure they wouldn't take the next one from her. She knew how to play them after the last carry on – the army of social workers that trooped in and out of her house week after week, checking up on her family, filling out forms, ticking boxes, making sure there were no more broken bones, no more bruises or superficial damage. They were too stupid to see it all though, too rigid in their beliefs and too naïve to see beyond the lies. They thought that if each and every form was neatly filled out, every box ticked, every piece of paper filed away, then everything was fine. They couldn't see the internal hurt that her family carried. Just as well, really. The internal stuff was far worse than any bruises. It didn't heal. It simply festered and rotted, seeping into their bones, killing them slowly from the inside out.

She looks up again at the family picture sitting on the fireplace, then stares down at the photograph tucked tightly between her liver-spotted hands. It's blurry and her eyes aren't as sharp as they used to be. She wishes she could feel something – anything at all – as she waits for the image to come into focus. But there is nothing. She died inside a long time ago. It will take more than an old photograph to stir up any deep-rooted emotions inside her cold, dead soul. Just people, that's all it is on there: pictures of people from another life. A life that took place so long ago, it doesn't even feel as if any of it actually happened. It means nothing to her.

She won't allow herself to get sucked into feeling pity or sympathy for anything or anybody any more. All those memories, all those years, they're behind her now. No point in reminiscing over things you can't change. What's done is done. It doesn't even look like her. It's a tiny, creased print, so grainy and blurred, it could be anybody. Except it isn't anybody. It is her, and now it's here, in her house: a throwback to another era. An era she would sooner forget. An era that saw her life turn upside down, never to be righted or balanced properly again. She has been on a seesaw ever since, tipping from happiness to abject despair and back again in a heartbeat, living life slightly out of kilter, like a watch that keeps losing time.

She no longer knows what a conventional life is. She can't remember normality and she cannot for the life of her remember this photograph being taken. She remembers the events that took place afterwards though. Oh dear Lord, she remembers those with frightening clarity. Even the drink has failed to dull those first few days after she was taken from her; the dark and depressing times that closed in on her after her firstborn was taken into care. She will never forget those torturous hours even though she has tried.

She swallows hard and stares outside at the cobalt sky and wispy clouds that hang like trails of candyfloss. She knows where this picture has come from. She has seen her daughter out there in the distance before, watching, waiting, biding her time. Her willowy frame silhouetted against the backdrop of the roaring sea, her long, auburn hair fluttering about in the breeze.

She bites down on one of her nails and winces as a small strip of nail comes away and takes a piece of skin with it. She didn't recognise her own child the first time they met and if that makes her a terrible mother, then so be it. It was only afterwards that she made the connection, the realisation hitting her like a thunderbolt, sending a hot dart of fear into her very core.

After the initial panic had subsided, she began to realise her child surfacing in town after all these years changed nothing. If her daughter is here then that's how it is and there's nothing she can do about it except keep a clear head and remain calm. And why shouldn't she stay calm? She did the right thing all those years ago, handing the child over, not taking her back. The girl has probably had a better life than she would have if she had come back, so it all worked out well in the end, didn't it?

This photograph, this *reminder*, has been posted through her door to stir stuff up, to make her feel guilty, to make her feel something. Well, it won't happen. She is too dead to feel anything. Too numb and jaded to care. She can post as many photographs as she likes; it won't change anything.

The knock at the door sends a small jolt of fear through her. It's been horribly quiet in the house since Russ died. His presence always made an impact, despite the fact he had quietened down towards the end. He simply ran out of energy. That's when she noticed the real change. In a perverse sort of way, she had got used to his loud voice and boorish behaviour and the sudden lull took some getting used to. Now since his death, any unexpected noise sets her nerves jangling. She has spent the last thirty odd years on edge and it's a hard habit to break. Life has changed so much lately and it's taking a lot of getting used to.

Shoving her feet into her fuchsia-pink slippers, she stands up with a groan and shuffles toward the front door where the knocking grows louder and more insistent until the sound of it makes her want to drive her nails over her bare flesh. Probably somebody who will try to sell her household items she neither needs nor wants, an ex-soldier or a reformed prisoner desperate to make a quick buck. She sees them all the time, trailing round the streets, trying to turn their lives around, asking for a second chance.

She grabs at the handle and flings it open, the weight of it causing the door to bash into the wall with a loud thud, the metal handle embedding itself into the smooth arc in the plaster: a lasting reminder of past slams.

She stares at the face before her. An unexpected flush of heat creeps up her spine and over her scalp. She reaches up and loosens the buttons on the neck of her sweater. The figure in the doorway watches her closely, not speaking, not moving. Silent. No words are needed.

They stare at one another for a short while, their eyes locked together, until eventually she gives a curt nod and steps aside to let the figure enter. She cannot let them see her nervous or ill at ease. This is her house, her rules. Anyone who steps over this threshold abides by her laws. She bites at her lip. She always knew this person would come to see her. She can sense these things. She knew deep down that at some point, they would find their way back.

They sit opposite one another in the eerie stillness of the dated living room, the figure clearly too ill at ease, too agitated to speak. She waits. She doesn't want to be the first to open her mouth. She has no idea why, that's just how it is. So many things to be said but no easy way to form the words and say them out loud. They always sound so much better in your head and once they are said, they cannot be unsaid. Better to stay silent than to go headlong into a conversation that she would rather not be having in the first place.

The silence goes on and on, a pregnant pause, making her restless and uneasy. Something is different. There is an air of anger about this person, a quiet rage that makes her anxious. This is not how they were. Something has changed and she doesn't like it. Perspiration gathers around her thinning hair and runs down the side of her face, a thin trickle of fear.

She lets out a rattling breath, looks around the living room and shakes her head slowly. This is nonsense. There is no need for fear, no need at all. She should have been prepared for this moment. It was always going to happen at some point. She places her hands over her knees and does her best to look unperturbed as she clears her throat and finally finds her voice, the person opposite watching her with dark, unforgiving eyes.

'So,' she says quietly, her voice low and soft with a sliver of anxiety running through it, 'at long last, you've decided to come home.'

LONDON

Before and Leading up to...

3

EVA

Have you ever felt as if your entire life is one huge fabrication – an assortment of lies so deeply embedded in your psyche you no longer know who you are? I have. I feel it every minute of every single day. Everyone thinks they know me. They don't. How can they possibly know the real me when I don't even know myself?

That's the problem, you see. The life I have now, the life I think of as mine, didn't start at the beginning. I have little, if any memories of my formative years, just fragments of thoughts too disjointed and ethereal to pin down. They meander around my brain, disconnected images, all parts of a jigsaw puzzle that refuse to fit together, pieces of my mind that simply won't mesh. I've tried over the years to work out what the images mean, but each time I end up more confused than before I began. It's like trying to catch the wind.

I dream about them – my parents – the ones I don't even know. I imagine their voices, what they're like, how they would sound as they call my name. I visualise their expressionless faces staring at me, their features bland and unrecognisable, like a pixelated image that never quite comes into focus. It's just a great big blank canvas where their faces should be. This happens regularly; my mind greedily salting away any clues that could allow me access to my past. I'm a person with no history, my previous life rubbed out, smudged into nothingness without my consent. I have no real identity.

There are days when I feel as if I'm a lesser version of me, someone who is just playing at being Eva Tweedie. Can you imagine how that feels? Have you any idea how soul destroying it is to have a great, yawning abyss where the very foundations of your life should be? No, of course you don't. You have no idea at all. Nor would I expect you to. Why would you be interested in me, in what I have to say, in what I have been through to get to this point in my life? Such interest would make you odd, a tad off balance. Such interest would make you as strange as me.

Anyway, I digress. This is something I do quite a lot – wander off on a tangent, teeter on the brink of a downward spiral – constantly reminding myself how unwanted I am. I need to stop the self-hatred and sort my life out. I do know that. I may be many things – melancholic, over analytical, even slightly out of kilter – but I'm not a complete idiot. I have to do one of two things: either I get over this, draw a line under it all and move on, or I do the unthinkable and open that particular can of worms. The latter is an unpalatable option and something I've avoided for many years, but not finding out is killing me. I have reached a point in my life where I need to know. I want to find out what happened. I just want to be me. The real me. Not an imposter. I want to be the real Eva Tweedie, to find out who I am, work out why I was abandoned at such a tender age. I think about it all the time. It obliterates everything I do, getting in the way of everyday life, hindering my ability to function properly. It has almost ruined me.

My car crash of a life isn't helping. Things haven't been great recently and there are times when I can't seem to think straight. I've also done some terrible things of late. Unforgivable things. I need to get some equilibrium back into my life, to restore the balance after I've tipped it so violently with my dreadful deeds.

I think of them all the time – my biological parents – I think of them living their lives without me, going about their day-to-day business, not giving me a second thought, carrying on as if I don't even exist. It never fails to get to me, to dent what little self-esteem I do actually possess.

And then there's my job. I hate it. It pays well and I'm aware that many would give their right arm to have it, but without the backing of a loving family, it is pointless. I know I sound like a grumbling pessimist who revels in being down on their luck, but you would have to fully understand my predicament to know where I'm coming from. I've had a shitty day stuck in a shitty office surrounded by even shittier people and now I'm going home to an empty house. Life doesn't get much more depressing than that, does it?

I pick up my pace and hurry down the escalators, gently nudging grumbling commuters aside. I reach the platform and slice through the crowds onto the waiting train to grab a seat before anybody else does. With every passing day, I hate this journey more and more. The stench of a nine-hour slog at the workplace oozes out of everyone's pores, masked by cheap perfume and aftershave. They all wear a grimace. Even the allure of heading home for the evening does nothing to lighten their mood or lift the misery that's etched into their inner core. They wear all their worry and anger like a dark cloak. It's written all over their faces: frowns and lines of disdain at their lot in life so deeply embedded in their expressions, they look as if they could murder one another at any given moment.

I hear a collective giggle and turn to see a group of tourists pointing at a map stretched out over their laps. They're nodding at each other and laughing at the weird and wonderful names on there – Seven Sisters, Elephant and Castle, Pudding Mill Lane. I pick up on an American accent and watch them closely, noticing how golden their skin is compared to the dozens of grey, dead-looking people around them, how animated they are and how their laughter tinkles through the carriage like stardust being scattered over the grieving masses. I remember being like that once – excited at the prospect of living in London, looking forward to carving out a new life for myself, being full of vim and vigour – but now I'm as jaded as the rest of the folk on this train. The big city that was once so full of promise and glamour has lost its shine.

Behind me, an argument breaks out. I turn to see a well-dressed gent being harassed by a pregnant woman who is demanding he give up his seat for her. She's wearing a purple velour tracksuit and her swollen belly sticks out from under her skimpy T-shirt like a huge beach ball. The skin on her abdomen is covered with bright red stretch marks as if the Devil himself has clawed at it, long jagged welts running the length of her entire midriff. Her stomach is horribly distended and looks fit to burst, the flesh translucent, shiny and raw looking and stretched to capacity. A gaggle of people join in with the fight while others turn away, their faces flushed with embarrassment at being privy to such an awkward display.

All this debacle does is provide me with another reason to leave this place, to get away from everything, to escape the noise and grime and mantle of discontent that seems to have settled on me. After last night's carry on with Gareth, I may just do it. There's nothing else to keep me here now he and I are no longer an item. I can do whatever I want, go wherever I please. As from 8 p.m. last night, I am officially a free agent.

The argument gains traction, with people standing up pointing and doing all the insane, irrational things that angry people do, even though none of it is any of their business. Perspiration breaks out on my face and my scalp prickles as the man next to me stands up and decides to get involved, gesticulating to everyone watching, shouting that he used to be a doorman and could wipe out everybody in the carriage if he so chooses. He shouts at the sitting man, his voice booming around the small space, bouncing off the walls of the carriage and rushing past me in a hot bubble of anger. I shift in my seat, my skin growing clammier by the second. I close my eyes and take a deep breath.

It feels as if an army of ants are crawling over my skin; the walls close in on me and every noise is accentuated as blood roars through my ears, thumping and growling through my veins, making me hot and dizzy. I need to get out of here, to get away from all of this. Horrible images fill my mind. I do my best to keep them at bay, to shake them off. I try to think of other things, anything at all to stop them. I bite at my nails and swallow the lump that has risen in my throat. All this shouting takes me back to the horror of last night, to the argument, until in the end, the quarrel close by disappears off my radar and my mind is totally focused on him: Gareth.

And what I did.

I blink back hot tears and stare out of the window. I cannot think about it. Thinking about Gareth is worse than anything, worse even than this dreadful fight. I wince as it gets louder and dip my head. Panic claws at me. Surely someone will fetch the guard or pull the emergency stop cord? Somebody should do something. I am consumed by an overwhelming urge to leave this train, to get away from these people.

The journey seems to go on for an age. The racket in the carriage grows ever louder around me and every bump on the track makes my blood fizzle with dread.

It's the shouting. I can't bear it. It triggers something in me. An unwelcome thought that I can neither see properly nor fully explain. I think about Gareth last night: our final words before we parted. My throat feels tight, restricting my oxygen. I need some fresh air. I have to escape from all of this. I have got to get out of here.

Suddenly, we're surrounded by blackness as we rush through a tunnel. My eyes water and my ears pop with the change in pressure. Still the argument with sitting man and standing pregnant lady rages. My pulse is a steady, thick beat in my neck as the doorman raises his voice another decibel. My chest becomes taut and my breathing laboured.

I cannot take this any longer.

We finally emerge out of the tunnel and the train rattles into my stop. Blinking repeatedly, I find I'm standing next to the warring crowd with no recollection of how I got here. I turn to see a blur of faces staring at me and feel vomit rise. I swallow it down. My face burns. I feel dizzy and disorientated.

Pushing past the queue of shouting passengers, I stumble onto the platform and gasp over and over again, sucking in the smoky, rubbery tang of the underground. My vision blurs and for one awful, gut-sinking moment, I fear I might pass out. I take a deep breath and gulp down the polluted oxygen, my upper body juddering with the memory of it all. It's haunted me all day: the vision of Gareth leaning over me, shouting, his face pale, leached of all colour. But it no longer matters because we're over, Gareth and me. I try to tell myself that lots of couples argue, lots of couples break up and go their separate ways and we are no different.

Except we are. We are very different indeed.

By the time I make it home to my tiny flat, I've come to a decision. It's the only thing left for me to do, something I should have done a long time ago. I have to go there, to the place where I was born. I need to go back to the beginning. Back to the start of me.

4

GARETH

Gareth scowls and downs another pint, his fifth of the night. His eyes scan the pub like a predator sizing up its next victim. He scours every inch of the place, his gaze shifting about, suspicious and narrow, his nostrils flared in anger.

'Easy, tiger. There are three prizes, you know.' Josh glances at his watch, then stares at his own full glass, comparing it to the rapidly disappearing pint of his friend. He watches as the amber liquid disappears down Gareth's gullet, amazed at the change in his usually reserved pal. He's hardly spoken since getting here and his face is like thunder, his eyes veiled and vaguely threatening, his body language defensive as he sits clutching his pint with tight, chalk-white fingers.

'What, so I'm not allowed a drink now then? Who are you tonight, Josh – my fucking father?'

Josh holds his hands up in mock surrender and lets out a small laugh, his voice a whisper in the sudden upturn of noise as Arsenal go one up two minutes before the half time whistle.

'Okay, keep your hair on, buddy. Just not used to seeing you drink so much. You're normally two pints a night kind of guy, not a bad-ass drinker with an attitude.' Josh laughs, hoping to lighten the atmosphere and inject a little levity into the conversation. His attempt falls flat as his friend scowls in return, his mouth sealed into a firm, mean line.

The noise settles down as the whistle blows and the commentary kicks in. A sudden rush to the bar ensues, leaving the two men virtually alone, the only two males in the vicinity who aren't there to watch the televised football match.

'People can change, can't they? Being the permanently nice guy gets you nowhere. Take my word for it,' Gareth hisses, his eyes dark with rage. He feels the alcohol take hold as he stares at the floor and tries to still his thumping heart. It continues to bash against his ribcage. Hardly surprising after the week he's had. He is tarred by it all, forever stained. Too late to turn back the clock now. Too late to go back to how it was before. And it's all her fault.

'Not sure what you want me to say, Gareth. Bad day at work then?'

'You could say that,' Gareth murmurs, keeping his gaze fixed on the glass clasped between his fingers.

'Ah well, not long till the weekend. Got much planned?'

'Nothing. Zilch. Got fuck all planned.' Gareth lifts his eyes and stares at his friend, his pupils tiny, black pinpricks of rage.

Josh shivers and looks away.

'Right. Well, me and Liv are thinking of going to that new Italian in town if you and Eva fancy joining us? Supposed to be amazing and the drinks are two-for-one if you get there before 7 p.m.'

Gareth doesn't reply. The glasses on the table rock as he taps his foot, the twitch spreading up his leg, his kneecap knocking against the wooden legs of the solid oak, causing the entire table to shake and shift about. Beer sloshes over the edge of both the glasses, spreading across the surface and dripping down the sides before splashing onto Josh's suede boots. He lifts his foot out and rubs at it with his fist, a deep frown etched across his forehead.

'Fuck sake, Gareth! What's up with you tonight anyway? You're as miserable as fuck and now you've just about spilled all the drinks. What gives?'

A silence grips the pair of them as Josh continues to mop up the spilt beer. Gareth sits motionless, his foot now still, his lips pursed in anger. Bubbles of beige ale creep along the table and drip onto the floor. Josh watches them and then stares at his friend before shaking his head, exasperated by it all. He doesn't need this. They all have shit days at work but you have to get your head around everything and just get over it. Passing on your misery to everybody else is bang out of order.

'Look, mate, I didn't mean to have a go at you but you need to get a grip. I've got no idea what's up with you but whatever it is, it can't be that bad. I'm not up to this at the minute. I've got my phone if you need me. You know where I am, yeah?' He stands up and straddles the pool of amber liquid spreading at his feet before shoving his hands deep into his pockets and nodding down at the dejected-looking male sitting close to him. 'Give me a call if you and Eva fancy the Italian thing, okay?'

No response. Josh sighs and shakes his head again. He bangs his wet boots on the floor to remove the final few drips of beer, shoves his hand into his breast pocket and leaves.

* * *

Gareth listens to the tip tap of his friend's shoes as he heads off towards the door, his shoulders hunched as he reaches for his phone, yelling into the handset that he's on his way to The George and for Andy or Chris to get him a drink in. He should follow him, tell him what the issue is, let him know why he's been so miserable tonight, what it is that's dragging him down. But he can't. No matter how hard Gareth tries, he simply cannot say the words out loud. He just can't bring himself to tell anyone about it. This is something that will always stay hidden. And already, he can feel it boring a huge fucking hole in his sanity. The secret of all secrets. The one he will never, ever be able to talk about. It's going to eat away at him, chip away at everything he ever thought he knew about his life. And he is so fucking angry about it he could punch somebody, doesn't matter who. He is so filled with rage, hatred crackling inside him like a furnace, white-hot fury scorching his insides, and there is nothing he can do about it, nobody he can talk to, to make any of it go away. He is tarnished now. The damage is done and no matter how long he thinks about it, no matter how hard he tries to erase it from his mind, it will always be there, a huge, black blot on the landscape of his life.

It makes sense with hindsight – Eva's endless questions about his life, her constant need for information. In the end, he pretended to not hear her or changed the subject whenever she asked.

He picks up the remainder of his drink and gulps it down in one go, the slightly bitter tang of ale hitting the back of his throat with an acidic kick. His body cries out for the next one. He needs it to numb everything, to make him forget. He longs for the alcoholic blur that another pint will bring, the gratifying numbing of his raging thoughts. He doesn't want to think any more; he just wants to drink himself into a blind stupor and forget.

The swarm of bodies head back from the bar, clutching their pints and roaring at the screen as the replays are shown and repeated over and over again, just a meaningless blur of images flickering about on the huge television. Gareth stares down at his shoes, willing the rest of the drinkers to disappear. He really should go. He's drunk more than he should, never mind having any more. He'll be in no fit state for anything in the morning, but right now, he couldn't give a damn. His life from here on in will always be shit. No amount of drinking or trying to forget what went on will ever erase it.

A buzzing vibrates through the pocket of his jeans. Leaning forward, Gareth slips his phone out and stares at it, his body locking into position, his skin suddenly clammy as the name flashes up on the screen. In a sudden swell of anger, he drops the phone on the floor where it spins in the sticky puddle of beer, small splashes of ale flying out like golden raindrops. Lifting his foot up, he places it directly above the flashing phone and brings it down hard, grinding the piece of machinery with his heel. The laminated screen cracks and fragments, the phone staying in one piece until he stands up and with a sudden, heavy thump, brings his foot down onto it, sending pieces of metal and plastic scattering across the wooden floor. A group of nearby drinkers watch him, their eyes wide with shock before a wave of clapping and jeering takes hold.

'Whoa, you go for it, man! Hope it was a Nokia.'

A hoot of laughter fills the room as they all stare at him in amazement.

'You fucking show 'em, man. Tell her to let you have a beer in peace.'

Gareth lets out a low growl as he bends down and scoops up the SIM card, leaving the rest of the pieces on the floor. He tucks the SIM into the breast pocket of his shirt and glances at the gang of onlookers who are already losing interest, their attention now fixed on the huge screen on the far wall where the second half of the match is about to kick off. He watches them, sees their blank expressions and thinks about how easy their lives are, so simple and free of the clutter and crap he has to put up with. He wonders if it would bother them, what he is currently going through. Or would they just shrug it off, put it down to experience? Maybe he's over-reacting. Maybe not. Everyone has their tipping point, don't they? And he's pretty sure he has reached his.

Without a second glance, he leaves the pub, his disappearance unnoticed by the spectators now enthralled by the imminent game of football. The cold air bites at his face as he steps outside. Under the murky, orange hue of the carriage lamp on the wall, Gareth does something he hasn't done for months. Grabbing a cigarette out of the battered packet that has been sitting in his jacket pocket since giving up six months ago, he shoves it between his lips and strikes a match, the tiny flame flickering ochre as he cups his hands around it and sucks greedily on the slim cigarette dangling from the corner of his mouth. His emergency pack. He knew he had done the right thing leaving them there for times like this. He closes his eyes against the initial dizziness that has him in its grip, then opens them and smiles, savouring the woody taste of the tobacco and enjoying the rush of nicotine as it hurls itself round his system, firing up his senses.

Fuck it all, he thinks as he strolls off down the street. Never again will he be taken in by somebody like that. He wonders if he should contact anyone back home, then shakes his head and lets out a sharp laugh. Is he mad? It hasn't been home for many years and it was anything but a home even when he lived there. There'll be no answers for him there. Nothing but heartache in that place.

He exhales loudly, picks up his pace and walks down the cobbled alleyway, sucking hard on the cigarette and blowing a long stream of smoke into the grey night air. From now on, Gareth will take care of Gareth and the rest of the world can go and fuck themselves.

WHITBY

Two months later

5

EVA

I wake to the soft, distant sound of the tide rushing over the sand. The metallic crunch of water as it hits land drags me from sleep. I open my eyes, wincing at the gritty sensation behind my eyelids as I blink repeatedly. Everything is distorted. My thoughts are muddled, crumpled and lost in an alcoholic haze after one too many last night. And the night before. There is always a good reason to have one drink more than I should.

I lever myself up and sit propped up against the headboard, my head lowered as the room spins. I keep my chin tucked into my chest, my mouth filling with saliva. I'm gripped by a wave of nausea and slump back down into the softness of the pillow, glad of the comfort and support beneath my aching neck. My head feels like a lump of lead, my throat as dry as sandpaper. I'd like to say I have no idea why I do it, why I insist on drinking more than my body is capable of processing, but that would be a complete lie.

I keep my eyes shut tight, waiting for the wave of sickness to pass. I know for certain that the room is in a terrible mess and I'm in no fit state to do anything about it. It doesn't matter. An untidy bedroom is the least of my problems.

I swallow hard, feeling overwhelmed by everything: the new flat, the hangover, how to begin my life all over again. It feels like it's too much for me to think about. I haven't the energy or the inclination to focus on it. I haven't the energy or inclination to focus on anything at the minute. I just want to crawl back under the duvet and sleep for a month.

I have a vague recollection of staggering up to bed, still clutching the wine bottle. I also recall eating a takeaway in bed, and as the memory of it creeps back into my brain, I'm not even sure if I put the pizza box on the floor or if it's still here, under the quilt with me; layers of grease and rotting food slowly soaking into the bed sheets and through to the mattress beneath. I doubt I even switched any of the lights out or locked the front door last night before collapsing in a heap on my unmade bed. I am a complete disgrace. But then I have every right to be. I've earned such an accolade.

More saliva fills my mouth as I make another attempt to sit up, and before I can stop it, a stream of projectile vomit sprays out of me, coating my gullet in a film of acidic bile. I watch through narrowed eyes as the contents of my stomach spills out over the duvet, spreading and pooling in a sickly pink and orange hue, a visible reminder of how much I overindulged last night. A visible reminder of what I have become.

I groan and gingerly step out of bed, grimacing against the shooting pain that sears across my skull. I lean forward, balling up the quilt until every trace of the vomit has been hidden away by lavender-coloured folds of fabric, and pull it onto the floor; a huge, purple mound of flowery satin material concealing my sins and shame within it.

Picking my way through the piles of debris scattered at my

feet, I head into the bathroom where I lean under the tap and rinse my mouth out again and again, the cold water soothing my burning throat and clearing the sticky residue from the roof of my mouth.

The room still swims as I swallow hard and stand upright, the floor tiles cold and unwelcoming under my bare feet. I dance about for a few seconds, trying to escape the freezing surface that cuts through my skin and clings to my bones, then stand straight and take a deep steadying breath. I need to do this, to get up and tidy this room and to freshen myself up. Hanging onto the edge of the sink for balance, I squint at the chinks of sunlight that are filtering in through the blinds, then stare at myself in the mirror. I am appalled by the sight that greets me. I look as if I've been pushed through a shredder. My face is puffy and red, and my hair is knotted and tangled and sits on top of my head like a huge haystack. Is it any wonder I'm on my own? Why would anybody want to be involved with somebody like me? Gareth is still in London and no longer loves me, and I can't say I blame him. I don't much like myself right now.

My head pounds as I force myself upright. No more drinking for me. I have to be stronger than this. After all, isn't this why I came here? To get away from it all, to start all over again, to find out who I really am? And yet here I am – alone – no further forward in my attempt to uncover my past, and slowly sinking into despair, a huge pit of misery that is gradually swallowing me up.

I stagger back through to the bedroom and slump onto the edge of the bed. I hold my head in my hands and tug at my hair in a bid to loosen it of the knots that are threaded through it. Moving here has proved to be more difficult than I thought it would be. At first, it felt like a big adventure, leaving the stresses and strains of the city far behind me, saying goodbye to work colleagues I couldn't wait to leave behind. Even selling my little flat didn't feel too traumatic. I was ready for this move. Every muscle and sinew in my body ached for it, and yet now I'm here, I feel weighed down by it all. Everything is so different, so much smaller.

Without even realising it, I had got used to the hustle and bustle of city life. All those things I had grown to hate are now conspicuously absent from my life and I feel as if I'm going through some sort of grieving process. Perhaps I should have stayed in York all those years ago, not skittered off to a place I knew nothing about, and not been so attracted to the idea of living in the capital. Hindsight is a wonderful thing though, isn't it? And now, after years of living in London, here I am, back in the north, rudderless and confused. But I had to do it. I just had to. Staying so close to Gareth was unthinkable. Come hell or high water, I had to get away. Truth be told, he wanted me gone and probably had a farewell party after I'd left.

Rubbing at my face, I swallow back tears I know I shouldn't be shedding. This is what I wanted, isn't it? I was so certain my problems would be sorted when I came here. I just need some time to adjust. That's all it is. The thing is, I don't think I expected the move to happen as quickly as it did. My flat in London sold within a couple of hours of it going on the market, so without further ado, I handed in my notice at the large accountancy company where I worked and now here I am, living in a rented flat in Whitby, on my own. No time to think about it. No time to change my mind. Perhaps that's a good thing. I've spent most of my adult life procrastinating, wondering, dithering, and now here I am, and I'm still doing all of those things. Nothing has really changed. Same emotions, different location.

It was a big step moving here and it all happened so quickly that I didn't have any time to plan. But then again, so was moving to London from York and I managed that, didn't I? For a while, anyway. I had a good job in London, a lovely little flat, friends and a social life. And I had Gareth.

Gareth.

I groan and chew at the inside of my mouth until the stinging sensation becomes too painful to bear and a trickle of blood gathers. This has to stop, this continual wave of self-pity. I *had* to come here. I have a plan. Or at least I did until alcohol and laziness took a hold of me.

I shower, doing my best to stay upright as the water sizzles over my skin. My head swims and I feel bile rise up into my throat with every movement I make. What was I thinking drinking so much last night? I'm not built for this. Back in London, I had friends who could down three or four glasses of wine on an afternoon, whereas I could hardly manage one without wanting to fall asleep on the spot. Drinking such large amounts doesn't suit me and yet I have consumed alcohol like there's no tomorrow since arriving here. It was sheer loneliness that did it; sitting here day after day feeling sorry for myself, going over everything again and again in my head, wondering where it all went wrong. Wondering why I am too terrified to make the visit. That visit. The one I should have made by now. The very reason I came here.

I almost made it a few times but I was too cowardly to go through with it, so instead I just stood there, over the road, gazing at the house, imagining what was going on inside instead of just summoning up the courage, marching over there and knocking on the door. Each and every time, I sloped off and consoled myself with alcohol and fast food, and sat around feeling sorry for myself, telling myself nobody has it as bad as me.

My jeans feel as if they are made of sandpaper as I dry myself off and pull them over my sensitive, aching skin. They brush against my legs, chafing and grating my thighs as I drag them up and wiggle my way into the coarse fabric. Everywhere hurts. I close my eyes for a second before pulling on a sweater and heading into the living room. The mess in the bedroom can wait. That's the one benefit of living alone; I can live like a slob and nobody will moan at me for being too untidy. I can do exactly as I please.

The toast feels like slices of cardboard as I swallow it down, grimacing as it grazes my throat on its descent. I sip my tea, mulling over the idea of going job hunting. Despite feeling like a herd of cattle has stampeded over my head, I need to get out there and find work. I can't continue living off my savings. I need them for a deposit on another property once I'm properly settled and gainfully employed. I have decent qualifications and plenty of experience, so it shouldn't be too much of an issue. The main problem is the location. Whitby is hardly the epicentre of the financial world. My knowledge lies in accountancy and number crunching, and this is a seaside town with amusement arcades and ice creams parlours aplenty but not so much in the way of fiscal institutions.

I stare out of the window and watch as a young couple struggle against the howling wind coming in from the sea, their bodies half turned away from the biting cold. Behind them, a group of schoolchildren troops along in a long, snaking line, excitement creasing their small faces. I envy them. I miss that innocence, the sheer exhilaration that comes with each and every new day. It's the growing up, the realisation that all is not as it appears, that is so damaging. That's what it is that stains our souls and dents our confidence in the world around us – the knowledge that those you love, cherish and yearn for, don't necessarily love you back.

I continue to watch the goings on outside. Once the sun makes an appearance, I will go out there and walk off this hangover. I'll be one of the tourists and disappear amongst the crowds. It will give me time to think, to clear my head of all the clutter. This flat is closing in on me. There is nothing wrong with it, and as seaside apartments go, it's a fairly superior property, but I've spent the last few days sitting in, pondering over what to do next and I'm tired of it. I am sick of sitting here wallowing in my own misery. I came here to begin a new life, to unearth my past and put to rest a few demons, and all I have done is stagnate and fill my body full of toxins. Enough is enough.

The room tilts as I stand. I need this walk. I need to start living and do what it is I came here to do, not sit day after day doing nothing, going nowhere. I have to tackle the past to plan for the future. And I have to do it right now.

6

EVA

The signs are everywhere to not feed the gulls, that you run the risk of being attacked if you brandish food in front of them, and yet there isn't one single street or alleyway or thoroughfare that doesn't contain fish stalls, candy shops or large groups of tourists gorging themselves on trays of battered fish or huge, swirling bundles of fluorescent pink candyfloss or ice creams or any number of sugary goods purchased from the many stalls and shops nearby. Above us, the seagulls hover and sway before bombing into the crowds, their beady eyes greedily scanning above everyone's heads for any morsel or scrap of food they can swiftly pick up and fly away with. The sound of their cawing echoes through the clear, spring air; their fat, white bodies filling the skies as they circle and swoop with alarming dexterity; their beaks a sharp reminder of how closely everybody should guard their snacks and cover their bare skin.

I make my way through the tourists that line each and every street. I dodge and weave through the mass of bodies packed together as they stare in shop windows or stop to take photographs, causing a major jam behind them. They saunter

ahead after a couple of minutes, unaware of the upheaval their
actions have caused. I weave my way through them all, a person
with a purpose, not a tourist, not someone who has come here to
drink in the history of the place, and not a Goth desperate to be
immersed in the darker side of Whitby's culture. Just me: an
anonymous individual trying to dig up her own history. An
unwanted nobody who is desperate to be wanted.

I consider stopping at the bandstand, allowing the mass of
people to get past me, but somehow get bustled along, buffeted
from all angles, pushed further and further into the centre of the
town until before I know it, I am standing in front of a collection
of huts and cabins. One small, pale-blue hut that is nestled
between a fish stall and a large, brightly painted board offering
boat rides around the harbour, catches my eye. I stare at it, trans-
fixed by the pale hue of the wooden slats and the garish sign
above. There is an uncanny serenity surrounding the place which
is in sharp contrast to the noise and hubbub taking place on the
harbour close by. Beneath and above us, the sounds of nature are
all encompassing, yet this tiny hut exudes such an air of calm, I
feel perversely drawn to it.

The door is open and inside sits a small lady of advancing
years. Her hair is a severe shade of black, contrasting sharply
against her pasty, slightly freckled skin. A grey cat sits by her side,
its back arched as she feeds it a small treat from the palm of her
hand. The sight is so predictable and surreal I almost laugh out
loud. Above the doorway, the amateur hand painted sign
proclaims her as Sylvia Rosa, a genuine Romany gypsy who can
foretell the future of anybody who enters. I want to roll my eyes
and tell her how ridiculous this all is, but find myself intrigued by
her, my curiosity piqued by her stereotypical appearance and tiny
cabin. A place of solace and tranquillity amidst the din and
crowds.

'All right there, are you, lovey?'

Her voice takes me by surprise as I stand for a few seconds, letting her sudden interest in me sink in. I feel as I'm being pulled towards her by an invisible thread that I am powerless to break. I'm intrigued by this woman. No, not intrigued. More than that. I am curiously drawn to her and yet all the while, my sensible inner voice is screaming at me to leave. There is something about her that arouses an emotion in me, something I can't quite put into words.

'You can come right in if you like, my darlin',' she says again and before I can stop myself, I find I am walking into her tiny cabin and sitting down next to her. The noise of the tourists outside seems so very far away as she stands up and closes the door with a quiet click, then sits back down in her overstuffed armchair. It's a crimson wingback puffed up with multi-coloured cushions and a large, patchwork blanket that is casually slung over the back of it. A small heater sits in the corner and the tiny window is covered with an intricately pattered net curtain. The table next to her contains a variety of crystal balls which for some strange, unfathomable reason fascinate me. Surely, they're just for show? I cannot quite believe that people actually fall for all this nonsense. And yet as I look around, I find myself wishing I could be such a person, let somebody tell me exactly what my future holds. How easy and convenient would that be. To allow yourself to be sucked into a world where a stranger claims they know what your life trajectory will be, how your destiny will pan out. How simple it would be to be led by another person's words, by their predictions and guesses that they come out with simply by looking at your face, or even more bizarrely, by studying the lines on the palms of your hands. I wish it were that easy. If only.

Without thinking, I sit on my hands, my defences now up. I won't allow myself to be led by this person. I'm better than that. I am a grown woman who always dismisses such nonsense. So why am I here? How in God's name did I end up in a fortune teller's cabin surrounded by a plethora of stupidly obvious artefacts designed to make her look like some sort of white witch? Why am I sitting next to a woman in a moth-eaten chair that she probably claims enhances her special powers? I make to stand up but she places her hand over mine and speaks in a voice so honeyed and soft, I feel compelled to stay.

'Don't dash off, lovey,' she whispers in a voice as gentle as silk. 'I don't bite.'

Her hand is cool on mine, her flesh thin and crisp like parchment. I feel as if I should pull my hand away, yet I don't. I remain seated, my back rigid, my skin suddenly hot and prickly. My heart jumps about my chest as she scrutinises my face, searching me for answers that I refuse to give. I keep my mind blank, realising that by doing such a thing, I am entertaining the idea that she can actually read my mind.

'I can do you a cheap reading if it's money that's stopping you,' she whispers and meets my gaze, our eyes locked together in the dim light of her tiny cabin.

'I have money,' I find myself saying and immediately regret my decision. A slight twinkle takes hold in her azure eyes as she leans even closer to me and pats my hand. I have just entered into an agreement without even realising it. This is how they operate, these people. They are adroit at understanding how others work, how the human psyche responds in certain situations. I have been cornered, trapped like a wild animal and now she is watching me to see how I'll react. Will I fight or take flight and just up and leave? I do neither. Instead I reach into my purse and take out a crisp £20 note which I place into her hand. She snatches it away and shoves it to one side, her face full of disdain as if I have just given her a handful of insects or a severed limb.

A noise behind me causes me to shift in my seat and turn around.

'Oh, pay no attention to her,' she says as a young girl of no more than eight or nine clambers out from under a pile of brightly coloured silk sheets stacked up in the corner of the cabin. The child sits there, eyes wide, her black hair and grubby clothes askew, watching our every move. I feel nervous. Sweat coats my back and I have no idea why. I feel as if I have been caught out doing something wrong, as if this child can see through all this nonsense and is wondering why I am here, wasting my money on such claptrap.

'You make sure you sit there quietly, young 'un,' the woman says in a clipped tone, 'none of your silly stuff now, little missy.'

The girl nods submissively and catches my gaze. I give her a small smile and she widens her eyes at me and slinks back onto the sheets like a frightened rabbit. Embarrassed by it all, I turn away and wait for the woman to do her thing. This is all very silly and I am tempted to get up and leave but she obviously senses my mood and takes my hand once again, dragging her cold fingers over my hot sticky palm, soothing me with her cool skin, calming me with her soft warm words.

'You've had a difficult journey,' she mutters quietly and suddenly the spell is broken. I almost want to laugh out loud. Such a glib, sweeping statement; words that could be applied to quite possibly anybody, anywhere. We all consider ourselves hard done by at one point or another. I know I do.

Seeing the look on my face, she continues, 'And it isn't over yet. But you have a kind, supportive family behind you to help you along. I can also smell roses. Did your grandma have a rose garden, lovey? Or was there an older lady in your family who was a keen gardener? She's with you right now, keeping an eye on you. Said she's very proud of you, she is.'

I remain mute, still steadfast in my belief that I will give nothing away. A nod, a slight smile or tilt of the head and she will take this as an indication that I believe her. Which I don't. Nothing she has said resonates with me or my life in the slightest. She cannot know my life or work out what I'm thinking. I barely understand that myself.

'And you have a good man in your life. Your relationship is strong and you'll never be parted. Am I right?'

Again, I do nothing. Silence is my friend.

'Lastly, always remember to be true to yourself. You have a chest problem. Asthma perhaps? Is that right, lovey, you have asthma?'

I nod and grin to convey my agreement. It's easier to let her believe she has won with this one. To contradict her or disagree would be embarrassing. I've never had any type of cough or chest infection in my life. She couldn't be more wrong about me. This purported fortune teller is out by a country mile.

She leans back in her chair to indicate that the reading is over. So many words that say or mean nothing. I stand up and smile at her. If nothing else, this time spent here has proven to me what I already knew – that the whole thing is a complete farce. I actually feel vindicated in spending £20 of my hard-earned money to prove to myself that nobody knows me as well as I know myself, and that nobody can predict how my life is going to turn out. I am the only one who has control over that particular minefield.

'He'll never forgive you, you know. He hates you now, after what you did.'

The small voice freezes my blood. My stomach tightens into a small knot of apprehension as the girl speaks again.

'You shouldn't be here. They don't want to be found. They don't want you, never did. You're nobody to them. You should leave this place and go back home.'

'Oi! Told you earlier to keep this shut, didn't I?' Sylvia Rosa, or whatever her name actually is, points at the young girl with her long, skeletal-like fingers, her eyes ablaze with anger, her other hand pointing to her mouth which she pretends to zip up. Her lips purse into a firm, solid line, her face puckering in disapproval.

The child shrugs apathetically and I watch, frozen as she glares at me and slinks back under the pile of sheets out of sight.

I breathe deep and hard, trying to still the arrhythmic beating of my pounding heart. My feet feel as if they're made of concrete as I shuffle out of the cabin without another word. I just need to gulp in the fresh air and clear my head. My eyes water and my head pounds as I step into the sharp chill of the sea breeze.

Staggering over to the nearby railings, I grip the cold metal, glad of its cooling effect on my hot skin. Just words. That's all they were. Silly words from a child who probably says the same things to all the unfortunate, needy souls who go in there. I quell my inner voice, the one that is screaming at me to go back and ask her how she knew about those things. She can't know. It's just a crazy coincidence. She could have said anything, and I would have made her words fit. That's what we do – us vulnerable people. We clutch at things, force them to meet our needs. That's all it was. Just words that resonated with me. They could probably hit a nerve with hundreds of other people around me today. We only hear what we want to hear, don't we? We all crave answers to our problems and will look in any place to find them, no matter how desperate that may seem. So how come the old lady's words meant nothing to me? She talked trite nonsense that didn't fit with anything in my life. How do I explain that?

I suck in a chestful of cold air and shake my head. I have to stop this. It's ridiculous to try to read anything into all this palm-reading nonsense. Therein lies the road to ruin. Any person with an ounce of common sense knows it's all complete rubbish. Utter poppycock. That's all it is. A perfect stranger cannot predict how our lives will turn out. It's our actions that define us, not the words of somebody who doesn't know us. We are all in control of our own destiny.

A flock of gulls circle above me, their loud screeching an echo in the wide, cloudless sky. I look up at the huge, white birds and dip my head to one side as one of them swoops down at me, its long beak only inches from my face. I watch, shocked and mildly scared, as it diverts to my left and heads for a group of nearby elderly people who are eating sandwiches and drinking coffee, unaware that they are about to be relieved of their lunch by a flock of scavengers. I stamp my feet and wave my arms about, shooing it away before it causes any damage or hurts anybody. An old lady nods her thanks at me and gives me a wide smile, immediately restoring my faith in human nature. Sometimes it's the small things that help us along and keep us sane, isn't it? A smile, an acknowledgement of a thoughtful gesture, kind words spoken: that's all we need to keep us on track.

Feeling steadier on my feet, I decide to continue my walk around town. I refuse to let the words of a small child ruin my day. I like to think I have the strength to rise above such twaddle.

Very slowly, I make my way down the pier, a yawning stretch of concrete I haven't yet been down since moving here over a month ago. The wind is powerful and does its utmost to stop me making the walk, but like everyone else, I persevere. We push back against the strong breeze, our bodies bent over as we fight against the tremendous forces of nature. The wind whips the sea up into a white line of froth. It bashes against the harbour walls, ferocious and unrelenting, sloshing up over the sides before dispersing into tiny beads of foam that splatter over the seating area. Despite its brutality, the view of the sea really is quite beautiful. I can't help but be moved by its strength and the way it shapes everything around it.

I resist the urge to go all the way to the end of the pier, my skin already numb with the cold and instead, flop down onto a damp bench to take in the view of the church and craggy looking abbey that sit high up on the cliff, the church perched so perilously close to the edge, it looks as if it will slide down the embankment at any given moment. People drag themselves up the steps, all one hundred and ninety-nine of them. From where I sit, the people look like ants, their small bodies twisting and turning as they stop to rest or take in the view. I have yet to do the iconic steps even though I've lived here for six weeks. I am not a lover of heights so not seeing that view is no great loss to me. Perhaps once I'm more settled, I'll do it, but as it is, I have other more important matters I should be dealing with.

I feel a slight pressure build in my head at the thought of why I came to live in this town. I have yet to do anything about it. It feels like a lifetime ago when I first made the decision to come here and in that time, I've done nothing worthwhile. Instead, I have hung around my flat, miserable and full of self-pity, drinking myself into a stupor and generally being utterly useless at everything. I couldn't even make the move to knock on the door of my parents' house. Such a pathetic, weak soul.

I rub at my gritty eyes that ache as if I've been punched and let out a wavering sigh. This is it. This has got to be the turning point in my current predicament. I have to change, to get some sense of direction back in my life. No more fast food and alcohol. I've done more than enough damage to myself. I have drunk, cried, drunk some more, even passed out and woken up unable to remember where I am, but the one thing I haven't done is make any kind of headway with what it is I came here to do. Alcohol has taken hold of everything, twisting my life into an unrecognisable scrap of nothingness and I need to stop it. I need to get back on track.

I stifle an involuntary sob as the memory of calling Gareth comes back to me. Not just one call but a couple a night for at least a week, probably even longer. He didn't answer them, of course. I'm not even sure what I would have said if he had. I was a bumbling wreck each time I rang him, my misery and angst fuelled by drink and loneliness. He did me a favour by ignoring me, saving me from a great deal of humiliation. I don't mind admitting that I miss him, although I know he doesn't feel the same way. He made his feelings towards me crystal clear the last time we spoke. A lump lodges in my throat. I swallow it down. Too late for regrets. What's done is done. This is my new beginning.

This is the start of the new me.

Standing up and striding back towards the bandstand, I make the decision to return to my flat. If I am going to finally unearth what has been hidden for too long, I have to do it now before the downward spiral of my life becomes a permanent pattern; a groove I become too familiar with to break.

Pushing back through town, through the crowds that fill every available space, I sense the ghosts of my past behind me, forcing me on, whispering to me that I need to do this thing, telling me that if I don't take this chance and do it now, I never will. It would be stupid and cowardly to come this far and then do nothing. I can crack open my past and find the real me, and isn't that what I've wanted for so many years?

By the time I get back home, I am beside myself with excitement and apprehension. I'm finally going to meet my parents. At long last, I've summoned up enough courage to see it through, and it feels good. I try to imagine what my first words will be when they open the door, what it is I should say to make that all important first impression, a good one. It's so close I can almost touch it.

I unlock the door and all but fall in, stumbling over the bunched-up rug in the hallway, and land in a heap on the sofa, tears threatening to spill over, my head tight with churned up thoughts of my parents: the ones who didn't want me. Even after all these years, the hurt of rejection still burns.

I close my eyes for a second; just a short while to allow the memories to fade. That's all I need. Just a bit of breathing space to clear my head so I can think straight.

* * *

The pressure on my chest is intense, my limbs locked into place, too relaxed to move. I try to twist and turn, to spring free out of this position, but it's all too much. Easier to let sleep do its thing. No matter how often I experience this, I am always convinced I will die if I don't move. It's like slipping into a deep, deep hole, allowing myself to be enveloped by the darkness, by the terrifying paralysis that has me in its grip.

It always happens when I'm over-tired or stressed and desperate to wake up from whichever dream I want to escape from, but it's not always that easy. My brain is alert but my body is exhausted, still trapped somewhere between the realms of the deepest sleep and wakefulness, and it refuses to move no matter how hard I try. Even after all these years of suffering from this condition, panic still sets in. This is how it must feel to be paralysed, to be unfortunate enough to have locked-in syndrome. A living nightmare. The world continues to spin, life goes on as normal, but you are not able to be a part of it. You are fixed in position, your body rigid, your mind screaming out for help while your own body holds you hostage.

I give it one more go, my core strength pushed into moving my right arm, to no avail. It's futile, so instead I relax and let the dream continue, the one where I am chasing my past. I race along the street. Ahead of me is a figure dressed in black. I have no idea whether it is male or female. All I know is I am desperate to catch up with it, to spin it around and see who it is. As I run through the crowds of people, I can hear them laughing at me, yelling that I should go home, forget about the chase and just leave. I stop and cry, screaming at them to leave me alone, hollering about how they need to help me catch this person.

When I run again, the figure has gone. They have been spirited away into thin air as if they never existed. The laughing gets louder. I turn tail and head towards the crashing sea where the mocking voices are drowned out by the almighty roar of the frothing ocean as it crashes against the immense rocks and boulders. And then I see him: Gareth. He is there at the foot of the cliff, beckoning me to go to him. I head over but by the time I get there, he's gone, disappeared into the ether as if he was never there to begin with.

Out of nowhere, one of the rocks bounces down the cliff wall and knocks me over. I lie there with it trapping me, pushing every last pocket of air out of my lungs. I pant and gasp for breath, terror enveloping me. I push and push with all my might, my body rocking and shaking with the effort, and then suddenly, the huge boulder shifts and falls to one side and my body is free of the weight. I spring up off the floor, my head throbbing, my muscles as light as air. I am ecstatic to be able to finally move.

I sit up, startled and fuzzy with fear and look around the living room. I am awake.

7

EVA

I wake up with the mother of all headaches. Blood roars through my ears, and my neck is stiff where I have lain at an awkward angle. Disorientated, I struggle to my feet, staggering on liquid legs towards the kitchen where I grab a glass and fill it to the brim with freezing water. I stare at it for a few seconds, trying to get my bearings and pull myself round. Its sheer clarity mesmerises me. I watch bubbles froth up and disappear then tip my head back and glug it down as quickly as I can, enjoying the icy sensation as it coats my throat and alleviates the nagging ache that has set in at the back of my jaw.

Jesus, I feel groggy and marginally sick. Nightmares like those never get any easier to deal with. In fact, with a little knowledge of how bad they can be, each one gets progressively worse. I dread them. There have been times where I have tried to stay awake to avoid having them, and then ended up falling asleep and slipping into the most horrific dreams imaginable where I'm unable to move and am paralysed, my limbs refusing to budge no matter how hard I push them. It's a living hell. Even my own body wants to punish me.

I have no idea how long I have slept for and swing round to stare at the clock. I squint, waiting for the numbers to slowly come into focus. It's two o'clock. I've slept for over an hour and yet it feels much longer than that. My body is like lead. I feel as if it has gone into some sort of shutdown, my mind and limbs refusing to work as they should.

Slumping down onto a nearby chair, I rest my head in my hands. A long line of drool stretches over my cheek, warm and sticky. Using the back of my hand, I wipe it away and wince at the sour odour it leaves on my skin. I rub at my eyes, feeling like an overtired, petulant child. I have got to pull myself round both physically and mentally. Afternoon naps are for the elderly and the infirm and I am neither. What I am, however, is an old soak who is utterly useless at pulling herself together, making sure my life has some sort of focus. I have sought refuge in the bottom of a bottle and this is the net result – me sitting here at my kitchen table, covered in spittle, body like lead, head as tight as a drum and generally feeling like shit. I mean, I even visited a fortune teller, for God's sake. This is not how I want my life to be: alone, unemployed and permanently hungover. I've spent the past six weeks or so wandering around in a daze. It has to stop.

I drink some more water and give myself time to come around. Slowly, my head clears, the fog inside it dissipating, allowing me to think properly. I decide that now is as good a time as any to root through all my things: all the documents and certificates that I stashed away in a box when I first moved here. I've put it off for too long, using every excuse under the sun to avoid doing what it is I originally came here to do. This is where that all ends. Headache or no headache, I am determined to tackle it. It scares me, I don't mind admitting that, but I will fall apart completely if I don't go at it head on. I am already well on my way to unravelling. It's as if I have some sort of self-destruct mechanism hidden deep inside me and misery and angst are my default emotions. I want to be happy. I really do. You wouldn't think so to look at me, but deep down, I am actually a really positive person. It's just that somewhere, somehow, along the path of this thing we call everyday life, I have lost my way.

Dragging up my weary bones, I reach on top of the kitchen cupboard and pull down the small box that contains everything I need. All the addresses, numbers, photographs and general documentation detailing my past, my other life. Not that I have much in the way of paperwork: just an address, some certificates and a couple of photographs.

I run my fingers through my hair and yawn loudly, yet another way of procrastinating. It is my forte. I suppose I have to be good at something, don't I? While my life is falling apart, at least I can say that I completely mastered the art of putting stuff off that I should have sorted out many years ago.

I lift the lid off the container and my fingers hover over the first thing I see: a black, velvet pouch no bigger than my hand. My eyes fill up and my face grows hot. I had forgotten it was in here. I lean down to touch it: the pouch that contains my bracelet. I stroke it carefully and swallow back unexpected tears, then place it to one side and look back inside the box. A grainy photograph stares up at me from the top of the thin stack of papers. My breath catches in my throat and a film of something foul tasting coats my mouth. The picture. *My picture*. I clear my throat and snatch it up, grasping it firmly between my thumb and forefinger. It's a photograph of me as a toddler. I have no recollection of it being taken but know it is definitely me as I've looked at it thousands of times over the years, glancing at it each and every day, hoping for some hidden memory to resurface and unlock the mystery of my past. It's one of the few photos I have of me with my parents – my biological parents – the ones who dumped me then forgot I existed.

I keep my eyes glued to it, still hoping it will release a memory or a fleeting thought hidden somewhere deep inside my brain, but nothing comes. It's hard to believe, looking at such a happy, family snap, that our home, the place where I was born, contained such heartache. The barely visible image is of my mother staring up at my father adoringly, her head tipped back, her shoulders hunched as she smiles at her husband. I am balanced on my father's knee and he is grinning at the camera like he doesn't have a care in the world. A man who has everything going for him. A man who, only weeks after this picture was taken, beat my mother black and blue and broke my arm whilst in a drunken rage, one of many from what I have gathered from the bits of information I've managed to glean out of the social workers over the years. I've been told that I'm lucky to not have any recollections, that it was a bleak time for everybody involved and being removed from the family home was the best thing that could have happened to me.

I grimace and place the photograph to one side then rummage through the pieces of paper, knowing the particular one I'm searching for. I am almost certain I have the details correct in my mind but need to check just one more time. I can't afford to make any mistakes. Not when I've come this far. I may have wasted lots of time and done some stupid things in the past, but my mind is made up about my next move. There is no way I'm about to bugger it up. Not a hope in hell.

I trace my fingers across the brittle wad of papers, leafing through them all until at last, I find it nestling at the bottom of the pile. The one I've been looking for, the one that will put an end to all of this. Dust motes swirl lazily in the air as I lift it out and place it on my knee, my fingers trembling slightly as I flatten it out and watch as the words on it blur and merge, my eyes misting over, my chin trembling. Everything in my life, all the worry and the loneliness, the mistakes and the clawing sense of dread I feel, it has all come to this point. I hold the answers to both my past and my future in my hands. It's all down to me from here on in. How I manage this next step will determine what lies in store for me. So far, I haven't done so well, but I can change. I have it within me to adapt. I am a chameleon. I've had to be.

Leaning back, I lift the paper up to the light, reading and re-reading the words on it as if they are about to change in some way. I smile as I trace them with my index finger, looping around the cursive script with absolute precision.

I stop and take a deep breath, the cold air hitting my nostrils as I slowly inhale. I can do this. All of a sudden it feels within my reach. For so many years, it was an unattainable dream. I had neither the courage nor the wherewithal to see it through. But now, it's here, right in front of me. This thing is mine for the taking.

First off, I need to tidy myself up, snap out of this slovenly lifestyle I have managed to slip into since moving here. When I meet them, I want to be presentable, not turn up on their doorstep, hair and clothes askew and reeking of alcohol. They would slam the door in my face if I were to do that, and I wouldn't blame them one little bit. But once I present them with my birth certificate, there is no way they can deny that I am their daughter. I will show them every piece of ID I can think of: this birth certificate, my driving licence, my passport. Hell, I'll even present my Nectar card if I have to. There is no way they are going to escape from me. Not this time. I can't wait to see their faces, to study them closely and see if I look like them. The picture is too small to see them clearly. They are no more than a pair of grainy looking individuals with blurry faces and indefinable features, but that doesn't matter because very soon, I'll be able to see them up close, work out which one of my parents gifted me with my slightly crooked nose. I wonder if my blue eyes match those of my mother? Mixed emotions bubble up inside me: fear, excitement, resentment. All those years I was ignored, forgotten about.

I place the certificate down on the kitchen counter, put the box back, and go about tidying up the flat. I start in the kitchen, scooping up armfuls of empty bottles and discarded food wrappers that I have studiously ignored over the last few weeks, and push them into the bin. I wipe surfaces until they gleam and I even wash the floor, getting down on my hands and knees, and scrubbing at it until my hands are raw, dragging a bleach-covered brush around the edges one last time before standing up and surveying my handiwork.

Next, I tackle the living room, shaking cushions and gathering up magazines and old newspapers before placing them in the recycling box in the alley outside the door. Even my dustbin of a bedroom doesn't faze me. I enter it, a ball of positive energy. It seems that the more I clean, the more determined I am that I will take back control of my life. I bundle the reeking, vomit-stained duvet into the washing machine and clean every corner of the room, not resting until it's complete.

By the time I finish, every muscle in my body aches from the effort but my mind is clear, my thinking back on track. I can't remember ever feeling so excited or filled with such a sense of purpose. It's as if by ridding myself of the outward clutter, I have helped to cleanse my mind in the process, streamlined my thoughts and pointed myself in the right direction. I know now what it is I have to do. I will get cleaned up, make myself thoroughly presentable and make that visit – the one I have dreamed about for as long as I can remember; the one that has haunted me for all of my days. I will do it now before this surge of adrenalin dissipates and the demons begin to bite once more.

I am almost running as I head back into the bedroom and strip naked, pulling my clothes over my head. I step into the shower and let the hot water pummel my grimy, filthy skin, ridding me of the dirt that has clung to me as I cleaned the flat, swilling away the oil and sweat that coated my skin and made my hair stick to my forehead in little, wet ringlets.

When I finally emerge, hot and clean and smelling of mint shampoo and magnolia shower gel, I feel strangely refreshed, ready to take on the world. Funny isn't it, how feelings and situations can change so quickly? One minute, you feel down in the depths and the next minute, you're ready to face anything.

I dress quickly and tie my hair back, my hands shaking as I grab the certificate and photograph, and stuff them deep into my pocket.

I pull on a fleecy sweater and head out, so sure, so certain that this day is the one that will change the rest of my life. I have finally taken the plunge and am now about to meet the people who left me behind. In just a short while, I will be face-to-face with the parents who didn't want me. Whether they like it or not, I am on my way to their home so they had better be ready. I want to know the truth about my past and I want it now.

LONDON

8

CELIA

Celia turns her fist sideways and hammers on the door once more. No answer. This is the right address; she is sure of it. She checked it over and over again before setting off and timed her journey to get here for early evening so she would catch her friend when she returns home after work. She turns and looks around. Up and down the long avenue, people scurry along, keen to get indoors. Cars park up, squeezing into the tightest of spaces, doors slam, children chatter as they clamber out of vehicles, arms bulging with schoolbags and pictures, and all manner of belongings. Celia watches them as they slink off into the warmth and security of their homes. She considers stopping them, asking if they've seen the lady who lives here, but doubts that many of them know who their neighbours even are. Such a long road with so many houses and everybody too busy with their own lives to worry about anybody else's. The place has a business-like feel to it, not the sort of street where people stop and chat or knock to borrow a cup of sugar. They look too official for that sort of thing, too active and aloof to become involved in the minutiae of one another's lives.

Stepping over the gravel, Celia cups her hands together and

peers in through the living room window, her breath misting up the glass in small, pulsing waves that grow and retreat in a fine circular motion. She stands for a while, her eyes narrowed in concentration. Something is wrong but she can't quite work out what it is that's amiss. There is something about this place, something that doesn't quite feel right, like misshapen parts of a puzzle forced into place. A small tic starts up in her jaw as a flicker of a shadow darts out of view in her peripheral vision: a grey, indistinct movement that sets her pulse racing. She twists around to look, but everything appears the same as it was a few moments ago. Nothing has moved. There is nobody in the room.

Stepping back from the glass, Celia rummages in her pocket for her phone. She's tried ringing a few times but hasn't received a reply and is getting concerned. This isn't right. It's not like her friend to just disappear like this, not like her at all. She usually gets in touch every couple of days to let Celia know how she is, and now her absence has set alarm bells ringing.

Holding out her phone, Celia squints down at it, wondering if she should call somebody. She has no idea who that somebody would be. Apart from Greta, their one-time foster mother, they don't really have any mutual friends or acquaintances. They only have each other in common, fused together by their past. Thrown together by their warped history.

Scrolling down the list of numbers, more for inspiration than anything else, Celia feels the hairs on the back of her neck stand up in fear. A prickling sensation covers her skin as she slowly places her phone back in her coat pocket and turns around, her chest closing up with unease. She lets out a small shriek as a pair of dark eyes stares out at her from the corner of the bay window. Holding her hand to her neck, she watches as a large, black cat hisses at her then arches its back and leaps away from the glass, slinking its long body over the back of the armchair next to the window. Celia lets out a nervous laugh, her legs suddenly watery as she silently chastises herself for being so easily frightened. After an arduous train journey down from York, where she was forced to stand because somebody took her reserved seat, she is feeling rather fragile and could do with a sit down and a cup of tea, but instead is standing here in an alien environment with no idea how to get to her hotel, where her friend is, or how she should even go about finding her.

Fighting back tears, Celia sits down on the step, worry and fear consuming her. It was possibly too rash a move coming here. She should have stayed in York, rung the local police station, made them aware of her concerns, but as it is, she is here, sitting on Eva's doorstep with no idea of what her next move is going to be. Greta always chastised her for being too impulsive. And she was right. Greta was always right.

Celia puffs out her cheeks and runs her fingers through her hair, suddenly weary of it all. Why would Eva stop calling, not reply to her texts and simply disappear out of her life? It doesn't make any sense. They are friends, their bond too strong to break, united by fragmented childhoods, strengthened by their need to leave it all behind. And yet Eva is so fragile, so easily dented. She appears confident to those who meet her, but Celia knows her better than anyone. Underneath her tough exterior is a desperate, broken, little girl waiting to be healed.

Celia feels her heart thrum out an uncomfortable, erratic beat. If there is one true thing she knows about her friend, it is that she is also prone to bouts of anxiety and depression and... she doesn't want to think about the other things. The things that they have worked hard to break away from. It was all such a long time ago. They're now both fully functioning adults with decent jobs and busy lives. They are not the children that were abandoned by their parents, those hurting, damaged kids who struggled to cope with their lot in life. What they were does not define them. It's what they are now that matters. And they are both hard working, conscientious members of society who, despite their ragged upbringing, have made it. Against all the odds, they have remained stoic and positive and are getting on with their lives. They keep in touch, helping one another with the day-to-day problems that life often throws their way, seeing it from the same perspective. Their lives have always ticked along fairly nicely since leaving home, getting half-decent qualifications and better-than-expected jobs. They have survived. Eva even made the move here to London from York on her own. No job to go to, no place to live. She just took the plunge and did it.

So, where is she? Why has Eva suddenly gone to ground?

A small pulse taps at Celia's neck, making her shiver. She digs her nails into her palms. This definitely isn't right. Eva needs her; she needs to be kept in check.

She can't manage on her own.

Dropping her hands by her sides, she drums her fingers against her thigh, then stands up, turns once more and stares in through the living room window, her eyes sweeping over the furniture and bric-a-brac dotted around the place. That's when it dawns on her. It's the picture on the fireplace. It's wrong. It doesn't fit. The photograph is the puzzle piece that spoils the whole image. It isn't the one that Eva has talked about for so many years, the one that Celia feels as if she knows every inch of. The image sitting there doesn't match her friend's description. It's a sharp black and white picture of a young, fresh-faced couple, arms slung around each other, hair whipping into their smiling faces as if they don't have a care in the world; not the small, blurry image of her parents that Eva has described to her in such great detail Celia feels as if she took the picture herself. Her heart starts up again in that irregular, sickly beat that makes her feel mildly dizzy and disorientated. Where has the picture gone and more to the point, where is Eva?

'Can I help you?'

The voice sends a streak of electricity coursing across her skin, an uncomfortable, tingling sensation that pierces her flesh and races through her veins. Celia whips around and finds herself standing face-to-face with a lithe, glamorous woman in her late twenties. Her blonde hair is scraped back into a loose ponytail accentuating her smooth, angular features. Her face is free of make-up and her eyes are creased ever so slightly at the corners as she watches Celia intently, waiting for her reply.

'Erm, sorry, yes. At least I hope so.' Celia stops and clears her throat, suddenly embarrassed by her stance. She feels like a naughty schoolchild caught red-handed. She was so sure this was the right address, so utterly certain. 'I'm looking for a friend,' she says quietly, fatigue gripping her, 'but it appears I'm at the wrong house. I'm so sorry,' she whispers, her voice croaky with shame.

A thousand thoughts whirl through her head. She no longer wants to stay in London tonight. She has travelled all the way down here from York and wishes she had stayed at home and gone with her initial, gut instinct to contact the local police station. But even doing that would have felt silly and foolish: an over-reaction from an anxious friend. She should leave here, get the next train home. This is ridiculous. She feels like a prize idiot.

'It's not Eva you're looking for, is it?' the woman says quietly, her chiselled features softening into something more welcoming, a look that makes Celia want to cry. She has passed a sea of indifferent expressions on the way here, everybody busy, everybody on their way to somewhere else, bustling past her with such a sense of purpose she felt as if she were invisible.

Celia nods and swallows down a hard lump that has risen in her throat. This is perfectly ludicrous. She is a grown woman with the means to get back home should she decide to, an independent, sharp-minded individual, so why does she always feel like the damage she carries on the inside is visible on the outside? No matter how hard she has worked at leaving it all behind, her turbulent childhood follows her around, a constant reminder of what sort of person she really is: broken and vulnerable. That's what she and Eva have in common: their scars. Hidden from the world but glaringly obvious to one other.

'Would you like to come in for a cup of tea? You don't look too well,' the woman says quietly, and before Celia can answer, she finds herself being ushered inside by this fair-faced lady who insists she take a seat in the lounge while she boils the kettle and locates Eva's forwarding address.

Celia stares around the carefully furnished living room, drinking it all in: the matching grey fabrics and contrasting black throws, the modern art hanging on the walls. She doubts this is how Eva would have had it, although she doesn't know for certain. She never visited her in London after Eva moved. They often made promises to one another to meet up but it never ever came to anything. And now, the one time she does make the effort, Eva isn't even here.

Celia nibbles at her nails as she listens to the familiar clink of crockery coming through from the kitchen, all the while doing her best to stem the uneasy sensation that has settled in the pit of her stomach.

Eva has moved?

The feeling she had that something was terribly awry has proved to be correct. The Eva that Celia knows needs stability in her life. She craves a day-to-day routine and the last time she spoke to her, Eva made no mention of moving. She talked of her job and a handful of close friends. She even mentioned having a steady boyfriend. Her 'soul partner'. Those were the words she used. That was what she had called him. Celia has no idea what his actual name is. Eva was pretty coy when it came to revealing any details about him but it was obvious that she was happy. So why would she suddenly up and leave?

Celia closes her eyes for a second and exhales, her nostrils wide with worry and exasperation. Everything was normal. *She* was so normal. Not the frantic, rash Eva of old, but a measured, well-balanced woman with everything to look forward to. Or so it seemed. That's the thing with Eva. She always did excel at lying. Maybe Celia doesn't really know her at all. Maybe after all these years, everything she thought she knew about her friend is way off beam: a complete tissue of lies. After all, Celia only knows what Eva has chosen to tell her.

Before being placed together with Greta, they had lived separate lives, mysterious, fragmented lives that were so chaotic and jumbled and miserable, they were only too happy to throw off those shackles and reinvent themselves the first opportunity they got. Celia told the odd untruth but was always plagued with guilt and retracted it almost as soon as she said it. Nothing major. It was more a case of building up her past, pretending it didn't happen. All she ever wanted was the normal upbringing others had had. What was so wrong with telling everyone her dad worked in a bank and her mum was a fashion designer at a top retail outlet? It was better than the truth. Better than telling people her dad was in prison for murder and her mother was a raging alcoholic who barely even recognised her own children. And she was glad to be with Greta. It was a happy place to be, full of warmth and laughter and security. Celia welcomed being in such an environment, whereas Eva railed against it. She hated every foster parent she had ever been with. And apparently there had been many. Despite the attempts of a string of social workers, Eva couldn't settle anywhere. All she talked about was being back home with her own parents, even though her father was violent and her mother was ineffectual, making no attempt to protect herself or her child from his blows, often becoming embroiled in it, instigating many of the quarrels and arguments. Eva had been removed when she was no more than a toddler and had erratic contact over the years which had soon petered out.

Snatches of Celia's teenage conversations with Eva come back to her as she sits and waits for the tea. There was another child. Or at least she thinks so. So much had happened in the intervening years, a lot of her early memories seem so blurry and intangible, half hidden in the shadows of her mind. She has enough issues piecing together her own formative years, never mind anybody else's. And Eva told so many awful lies that even now Celia still can't sift through the untruths to the actual facts. Eva never did realise or appreciate that living with Greta was a blessing.

'Here you go.' The voice snaps her back to reality as a cup of hot tea is handed to her and a small plate of biscuits is placed on the coffee table next to her chair. Celia smiles and sips at the tea, glad of its warmth and familiarity. The thought of eating a dry biscuit, however, makes her want to heave. But tea... She smiles; why does tea always make everything seem so much better?

'Thank you,' Celia murmurs, a sudden flush creeping up her neck and over her face. Lifting her hand, she brushes it over her forehead and runs her fingers through her hair, pushing auburn locks back out of her eyes.

'Oh, and this is the forwarding address she gave us. I clipped it to a magnet on the side of the fridge, along with all our other stuff. We haven't received any post that needed forwarding on so I almost threw it out. So glad I hung onto it now.'

Celia reaches over and takes the piece of paper. 'I'm Celia, by the way.' She almost adds that she is a friend of Eva's but stops in time, realising how ridiculous that would sound. What sort of person would turn up on the doorstep not knowing their friend had moved house? It would make her appear foolish, perhaps even a little bit unbalanced, and that's the last thing she is. Celia prides herself on being staid and sensible. She is the thoughtful one, the honest one.

'Jesus, how rude of me!' the woman replies, her smile lighting up the room as she slaps a hand over her forehead to indicate she is a complete klutz. 'I'm Marie. Pleased to meet you, Celia, even though you did scare the living daylights out of me out there.'

Celia flushes even hotter, remembering how she clambered over the gravel and peered in the window like some sort of stalker.

'Yes, sorry about that,' she whispers, feeling her strength slowly being sapped away at the lies she is about to tell, 'I got the dates wrong. I somehow thought Eva was moving next month and not this one.' Celia turns away, pretending to scrutinise the goings on outside in the street. A car pulls away and an elderly couple walk arm in arm, their bodies hunched with age and weariness. She knows how they feel. It seems as if she has aged a good ten years in just one day, coming down here chasing Eva, worrying about her, trying to work out what she is up to. Celia takes a shuddering breath and swallows back her fear. If she is being truthful, she has a fair idea of what Eva is up to. That's what scares her. She hopes she is wrong.

'She's moved a long way, hasn't she?' Marie chirps, 'Not so sure I could do that. I really like living in the city. I love its vibrancy and the cosmopolitan feel, and there are so many great places to visit. So many fabulous galleries and coffee shops. Everything is at our fingertips here.'

Celia nods in recognition even though this is only the second time in her life she's been here. She opens the folded piece of paper and reads the words written there, feeling the blood drain from her head. Doing her best to remain composed, she stares at the address, the location jumping out at her. She was right. Her fears have been confirmed.

Eva has done the one thing Celia has always tried to talk her out of doing. So many times over the years, she has begged her not to go through with it. So many times, she has told her to leave it alone, to get on with her life and not rake it all up again. And now she has done just that: opened up a very nasty can of worms that once cracked apart, will be almost impossible to put back together. Eva is ripe for the irreparable damage a move like this could cause. She already *is* damaged. This will only increase her chances of free-falling into a deep depression.

Celia takes another gulp of hot tea, a tepid panacea for her current predicament. It's clear now why Eva didn't tell her of the move. She would have done everything she could to stop her. No good will come of it. Eva knows this and yet she has given up everything she has worked hard for, put everything on the line to unearth her past, a past that she is better off without. A past that didn't want her.

Fighting back tears and a wave of anger at being kept in the dark, Celia straightens her back, drains her tea and stands up.

'Thank you so much for this. I do feel like such a fool for getting it all mixed up.'

Marie cocks her head slightly to one side and smiles sadly at her, as if she is a small child. 'No worries at all. When you do see her, tell your friend I'm remembering to water her azaleas and that they're still going strong.'

Celia nods and scrunches the paper into a tiny ball before thrusting it deep into her coat pocket. Stupid Eva and her desperate need to go chasing what went before. A disturbed woman in pursuit of people who never wanted her. Celia shakes her head sadly. She has no idea why Eva has done this *thing*, made this rash move and not informed her, but Celia knows now what it is she must do. She will put her own life on hold to go after her friend. And she will find her. She has to. Leaving her to do this on her own isn't an option. She knows what she must do to save Eva from herself. She has always known.

9

CELIA

Feeling as if she is choking on thin air, Celia makes her way down the tree-lined avenue, her fingers clutched around Eva's new address. Her head spins as she staggers towards a nearby bench and slumps down on it, her stomach a tight knot of anxiety. She still can't quite get her head around it all. Eva has gone. Upped and left without a word, and now Celia has to make a decision – spend the night in London, or head straight up to see her. She knows what's sensible, but sensible doesn't always get things done, does it? Sensible is what people do when their lives are untroubled and peaceful, not when they have had the upbringing she and Eva have had. And yet, she has spent so many years doing the right thing, being that sensible individual, trying to fit in that she is sick of it; she is tired of living her life in a straight line. So what harm would it do to break the pattern and once again be one of the damaged souls whose behaviour is unpredictable and spontaneous? It might help locate Eva, for one thing.

Pulling out her phone, Celia calls her friend once more, her breath suspended in her chest, the world at a standstill as she prays for Eva to answer. As expected, it goes to voicemail, the long, drawn-out beep at the end of the message irritating her beyond reason.

Pursing her lips, Celia lets out a stream of hot air and briefly closes her eyes. She has a small, overnight bag with her; just enough to see her through until tomorrow. Pretty soon the last train will be leaving for York. She could jump on it, then make the changes for Whitby. It's now or never. She needs to decide what her next move will be. Should she stay here or not? Should she do the sensible thing and face it all tomorrow with a clear head, or go racing off up north in pursuit of her friend?

She checks her phone again, eyes narrowed in concentration. Shaking her head in exasperation, she wonders why trains are so bloody complicated and why nothing is ever easy when it comes to using public transport in this great nation of ours. If she catches the next train, she won't get into York until after nine p.m. She is tired. Not just physically tired, but mentally drained by it all. Suddenly, the hotel room seems appealing. She can check in, have something to eat, sleep on it and make a decision in the morning as to what her next move is going to be. She doesn't want to do anything too rash right now even though every nerve in her body, every sinew and fibre is screaming at her to drop everything and head straight to Whitby. The train there stops at York. It's one of the two changes she has to make, and it will take her ten hours with all the waits and changes.

Even as she goes through all the facts in her head, she already knows her mind is made up. If she stays the night in London, she can catch a mid-morning train tomorrow and the journey to Whitby will be much shorter. Still two changes but no waiting around for connecting trains. No hanging around on cold, dark platforms in the middle of the night, doing her best to avoid eye contact with everybody around her; everyone tired, everyone mildly scared of being out at night, surrounded by perfect strangers. All of them watching the shadows and feeling exhausted and fearful.

Celia blinks and feels her chin tremble with both fear and relief: fear at what may lay ahead and relief at finally coming to a decision. Clambering up to her feet, she slings her overnight bag onto her shoulder and heads out of the avenue towards the tube station feeling marginally energised after finally coming to a decision.

* * *

The hotel is a welcome sight after navigating her way through the tube stations and myriad of unfamiliar streets to reach it. She is flooded with a sensation akin to smugness at actually making it back to where she started. It's a Premier Inn close to the station: the perfect location for a rapid exit first thing in the morning. She wants to get going as early as she can. No time to waste now she knows exactly where Eva is. Every second wasted puts Eva at risk. Not that wasted time will do any more damage to Eva than she already does to herself. Eva is, always has been, and probably always will be, her own worst enemy. God knows Celia has tried over the years to help her, to make Eva see that she now has the capacity to forge out a good life for herself. She is an intelligent woman and yet so delicate and breakable. Her emotions oscillate constantly; tipping one way or the other with no in between. And she did have a good life by all accounts: a good, solid job that paid well, a handful of friends, and a boyfriend. A soul partner. But her blighted upbringing has always overshadowed everything she has done. It has always been there, obscuring the good stuff, darkening her vision, convincing her that she can bring an end to it all and be reunited with her family. Celia puffs out her cheeks. Perhaps they can. Perhaps after all these years, her parents have sorted themselves out, become half-decent citizens and developed a conscience. Maybe when she finds them, they will feel guilty enough to welcome her back. But she doubts it. If they had wanted her back, they would have come for her, taken her back into the fold and given her the decent upbringing and stability Eva so desperately craved.

They did none of those things.

Instead, they let her down time and time again, not turning up for contact appointments, giving insipid, pathetic reasons for their absences, turning Eva into the vulnerable, needy individual that she is now. Not everybody sees it. Eva is a chameleon. She has developed the ability to morph into whatever people want her to be. Friendly. Euphoric. Suicidal.

Eva is a disaster waiting to happen.

The receptionist is a brisk, efficient creature who has Celia checked in within a matter of seconds. She gives her clipped instructions as to what time breakfast starts and an impossible route of how to locate the restaurant.

The room is clean with the splashes of deep purple everywhere, a constant reminder of which hotel chain Celia is in. She drops her bag on the floor and throws herself on the bed, her need for food only fractionally overtaking her exhaustion by a hair's breadth. Her stomach lets out a loud growl. She sits up and grabs at the menu on the dresser next to the bed. Everything looks appetising. She hasn't eaten for hours. In fact, she hasn't eaten since breakfast and is in dire need of some sustenance.

Outside, a noise draws her attention. Standing up, she stares out of the window at a growing fracas taking place on the pavement outside. An elderly man has fallen over and a crowd has gathered around him. On the periphery of it all is a young man who has his phone out. He is holding it up to indicate he is calling an ambulance, Celia assumes. Tall and swarthy looking, he is a striking sight. Handsome for sure but he is frowning; his forehead furrowed into a deep, concerned line. Celia looks up at the sky. The earlier downpour has probably made the pavement slippery. She catches a glimpse of the fallen man as the crowd parts for a second. He isn't moving and if she isn't mistaken, there is a pool of blood gathering on the pavement.

Celia watches, her breath stilted as she waits for him to move. Time seems to stand still as she watches the people bustle around the fallen man.

In the distance, a wail of sirens pierces the air, bringing her round to the present. Everybody disperses as an ambulance screeches up and a team of medics spill out of it, their movements swift and effortless. The young man with the phone speaks to them, his face the picture of concern as he shakes his head and looks around helplessly before the medics pat him on his arm and get to work, kneeling down next to the man on the floor, speaking to him as they lean in close to his ear.

He nods and Celia is awash with relief. She has no idea why. She doesn't know the fallen man. He means nothing to her. It's just that suddenly, everything feels so fragile and unstable, as if things are about to come crashing down upon her. Her routine has been disturbed and she has no idea what the next few days will hold. She feels anxious and uneasy, enveloped by a sense of doom that everything she knows is about to come to a grinding halt.

The injured man is placed on a stretcher and Celia watches as he is hoisted into the back of the ambulance. She feels a strange sense of solace and watches as the young man who called the ambulance turns and walks away.

Her stomach lets out another growl of protestation at being deprived of food for so long. She needs to eat. Everything will seem better after a meal and a glass of wine. She will sleep well, get the early train back up north and find Eva, who will try to assure her that everything is okay and try to apologise for her behaviour. All Celia wants to do is make sure she is safe. Then Celia can settle. Then she can go back home and get on with her life. Perhaps she can even persuade Eva to go with her. The thought buoys her up, makes her feel as if she can sort this thing out. She hopes so. All she wants is to find Eva and keep her safe. All Celia has ever wanted to do is save Eva from herself.

* * *

The shower is hot and the restaurant relatively easy to find. Celia eats heartily and limits herself to two glasses of Pinot Grigio. She needs a clear head for tomorrow. Missing her connecting train is the last thing she wants to do. She has to be on her mettle, find Eva and work out what is going on in her head; ask her why she thinks finding her parents is a good idea. It isn't. It's a bad idea. The worst.

Celia drains the last of her wine and heaves a sigh of resignation. Perhaps Eva has already found them. Celia hopes not. She hopes to God they saw her coming and avoided her, or were out, or any number of things that will stop them from meeting up with their estranged daughter, because if they do actually open the door to her, Celia knows exactly what Eva will do. She has been planning it for years, dressing it up as a need to find out about her childhood, telling everyone she has an overwhelming urge to be reunited with her parents, to play at being one big, happy family. But that's not it at all. Eva is damaged goods and it was her parents who damaged her. For years, Eva has spoken at length to Celia about her hatred for the people who left her behind. She has screamed and wept at the injustice of it all: at how they have continued to live their lives without her, never giving her a second thought, never once making any attempts to get her back.

And she has never forgiven them.

Her loathing of them is so deep rooted, so unwavering, Celia fears for her. She fears what Eva may be capable of when she finally meets up with them. Which she will. Eva has watched them from a distance for years, always checking to see if they have moved house, even dragging Celia to Whitby for the day a few years back under the guise of spending a day at the coast. Celia went along with it, knowing all the while what her game was, but too apprehensive of what Eva's reaction would be if she refused.

Celia knew exactly why they were going and tried to talk Eva out of it, but she was so wound up about the whole thing, so ready to implode, that Celia didn't have it in her to refuse. So she accompanied her and they spent the whole day standing and watching their house from a distance, the howling wind biting at their skin, the cruel north-easterly weather freezing them both until they were chilled to the bone, unable to feel their fingers and toes. And they didn't catch even one single glimpse of Eva's parents. Not one.

They returned home in silence, Eva too distressed and frustrated to speak, Celia too embarrassed and upset to make her. It took Eva three weeks to recover from that particular incident. So, when Celia heard that she has returned there to seek them out, it sent a shiver down her spine. She hopes to God that Eva is going through one of her better moments, one of the times when she is upbeat and positive. At least then Celia may be able to talk to her, to sit her down and make her change her mind. If she isn't... well, Celia doesn't want to think about it. She will cross that particular bridge when she comes to it.

The hotel room is bathed in a welcoming, amber glow when

she gets back to it, and a bed has never looked more inviting. Despite feeling mildly sick about what tomorrow may bring, she strips off her clothes and all but falls onto the bed, wrapping herself up in the taut, crisp, white sheets, her body cocooned in the warmth and safety like a pupa waiting to be reborn.

10

GARETH

The fine drizzle turns into a downpour as Gareth dodges into a shop doorway, his head dipped down into his upturned collar. Such an awful fucking day and it doesn't look like it's about to get any better. Josh and Andy have texted him to tell him to pull his head out of his arse and stop mithering about the break-up with Eva, and his boss has just informed him that he needs him to work this weekend on the new project for Camden Council. And now it's pissing down. Marvellous.

He had to tell his friends about the split with Eva. They would all find out anyway once the tongues of the bored and the spiteful get to work; so, he figured it was better coming from him than from the gossip mongers who would only embellish on it, adding their own bits of made-up nonsense until it was so far removed from the truth, it would be laughable. Of course, none of them know the real story. And they never will. Not as long as he has a say in it. Eva has gone, sold up and left the area, which is good. Safer that way. Less chance of the real story leaking out and ruining his life. He knows where she has gone to, and why. He didn't even bother trying to talk her out of it. She isn't worth the effort. None of them are. They deserve one another.

He steps out of the doorway and braves the rain, dashing through the crowds of shoppers as it bounces off the pavements in huge splashes and runs into drains, bubbling and gushing, traversing its way across the concrete and down the metal slats of the drain cover at the edge of the road.

There was no way to tell in the beginning that Eva was anything but who she seemed to be. He met her at work. She was thinking of setting up her own business and came to him for software advice, asking all manner of weird and wonderful questions that he found endearing. The attraction was immediate. There was a spark, a chemical reaction that triggered all kinds of deep-seated emotions in him. He doesn't mind admitting he was captivated by her, from when she sashayed into his office, how her mouth moved as she spoke, the strange and erotic way she had of constantly flicking her long, auburn hair back over her shoulders without it appearing contrived or attention seeking. He's seen the way other girls do it – constantly batting their eyelashes and tipping their heads this way and that to attract the eyes of all the men in the room. But not Eva. Everything she did seemed effortless and natural. Now the thought of it sickens him. The very idea of her repulses him. He cannot believe he was ever attracted to her. What in God's name was he thinking?

Shoving his hands deep into his pockets, he makes his way over the road and heads into a newsagent, more for shelter than anything else. Pulling a note out of his pocket, Gareth grabs a magazine and a packet of mints and hands the cash over to the man behind the counter who looks as if he would sooner gouge his own eyes out than serve customers. With a scowl, he slaps the handful of change into Gareth's palm and looks beyond him to the next person in the queue, his eyes scanning the snaking line of people with complete contempt. Gareth feels like telling him to cheer up, that there are far worse ways to earn a living and that everyone has problems, including plenty of the folk currently lined up waiting to be served. Everyone has their issues that they have to deal with. But, of course, he says nothing. He doubts very much that this man has ever had to deal with what Gareth is going through.

The rain has eased up by the time he steps back outside. A small crack in the clouds has allowed the sun to peep through, flooding everything in a sudden burst of unexpected warmth. He raises his arm and stares at his watch. He might just message Andy and see if he fancies a drink before heading home; let him know he has actually managed to retract his head out of his arse and is well and truly back in the land of the living. Fuck Eva and her stupid, thoughtless antics and strange behaviour. It feels good to be single again. It feels even better to be away from her.

Stopping for a second, he slips his hand into his pocket to retrieve his phone and looks down at the screen. This new one still pisses him off every time he uses it. He had got used to his other one. It was easy, manageable and familiar. He doesn't want to wish that he hadn't smashed his other one: that would mean she had won. And he never, ever wants her to have the upper hand in his life. It's bad enough waking up every morning, remembering the whole sickening incident, raking over it again and again in his head, but he should at least be able to piece back the other bits of his life. He refuses to let her have everything. He will salvage what he can and do his best to move on. He swipes the screen and punches in a number.

It happens so quickly. He has no idea how he didn't see him. Such a stupid thing to do, stopping in the middle of the street. If he saw anybody do anything like that, he would think them selfish or mad, but by the time Gareth realises his mistake, the old guy is on the floor, a lump forming on his head where he banged it on the pavement as he fell. Gareth wants to kick himself. What an idiot.

Almost immediately, a crowd of people are at the man's side, covering him up with coats and stroking his hand, leaning in and telling him it'll be all right and to not move.

'We need an ambulance!' a voice hollers above the deep thrum of murmurs emanating from the gathering of helpers.

'I'm on it!' Gareth shouts, his fingers shaking as he punches 999 into his phone.

His heart hammers around his chest. What if the man's unconscious, or worse? How did Gareth not see him? More to the point, why the fuck did he stop in the middle of a busy street to call a friend? His mind was elsewhere. That was the reason. His mind was preoccupied trying to work out how to use his new phone, the one he had to get because of her relentless calls to him, the one she made him smash in a rage. This is all her fault. It's as if she will forever be in his head, clawing at his senses, dulling his reactions, slowly killing him day by fucking day. If this poor old guy is seriously injured, it will all be her fault. Fucking Eva Tweedie and her insidious, warped ways that permeate everything and interfere with every bloody thing that he does. Will it always be this way? Is this thing going to follow him around for the rest of his life?

Shaking his head, he speaks to the operator on the other end of the line, relating everything that happened. No point in denying it, is there? The entire street saw it all. It was an accident, obviously. It's not as if he pushed the old guy to the ground on purpose. He can't be blamed completely for what has just taken place. It was just a stupid, careless mistake on his part and now it's just another fucking thing to worry about.

It doesn't take too long for the ambulance to turn up. It

screeches to a halt beside him and the crowd parts as if by magic, allowing the medics access to the bleeding, elderly man on the floor.

'It was my fault,' Gareth stutters, feeling awkward and embarrassed by the whole thing. He may as well have taken the old man's head and smashed it against the tarmac. This is all Gareth's doing. It seems lately as if life is determined to rain blows down upon him. He clears his throat and thinks how a beer would be most welcome. He wishes he had taken a different route, gone straight to the pub rather than go past the station with its rush of commuters and packed pavements. He could be standing at the bar, ordering his first drink of the evening, but as it is, he is here, soaking wet and staring down at an injured person he has never met before who has an egg-sized lump on his head and who is about to be rushed off to hospital. And it's all because of Gareth. All of this is his fault. Shit. What a bastard of a day.

'Accidents happen,' the medic replies softly, touching Gareth on the arm with a gentleness that makes his head ache with guilt. God, he would kill for a pint and a cigarette.

'Do you want any details from me?' he asks, feeling both helpless and ridiculous.

'We could do with contact details for the patient if you have any?'

Gareth looks at her blankly, unsure how to respond. It hadn't crossed his mind they would want him to know anything about the old guy. He has no idea what to say. He mutters, feeling useless and deeply self-conscious.

'Erm, sorry. I don't know. You could maybe try looking in his pockets?'

She smiles at him, and once again her kindness catches him off guard, hitting him in his gut: an unexpected punch to his solar plexus. He's used to misery and shit being thrown his way and has forgotten how to deal with thoughtfulness and consideration.

'It's fine. We can take it from here. You did a good thing, you know, calling us. Many wouldn't.'

Gareth lets out a low whistle and shakes his head.

'It's true, I'm afraid,' she says sadly. 'You wouldn't believe the hassle and abuse we get on a daily basis. Some people can be so incredibly mean and selfish. When I retire, I plan on seeking them out and giving them a piece of my mind. It's not healthy keeping it in, is it? We all deserve a good blow out and a chance to put right all those wrongs people have put our way.' She smiles a wide, fresh smile and clicks her tongue. 'It helps restore the balance, you know? Like yin and yang. But in the meantime, I'm just going to get my head down, get on with my job and save more lives. I'll start by getting this poor man to the hospital to get that bump looked at.'

Gareth nods. He knows first hand how awful people can be but says nothing. Instead, he steps back from the general melee and lets the medical team do their thing.

One by one, the onlookers slowly disperse, spreading far and wide as they head off in different directions, eager to get home. Gareth follows a large crowd, unsure of where they are heading. The pub seemed inviting for a while back there but now his mind is elsewhere. He is distracted, his thoughts full of itches he can't scratch. He needs to do something to get rid of the edgy feeling that has suddenly settled on him. His mind crackles with pent-up energy, his limbs are twitchy with a slowly building rage. Every time he thinks he has it sorted, every time he feels calm and starts to develop a resigned acceptance to it all, it creeps back up on him, riling him, niggling at him, reminding him of what he has done. What *she* made him do.

Sweat prickles his scalp as he picks up his pace. A thought

plants itself in his head. He dismisses it. Madness, that's what it is: complete and utter madness. He should go home, forget about everything, or go to the pub, get as drunk as he can and sleep it off. And yet... He shakes his head. He has to stop thinking like this. He left all that behind him many years ago. He has a good life here. Or at least he *did* until that mad bitch stepped into it and turned everything upside down.

He continues walking, his mind a forced blank and with no idea of where he is going. He should stop and think about this. He needs to be on top form, to keep a clear head. He has work in the morning and a complex project to focus on. The sun beats down on him and water from the earlier downpour trickles down his back. He shivers and looks around, his brain unable to register his whereabouts. Perhaps he's having some sort of breakdown. How would he know? Do mentally ill people know they're mentally ill? Do they still have the capacity for self-analysis? His head aches with the thought of it all. The noise in the street seems to grow and booms in his brain. Birds squawk overhead, traffic growls past, spraying water everywhere. The inane chatter of people's voices roars in his ears, making him suddenly hot and uncomfortable. Where the hell are they all going to, anyway? All he wants is some time to think, just a few minutes of quiet. Is that too much to ask?

He finds himself being pushed along by the crowds of commuters, his feet struggling to gain purchase on the pavement. His head buzzes, his armpits are wet with sweat. There is so much noise, so much heat and humidity. Bringing his hand up to shield his eyes against the glare of the low sun, Gareth looks up and stops abruptly, letting out a small gasp. This isn't where he wants or needs to be. Somehow, he has let himself get dragged along with the rush of the crowd, be carried along by their momentum, and now he is here and he feels confused and tired and all he wants to do is sit down and gather his thoughts.

His legs feel weak as he staggers inside and looks around. The lights and the noise and general hubbub annoy him, pricking his senses, filling him with a slowly augmenting rage. He breathes hard, and almost turns around and leaves. Except he doesn't. He keeps on going, his feet directing him towards the place he always knew he would go to anyway. Circumstances made the decision on his behalf while his mind was elsewhere. Maybe this was always going to happen. Maybe this is just how things are meant to be.

Before he has time to change his mind, Gareth reaches into his pocket and pulls out his wallet then flips it open. He eyes up his credit cards, driving licence and a small wad of cash. It's all here; everything he will ever need to travel the length and breadth of the country. He can do it; he can put an end to it. All he needs to do is pull himself together and keep walking...

WHITBY

11

EVA

I take the long route there, away from the crowds. Sometimes the swarms of tourists provide a place to hide, giving me a sense of security. But not today. Today, I want to be alone, to allow myself some time to think, to be fully prepared for what I am about to do. The noise and commotion will only cloud my thinking and judgement, and I don't want that. I need to remain sharp, critical. I have to be in complete control when I get there, not some shambolic wreck who can hardly think straight. I want to be precise. I want to fire questions their way. I want to be wanted.

Turns out even the back streets are busy. I weave through the bodies and try to stay calm, to imagine I'm out for a saunter, just another tourist taking in the sights, and all the while, my stomach is churning and my skin is hot with anticipation and fear. No, not fear – more a sense of apprehension. It's not a feeling I've encountered before, which is to be expected, really. I've never been in this position before – about to confront my biological parents and take them to task over why they abandoned me, because that's what it amounts to: being left alone. Thrown to the wolves. You can dress it up any which way you like by saying I was cared for by foster parents, that I was nurtured and survived it. I'm here to tell the tale, aren't I? But at the end of the day, my parents – the ones who should have taken me back – chose to live their lives without me. I don't care what social workers felt was best for me; *I* know what was best for me, and right now, finding my parents is what I need to do. I have a missing life, a black void that needs to be filled and until that happens, I am incomplete, half a person, and I so desperately want to feel whole again.

I pause in front of an old auction house to catch my breath and still my thumping heart. Without realising it, my suppressed anger has risen to the surface. It's something I have had to work hard to control over the years, and most of the time I manage it pretty well, but I can hardly be blamed if it gets the better of me every now and again, can I? I've led a fairly decent life for the most part so I think I'm allowed the occasional slip up.

I stare in at a nearby coffee house, thinking how a cappuccino would be most welcome, then think better of it. More delaying strategies, that's all it is. I stare in at the smiling faces of the happy people inside, mingling with friends and family, discussing everyday things, chatting about inconsequential stuff. I am insanely jealous. I want to run in there and ask them if they fully appreciate what they have. I don't. Of course, I don't. Everyone would think me mad, which I am most definitely not. Unhappy, stiflingly unhappy at the hand life has dealt me, but definitely not mad. Instead, I continue walking, taking the narrow path and then up the steps that lead to West Cliff and the place where I would have grown up had I not been ripped from my family at such a tender and impressionable age. I could have spent my childhood here in this beautiful place, *if they had bothered to take me back.*

With a fire in my belly, I stride over the grass towards the row of Victorian buildings that stand tall and proud, and up to their house, my house. I stare up at the yellowing, lace curtains hanging from the windows and the peeling paint on the old wooden door, and swallow hard to still the hot breath that is now pumping out of me. I bring my fist up, knocking on the door so fiercely, my entire arm judders with the force of it, a wave of pain travelling upwards into my shoulder.

I wait, my breath continuing to come out in short, sharp bursts. No reply. I try again, this time rapping lightly with my knuckles, the soft trill of my knock echoing into the air around me. Still nothing. I lean in to listen for any sounds from the other side of the door but am met with a wall of silence. My stomach goes into a spasm. All the courage I had to summon up to come here and it's been in vain. Fuck!

Leaning against the door for support, I find myself fighting back tears. An empty house.

My planning and worrying has been for nothing. At long last, I find it within me to confront them and they're not even in.

I step away from the front door and stare up at the bedroom windows, scanning for any sign of movement. Anything at all. I just want some sort of indication that they are here, that they haven't moved house. I clench my fists and close my eyes for a second. They haven't moved. I know that for certain. I've tracked their movements for years, kept an eye on them online, checking the electoral roll to make sure they haven't moved house. I would know if they had suddenly upped and gone.

I would fucking well know!

A vibration buzzes against my chest, making me jump. I dread phone calls. They are rarely from people I want to speak to. I lean into my inside pocket and retrieve my phone, staring at the screen in the hope it might be Gareth. It isn't. Of course it isn't. Why on earth would he suddenly decide to contact me now? He hates me.

I stare at the name on there, then hit the decline button and slide the phone back into my pocket before knocking once more. I should return the call, I know that, but what I should do and what I *actually do* are two different things. Sometimes, we just have to go with our instincts, do what we feel is right for us at the time. And this is right.

Taking her call would spoil everything. I have no idea why she is so insistent on speaking to me, anyway. I'm an adult for God's sake: an able-bodied grown up who is perfectly capable of functioning on my own. It was all getting to be too much with her. Celia always did have a habit of overstepping the mark when it came to personal space and boundaries. And as for the way she has gone on over the years... well, everyone has their breaking point and I think that as far as Celia is concerned, mine snapped some time back. The thing with Celia is, she thinks she knows me and can see inside my head. She couldn't be more wrong.

I wipe away an unexpected tear, anger and disappointment bubbling up inside me, and turn away from the house. I head towards the grass verge on the opposite side of the road where there is a bench. I can sit there for a while, perhaps even wait to see if anybody goes in or comes out of the house. Maybe they saw me coming and hid? It wouldn't surprise me. Nothing they do will ever surprise or shock me.

Time has proven that they are every bit as hardened to the needs of others as your average, small-time criminal. So why do I want to meet up with them? Closure. That's all it is. I have a well of unanswered questions lurking deep inside me that refuse to go away. Believe me, I've tried to ignore them but despite my best intentions, they are still there. If anything, the urge for answers grows stronger by the day. I will get the information I urgently need, come hell or high water.

I start to make my way over to the vacant bench but am beaten to it by a busload of pensioners who plonk themselves down on it with their flasks of tea and chequered blankets which they sling over their laps for warmth while they take in the view. I have no option but to head back into town. I may even find a restaurant where I can sit and be alone to ruminate over what has happened and what I should do next.

The windy weather is behind me and propels me forward as I make the short trek back down the steps and around the winding path that leads into town. I pass rows of busy shops and arcades, my mind too full to even think about stopping or going inside.

She catches me unawares, the very sound of her voice sends a needle of dread down my spine as I hurry past her cabin, my eyes half closed against the bracing wind that is coming in from the sea.

'All right there, lovey? In a rush, are we?'

I stop and stare at her, unsure if she recognises me from my visit earlier. It feels like such a long time ago, not just a few hours. Her eyes have a glazed look to them and before I can even think about replying, her eyes are elsewhere, her gaze shifting to the mass of faces behind me. She scans the throng of tourists, hoping to land upon another vulnerable person, someone she can prey on. This is her livelihood. She isn't a friendly soul hoping to make chitchat with passers-by; she is a grasping, soulless predator who knows no other way to bring in money.

I pick up my pace, my heels clicking loudly on the pavement, and stop dead when I hear the voice behind me.

'Turn around and leave. It's bad that you're here. You should go.'

A sharp pain cuts its way up the base of my skull and over my left eye. I swallow and clear my throat. Just a child. That's all she is. A child who has seen more than she should have and is now mimicking the things she has witnessed. I should pity her, not fear her.

Suddenly enraged, I turn around and march up to the pair of

them, the older lady leaning against the door of her cabin as if she doesn't have a care in the world. This infuriates me all the more. I point my finger at the young girl who is staring at me intently, her hair an unruly mass of knots and curls.

'Why isn't she at school?' I bark, my voice reedy and accusatory.

The lady smiles and rolls her eyes as if I am some sort of imbecile. I don't look away from her. I am determined I will not let either of them get the better of me again.

'Looking after her for a friend, aren't I? Go on, Bella, show her. Show this lady your tummy.'

Without missing a beat, the child lifts her sweater up to reveal an abdomen full of angry-looking spots. I narrow my eyes and try to think of something positive to say, something that will help alleviate the uneasy, uncomfortable feeling that has settled over us.

'See. Chickenpox. Covered she is, aren't you, Bella? And her mummy has to go to work so she's staying with me while Mummy brings the pennies in. Work can't just stop 'cos kids get ill, you know.'

The child nods and gives the lady a huge smile. She is rewarded with a handful of boiled sweets which she munches on hungrily as if she hasn't eaten for a week.

I shake my head to show my disgust and shrug helplessly then turn away and hurry through the horde of sightseers before she can say anything else. I make a mental note to avoid walking past her hut in the future. I'm pretty certain she sees me as a figure of fun: somebody wet behind the ears that she can mock and manipulate each and every time I pass by her stupid little gypsy hut, with its awful, frilly curtains and piles of stinking blankets. Well, she can think again. I have more street cred and common sense in my little finger than she has in her entire, ageing body. I have put up with enough shit in my life to know when to turn my back on people who have a hidden agenda. And she definitely has a hidden agenda. She thinks I'll be forever calling in, asking for advice on my future. I'm not about to line her pockets because I'm feeling down on my luck. Not a chance.

I half run along the path, eating now the farthest thing from my mind. The restaurants are almost full anyway. I can stop at the shop on the way back, pick up a meal for one and microwave it. The thought of consuming yet more processed food makes me want to throw up, but I can't seem to summon the strength or enthusiasm to cook a meal just for me. It's a harsh reminder of my current relationship status. Just another gloomy reminder of how lonely I actually am.

I stop and stare up at the sky, trying to stem the overflow of tears that are about to spill out at any given moment. The setting sun gives off an easy, coppery glow and I enjoy basking in its warmth, if only for the briefest time. I should do this more often. There are so many sights and places of interest round here and I haven't seen any of them. My head has been so full of plans and worry and heartache that I've forgotten how to live.

I allow myself one small thought that once I'm reunited with my parents, we will take in the sights together. They will show me around the town, let me know where the best restaurants are, perhaps even give me an idea of where I should start applying for jobs. Everything will be fine. That's my dream. Everything will turn out okay. It has to. I have too much riding on it. I've given up everything to come here. Everything. The least they can do is be half decent human beings and accept me. I refuse to consider any other possibilities.

I head back to my flat. I'll come back first thing in the morning and try again. At some point, I will catch them in. At some point, we will all be reunited. And then the real fun will begin.

LONDON

12

GARETH

It's madness. He knows it for sure, but something keeps driving Gareth on. This isn't like him. Spontaneity isn't in his nature. Perhaps it was the medic's words. There was certainly something about them. It was the way she spoke about retribution and revenge that got to him. It stirred his soul and made him feel that the effort this will take will all be worth it in the end. He could have listened to his inner, rational voice and walked away, he could have kept on fighting the overwhelming feelings of sickness that washed over him every time he thought about Eva, but he didn't. For the first time ever, he went with his gut feelings and reacted in a way he never has before. For all of his life, he has tried to do the right thing, follow the rules, be the good person that none of his family ever were, but the time has come for change. The time has come for him to develop a backbone and face up to it. It involves him deeply – this secret. This information that was denied to him has now surfaced and almost wrecked his life and it's about time his family faced up to their mistakes. It's about time they admitted their guilt and apologised. He was going to stay away, to leave his mother to rot in her own little pocket of self-made misery, but why should he? What she did was unforgivable. He had a right to know. And if he had known then maybe none of this would have happened. Forewarned is forearmed, and he wasn't. He was ignorant and unwittingly stumbled into a complete mess that almost wrecked his life.

Gareth reaches into his pocket for some loose change and buys a coffee, wincing as he takes a gulp of the steaming hot liquid. It's going to be a long night. He'll need plenty more of them to keep him going: a constant stream of caffeine to keep him awake and alert, to stop his mind from drifting and straying from what it is he is about to do. He is on his way and has to face it head on.

Gareth sits forward and stares around, his eyes narrowed against the trail of hot steam that billows up from the rim of the cup as he takes another sip. Only a couple of other passengers are scattered around him, which is good. He expected it to be packed but as it is, he is sitting on his own in a half-empty carriage. No need to avert his gaze when his eyes inadvertently lock with somebody else's, no need to listen to one-sided telephone conversations, no need to fight for seats. All of these things are positives. And it's warm and dry, which is more than can be said for his clothes at this moment in time. He is still drenched from the earlier deluge.

Standing up, Gareth wriggles out of his coat and gives it a shake before folding it neatly and placing it in the overhead compartment. Sitting down, he rests his head back, thinking how unlike him this unplanned journey is. He is usually methodical, enjoying the familiarity of his daily routine, and yet this impulsive decision sends a frisson of excitement through him. He feels empowered by his actions. Even the fact that he won't be available for work in the morning doesn't faze him. He's good at his job. No, he's better than good. He's bloody brilliant at what he does and has never missed a day so far. They will have to manage without him. He'll ring in sick first thing in the morning. It will kill him, having to lie, but there are worse things in life and God knows he should know.

Despite what his friends and colleagues might think or say about him, despite what he has let them think over the years, he hasn't led the blessed existence they all believe he has. It's been a struggle. He has worked hard at leaving it all behind him, pretending he is somebody from a different background, somebody better. It helps him forget the past, all the bad stuff that happened. He has done his best to stay focused on his career and work hard. He has made a pretty good job at building up his reputation as somebody who really knows what he is doing. People ask for him specifically. They trust him. Having that sort of reputation hasn't come easily. He has had to put some real effort in, always going the extra mile, working longer hours, always with a ready smile, and never making mistakes.

And then Eva came along and fucked everything up.

Just when he thought his life was ticking along nicely and he had managed to pile all the nasty memories away, she saunters into his life and drags it all back out again, his seedy secrets and messy history so close to being revealed to the rest of the world, it made him sick to his stomach. All his sins on display. The thought of it repulses him. He likes being perceived as being squeaky clean. It makes him feel strong and energised. It makes him feel like somebody else. Somebody who didn't have his upbringing. Because the truth is, if he could alter the past, he would. He is ashamed of who he is, ashamed of what he was. He has had to work hard at leaving it all behind.

None of his friends know, and he would prefer it stay that way. That's why he's making this journey: to see it all for one last time before he turns his back on it and gets on with the rest of his life.

She'll be there. He just knows it. If she isn't... He shakes his head and stares out at the blur of landscape from the carriage window. She'll be there. It's the only place she can have gone to. She'll be there and when he finds her, he is going to tell her exactly what he thinks of her and her warped little games. He will rid himself of all his demons and return to London cleansed and pure, free from her filthy little clutches.

He rests his head back on the seat and half smiles. They all deserve one another. Shit attracts more shit. The thought of turning up unannounced gives him a warm glow. He tries to visualise their faces, the look of horror and surprise as they open the door to him. For once in his life, he will have the advantage, the balance of power tipped in his favour. He deserves it after all the crap they have given him. He has earned this small piece of happiness.

The landscape passes in a mesh of distorted colours as the train picks up speed. They leave the redbrick buildings of the capital far behind them and rush through the greenery of the surrounding countryside with its vast tracts of neatly hedged farmland and distant crumbling barns and farmhouses.

Gareth sighs, the knots in his locked muscles slowly softening and loosening as the feeling of propulsion lulls him into a state of relaxation. He shuts his eyes and sighs, then opens them again, a sensation so close to a meditative state washing over him that he feels sure he has been drugged. He smiles and takes another swig of his coffee before placing it carefully on the table in front of him. It's been a long time since he has felt this way. Being uptight and permanently on edge has been part of who he is for so many weeks that it feels good to let it all go, to relax and kick back and not give a shit.

He pulls his phone out, toying with the idea of sending a few pre-emptive messages, but thinks better of it. Surprise will be his calling card. It will give him a head start. And God knows, he will need it. He thinks back to the last contact he had and feels a weight of darkness descend. He shrugs it off. He refuses to feel weakened or miserable any more. They have no right to do this to him. He deserves better.

A hot beam of excitement travels through him at the thought of seeing the look of shock on their faces. The look of abject horror as he churns out a few home truths. This is better: thoughts that stoke his excitement, set his senses alight. He now has the ability to push the dark memories away. If there is one thing he has learnt from all the crap he endured as a child, it's how to remain positive in the face of adversity.

He thinks of his childhood home and the scowling faces of his parents. *He* won't be there, of course. Good. The thought of that old bastard rotting in his grave gives Gareth a warm glow of satisfaction. He runs his hands through his hair, feeling the bumps and small scars there, remembering the nightmares he endured, the terror he felt at the slightest squeak of a floorboard outside his bedroom door and how he would lie under the covers, sweating and shaking, fear and revulsion rippling over and through him.

He remembers one particular time – he can't have been more than nine or ten. The rain was lashing the windows, the howling wind battering at the frames, rattling them until he felt sure the glass would shatter into thousands of tiny pieces. He had lain in bed, listening to his parents arguing in the room next door, his head buzzing with fear, his stomach taut with sheer apprehension and dread, when his bedroom door had burst open, slamming into the wall with such a racket, he had wet himself, hot, sticky urine covering his legs and groin. Seeing the dark patch spread like a blossoming stain on the bed covers, his father had ripped a young, terrified Gareth from his bed and half carried, half dragged him downstairs, roaring at him that he was a filthy, stinking waste of space, before opening the kitchen door and throwing him out into the back yard. Gareth had stayed there for almost an hour in the darkness and the cold while his parents continued their drunken tirade inside and the weather continued its fierce onslaught outside, soaking his young skin through his flimsy pyjamas and freezing him to the bone.

When his mother finally came to collect him and bring him back inside, he was huddled down the side of the old coalhouse, his hair slick with rain, his body shaking violently as he struggled to stay warm in the plunging temperatures and raging wind that howled its way in from the North Sea. It took three days in bed, a prescription for a chest infection and a whole host of lies to teachers and social workers to get over that evening of hell: just one of many.

And then his mother wondered why he refused to attend the old bastard's funeral. If he could, Gareth would have had the old man carved into tiny pieces and had his remains fed to the seagulls. Even that would have been too good a send-off for him. Gareth hopes he is currently rotting in the fires of hell with Lucifer stoking the furnace beside him.

She had rung Gareth full of woe after it happened, howling down the phone about how lonely she was now she was on her own. Her life choice. She made the decision to stick with her husband all those years, regardless of how badly he behaved. And it was bad. No amount of lapsed time will ever erase the hurt that man caused or repair the damage done to others. A heart attack was too swift. If Gareth had had his way, he would have wished a long, lingering disease on his father, one that caused pain on a scale too distressing and agonising to register. Then Gareth would have visited, just to see the suffering on the old man's wizened, puckered face and he would have smiled as his father writhing in agony. Forgiveness, as far as his father's behaviour is concerned, isn't on his agenda, and never will be.

He takes another sip of his coffee and swallows it down along with any misgivings he feels at this visit. He's on his way now, no turning back. He'll find a half-decent B&B and stay there while he does what has to be done. His mother will try to insist he stays with her. Not a chance. Her complicity in his childhood hell is never far from Gareth's mind. She allowed it to take place, not even acknowledging his bruises or the trauma he suffered from the beatings he received. She received plenty of her own so should have had an inkling of how it would have affected him; how it affects him still. How it ruined his childhood. How it almost ruined his life. But instead, she did nothing. She let it all unfold: the pain and horror that took place in her home. She is as guilty as her husband. If anything, she is worse. She should have protected him, taken care of him, loved him. She did none of those things.

Gareth blinks back unwanted tears and shakes his head, glad of the almost-empty carriage.

She could have left that place. She could have given up the drink and found a new place, somewhere they could have had a new life, free from the fear of violence.

Instead, she chose to stay.

The stone-sized lump in his throat refuses to shift, no matter how loud he coughs or how often he swallows. It's here to stay, like the memories and the damage from his childhood that he carries about with him, concealed from everybody, hidden too deep for anybody to ever reach. Or so he thought.

He stuffs his hands in his pockets, turning to gaze out of the window at nothing in particular. All of a sudden, the generous swathes of greenery and rushing scenery have lost their appeal. No matter how often he tells himself it's all behind him, the cracks of his past always seem to have a habit of reappearing if he lets his mind wander or if he dwells on it for too long. The only way it stays firmly in place is if he doesn't think. Work has been his sanctuary for so long, personal thoughts have been pushed down to the deepest reaches of his mind, exactly where he likes them. Until Eva came along, that is. Stupid Eva, unearthing what should have stayed buried.

He slumps down in the seat, wishing he had bought a beer instead of coffee. It's going to be a long night with a change at York and finding somewhere to stay for the night before he finishes the last leg of his journey in the morning. Christ almighty, this trip had better be worth it.

By the time he gets to York city centre, he is exhausted. It's after midnight and while he was on the train, he managed to book a small, functional hotel not too far from the station. After grabbing a sandwich and a drink from a vending machine, he flags down a taxi, already dreaming of hot showers and a soft, warm bed to fall into.

'Spending a few days shopping, are you?'

Gareth stares into the narrow strip of mirror at the taxi driver's eyes as they pull out of the station and swing out onto the surprisingly busy road given the lateness of the hour.

'Business,' Gareth replies and turns to stare out of the window. He's too tired for conversation, too deep in thought and too downright fucking miserable to bother replying. All he wants is that hotel room, a soft bed and a spectacularly hot shower to rid him of the day's filth.

Turns out the reality of the room isn't quite as comfortable as his dream, but it has hot, running water and somewhere to lay his head for the night. The last thing that runs through his mind before sleep whisks him off to a place of peace is Eva: her face, her voice, her expression when he told her exactly what he thought of her that final evening. The evening that she eventually told him. That one hurt. He actually had deep feelings for her that he has never felt for anybody else. And then she went and ruined it with her words.

Turning over, the cheap mattress creaking under his weight, he silently thanks her for finally giving him the courage to do what he should have done all those years ago, for helping him to grasp the nettle and face the past. He allows himself a small smile before falling into a deep and welcome slumber.

13

CELIA

The dash for the train after oversleeping puts her on the wrong foot for the rest of the day. By the time Celia purchases her ticket and finds a seat, tiny crystals of perspiration sit at the base of her hairline and her armpits are damp. She slumps down opposite a businessman who glances her way with a certain amount of scorn before turning away and returning to his laptop, tip tapping away methodically, the noise a sudden source of irritation to her.

Her face reddens and her body heat continues to rise until she manages to wriggle out of her coat, glad of the cool breeze from the vent close to where she is seated. She lets out a long, drawn-out breath. The sooner she gets there, the better. There are times when she could quite easily throttle Eva. She has spent so long looking out for her, being happy for her through the good times, crying with her through the bad, that it feels as if he has spent her entire life looking out for her, guiding her through every single event. Will it ever end? She bites her lip, idly nibbles at a loose piece of skin and thinks probably not. Especially given the way Eva is. She rests her head back and closes her eyes, already drained despite how early it is. The way Eva is. Such a phrase.

Words that cover everything and mean nothing. Unless you know Eva. Then you would understand.

Celia twists herself into a more comfortable position and enjoys the chug of movement as the train sets off out of the station. It lulls her into a state of near sleep, the smooth pull of the engine having an immediate soporific effect on her weary body.

A long-since-forgotten memory forces itself into her sluggish thoughts. She and Eva as teenagers, Eva the younger of the two by six months. Celia had bragged about it for weeks: hitting the big thirteen before Eva did. It gave her a strange sense of satisfaction being the older one, knowing she entered this world half a year before Eva did. She had no idea why it gave her such a buzz but when your world was as small and difficult as theirs was back then, you feel the need to cling onto even the tiniest of victories.

Eva had been with Greta for quite a while by the time Celia arrived, terrified and unsure of the dynamics of the place she would now call home. She spent many a sleepless night wondering where she fitted into her new family, how she should behave, what the rules were, what their general routine was. Celia's biological family didn't have any kind of routine worth speaking of so finding out that Greta set the table for breakfast every morning, complete with a jug of fresh orange juice and plates piled high with hot, buttered toast and scrambled eggs, was like stepping through the gates of heaven with a one-way ticket. No screaming arguments, no rooting around through a sea of stinking, unwashed laundry to find clothes that weren't stained and didn't smell as if they had been dragged through ditch water, while her mother stumbled around the kitchen, bleary eyed and smelling like a brewery.

Going to live with Greta was the best thing that ever happened to Celia. She can honestly say with a great deal of conviction that Greta saved her. She gave her a new life and showed her how to live it. Had it not been for her foster mother, Celia feels sure she could have easily fallen through the cracks of an overstretched system and ended up going down the same route as her mother. She didn't, and for that she will always be eternally grateful to the foster parents who went above and beyond their remit – nurturing, guiding, always being there with their wise words and loving ways.

Eva, however, did her utmost to spoil and ruin everything Greta put her way, whether it was new clothes, a lovely, clean bedroom or the tiniest of gifts. Like the matching bracelets Greta and Tony had bought for Celia and Eva. Tony, Greta's husband and their foster father, the man who worked so many hours at the local garage, regardless of how cold it was or how tired he was, that they barely saw him.

Celia feels tears prick at her eyes. Even now, after all these years, it still hits her hard: the memory of that day. The day that Greta took both girls out shopping into town telling them that if they helped her carry the bags back, they would both receive a hot dog and a milkshake as a reward for their efforts. The promised snack never happened. They went into town but there was a different purpose to their visit. It transpired that Greta had bought them both a silver charm bracelet as a gift for being the children Greta and Tony could never have.

Celia rubs at her eyes. Beautiful, thoughtful Greta and lovely old Tony, always with a ready smile and a dry, witty comment that entertained her no end and played to her unsophisticated teenage sense of humour.

'You're part of our family now,' she had told them as they were led through a mysterious-looking alleyway. Damp ran in tiny snaking rivulets down the dark, brick wall and both girls had stared at one another in mild horror as they followed Greta through it and out into a small, paved courtyard where the sun lay in dappled patches on the ancient, cracked flagstones. A diminutive jewellers shop was wedged in the corner, surrounded by a huddle of artisan shops that boasted unique, handmade goods ranging from moccasins to loaves of bread.

Greta led them across the courtyard and into the crooked, old shop where she greeted the owner with her usual sincere gusto. He had smiled at her and acted as if she were royalty, treating the girls with extreme care, his manner genteel and considered at all times. Celia had never known such grandeur and kindness and had cried when she was presented with the most beautiful bracelet that contained twelve tiny charms. Eva had lowered her head and complained that the shop smelt old and musty and that she was thirsty and needed her lunch.

'One for every month of the year,' Greta had said in that sweet birdlike tone of hers that always filled Celia with exquisite joy every time she spoke. It was in sharp contrast to her mother's gravelly voice that was permanently edged with sarcasm and anger. Hearing her mother speak had always made Celia's skin crawl with terror. It was usually an insult accompanied by a blow from one of her hard, bony fists. After years of enduring such goings on, having a conversation with Greta was like being immersed in a warm bath. Their chats were conversational opera which Celia treasured and stored in the deepest corners of her mind.

Eva, on the other hand, had taken the tiny, velvet bag and shoved it deep into her pocket with a scowl, her face a mesh of angry lines and creases.

'I hate jewellery,' she had whined as they threaded their way through the crowds of shoppers. She had pouted and muttered all the way back home, and Celia had wanted to cry at how embarrassing and rude she was, but instead remained mute, too frightened to say anything for fear of upsetting Greta even further. Greta had tried to keep the atmosphere light by regaling them with anecdotes from her own childhood, like the time her younger brother had run away and the whole street had gone out looking for him, only for him to be found hiding up the chimney in the old parlour later that day. She had tonnes of such stories; Celia thrived on listening to them, closing her eyes and imagining every inch of Greta's childhood home with its old-fashioned lace curtains and chintzy fabrics. Eva once told Greta while she was in the middle of one of her stories, that she was a stupid old bat and that she should stop telling such awful lies, which was horribly ironic when Celia knew fine well the myriad of fabricated stories that Eva herself regularly came out with.

Only when they reached Greta's vehicle did it become obvious what Eva had actually done. As Greta had unlocked the door, Eva had brandished the empty bracelet in front of her, her eyes glittering with mischief and menace. All that was left was the tiny, silver chain, bereft of any adornments. The small, intricate shoe, the highly detailed seahorse, the tiny, ruby heart. All gone. She had ripped each and every one of the miniature charms off one by one and scattered them around the cobbled streets of York as they had walked back to the car park.

To this day, Celia can still recall the look of abject hurt on Greta's face as the slim chain dangled from Eva's pale fingers. It hung there, taunting her with its broken links and twisted pieces of metal. Celia had swallowed down a huge lump and rubbed at her eyes with trembling fists. Eva, on the other hand, had laughed.

And then there was the time Eva decided she didn't like the bed sheets and duvet cover that Greta had chosen. They were a powder-blue colour that matched the new curtains and rug that Greta had purchased only two weeks prior, and even as a naïve, thirteen-year-old Celia could see they were an expensive item, possibly even handmade, to finish off their recently decorated bedroom. They lasted less than a week. In a fit of pique, after one of Eva's rages, she had taken a pair of scissors to them and by the time Celia had managed to stop her, the expensive fabric was in a hundred ragged pieces at her feet, the bedroom looking like it had been attacked by a pack of rabid dogs.

Of course, Eva wasn't all bad. There were times when she appeared so fragile, her moods so low and dark that both Celia and Greta feared she would do something silly, something permanent. She made idle threats about it that settled over them all like a heavy veil. The weekly counselling sessions she attended did nothing to alleviate her moods. Sometimes Eva would cry for days, her body wracked with sobs until she was so weak, Greta would tuck her up in bed and hand feed her pieces of boiled egg and toast like a mother starling feeding its weak, helpless chick.

That was why they always forgave her. That's why Celia is here, in hot pursuit of her fragile friend. Eva was, and still is, simply too breakable to risk ostracising her, regardless of how erratic and difficult and downright hurtful her behaviour was. So they managed her. Together, Greta and Celia, and whenever he could, Tony, looked out for her, tried their level best to steer her along the right path, a path Celia was only too happy to walk. Eva did it with a little more trepidation, questioning their motives and guidance every step of the way, lashing out if the mood took her, often screaming that she just wanted to be left alone and that Greta and Tony weren't her parents and never would be and that her real parents would be coming to take her back any day. They all knew it wasn't true. To this day, Celia still cannot work out whether Eva actually believed it or if it was simply a form of self-preservation to stop herself from unravelling completely.

Celia recalls Greta once telling her that she had been Eva's twelfth foster parent. That number made her hair curl; just the thought of being shipped from house to house, from family to family, made Celia feel physically sick. Greta was Celia's second foster parent. Her first looked after her well but became too old to carry on with her job and she was sent to live with Greta. That's when she realised that compared to Eva, she was truly blessed. She also knew at that point that she would always look out for Eva, make sure she felt wanted and secure. Nobody should have to spend their life being moved from place to place. As a child, Celia never questioned why Eva moved around so much. Only as the years passed did it become apparent.

Still... twelve homes. She wondered if that was why Eva despised the bracelet so much, with its constant reminders hanging around her wrist: twelve charms. She often wonders if Greta realised the connection with the bracelet. Then again perhaps not, because there were days when it seemed that Eva despised pretty much everything and everybody. That's just how she was. There didn't seem to be any triggers or pattern to her behaviour. Eva was and always will be an enigma: her own worst enemy.

Celia keeps her eyes closed. She prefers it that way. There are days when her thoughts are too sharp to bear and she always fears that they will show in her face, that people will spot her weaknesses and see her for what she really is. Then other days, she lives her life like any other person and manages to forget it all. Funny, isn't it, how the past closes in on you the older you get, tapping away at your brain, never letting you forget where you really came from.

She spent the latter part of her teenage years in a blur of parties and studying and hardly thought about her predicament at all. It was later that it hit her: the enormity of what she had been through. The gaping hole she had managed to crawl out of without being sucked back into it. Eva was also her benchmark. Celia saw in her what she could have become and always did her best to raise her standards. Every time Eva had a meltdown, no matter how low Celia was feeling or how bad the nightmares were of the life she had had to endure with her mother, she always managed to up her game and forge on with her day.

Of course, she hadn't been moved from place to place like Eva had. What Eva craved was stability. What Eva really wanted was her parents back, whereas Celia was only too glad to be away from hers. She once read that children can survive many traumas and escape relatively unscathed as long as they feel loved. But what if they don't recognise what love actually is? What if, like Eva, they are so full of bitterness and hurt that they reject the love that comes their way? Will they spend the rest of their lives searching for it, never resting until the picture they have in their heads, of what constitutes love, is complete?

Celia opens her eyes, tired of ruminating over what goes on in Eva's complex brain. All the years Celia has known her and she is still no closer to working her out. Nearly twenty years of being an armchair psychologist and yet here she is, chasing Eva halfway across the country to make sure she is safe. All of those thoughts and guesses and suppositions haven't helped her one iota.

The man sitting across from Celia snaps his laptop closed and stands up. He hoists his jacket off the luggage rack overhead and roughly slings it over his shoulders. She feels an element of relief. He was a mighty presence and she is glad he is getting off at the next stop. She much prefers sitting alone, especially since she has nothing to read and will end up locking eyes with somebody every time she glances around the carriage.

He doesn't get off. In fact, the train shows no sign of even stopping. Instead, he wanders down the aisle and sits elsewhere, next to somebody she presumes is a colleague. She hears him converse with another man about meetings and being late and how bad the Wi-Fi is on the train and feels only relief that he is gone. She notices two young women, who are wedged into a row of seats further up, grab their many bags and quickly stand up before heading towards her, the table and extra room for their baggage too good to ignore.

'You don't mind, do you?' they ask in unison before plopping down in a heap before Celia even has a chance to answer.

She watches as they shuffle about, arranging and rearranging their many bags and layers of clothing, making enough noise and fuss for a hundred people until eventually they settle themselves with a loud sigh and a gauche, embarrassed giggle.

Celia studies their faces as they reach into their respective bags for magazines and earplugs. They look about seventeen or eighteen but these days, she finds it so hard to work out the ages of teenagers, with their sophisticated ways and confident mannerisms that they could be even younger.

'Excuse me,' one of them says with such a cut-glass accent it takes her completely by surprise, 'I was wondering if you knew whether or not there was anywhere on the train where we can buy something to eat?' Her eyes sparkle with youthfulness and vitality and her voice is in stark contrast to her alternative black clothing.

'I think there's a trolley coming round later,' Celia replies softly, rapidly warming to both of them. They smile a lot and seem to exude and an air of kindliness and affability that Celia finds endearing.

She releases a breath she hadn't realised she had been holding in and returns the broad grin that both girls are displaying as they each thank her and reach in their bags for purses that are almost as large as the bags they were retrieved from.

'You off anywhere nice, then?' one of them says to Celia as she grasps a handful of notes and shoves them deep into her jacket pocket, pushing the purse back in place.

'Me?' Celia says with a slight upturn in her voice she wishes had remained inside.

'A weekend away somewhere nice, is it?' the red-haired girl says as she finishes tucking her purse back in place and rearranging a mountain of items around it before fastening the bag and stuffing it down at her feet.

'Ah, well not quite,' Celia replies, desperately trying to think up a feasible lie that has a grain of truth in it somewhere. 'I'm off to Whitby to visit a friend.'

It's not that far removed from the truth. Eva wouldn't give two hoots about telling the largest of lies but it never sits comfortably with Celia. That's the difference between them. Although she would never want to take the higher moral ground, both Eva and Celia know that that's what it is that separates them: Eva's propensity for causing untold damage, whether it be with her lies or her thoughtless ways. Celia has witnessed it first-hand over the years, seen the trail of destruction her behaviour has caused and grimaced inwardly, hoping against hope that one day she would change.

'Really? That's amazing! That's where we're heading too, isn't it, Lizzie?'

Celia closes her eyes briefly and lets out a heavy sigh. The other girl nods animatedly, her black locks swaying about over her shoulders with such ease that, for a moment, Celia finds herself envious of them. Do these young women realise they have the world at their fingertips and that they have the ability to be anything they want to be? She hopes so. She desperately hopes they aren't bound by past memories and horrors that interject their thoughts on a daily basis. Everyone deserves to be happy. She also hopes they leave her alone when they get there. As nice as they are, she wants to be able to meet Eva and sort out this sorry mess without being trailed by two youngsters who, despite being friendly enough, would never be able to comprehend her motives or understand her past.

'You probably guessed that by our attire, no doubt,' Lizzie giggles as she sweeps her gloved hand across their many layers of bizarrely arranged clothing. The red-haired girl is wearing a Victorian style velvet bodice of the deepest crimson and a black net shawl. Lizzie is wearing a military looking jacket and black leather gloves that reach her elbows. Along each one is a row of highly polished chrome buttons that gleam in the sunlight as she waves her hand about to fluff up her mass of backcombed hair.

'It's the Goth Weekend,' the other girl says quietly as she detects the look of bewilderment on Celia's face. The penny drops as the girl says it. Of course. Celia should have realised. Held twice a year, Whitby is the place where Goths gather for the bi-annual music festival. The town is filled with all manner of people dressed in weird and wonderful clothing, many paying homage to Whitby's vampire connections and some even dressed as the man himself.

'Tyler's got a set of amazing fake vampire teeth, haven't you, Tyle?'

Tyler responds by pulling out a set of the largest whitest fangs Celia has ever seen. They positively gleam in the sunlight that streams through the carriage window as they rush past a white-painted station where a smear of people stand. The concrete platform is a dot in the distance as Celia admires the fangs, incongruous in the relative calm of the carriage.

'Pretty authentic looking,' Celia says, unable to hide her joy at their eagerness. She finds herself hoping they have a blast at the festival. They seem really nice, these two. They are genuine people and genuine folk these days are thin on the ground. Celia knows all about that.

'Yeah, pretty cool, eh?' Tyler smiles as she places the teeth back into her backpack. 'Got fake blood as well. Looks like the real deal but I don't want to open it here as I'm a right Clumsy Clara and it'll end up all over the place.'

Celia laughs at her words, at their happiness and the innocence of it all. No hatred, no emotional baggage, just two young people out to have a good time and live their lives. The worry that was pressing down on Celia before they arrived lifts and it feels good. She could do with some light-hearted banter to ease her worries and take her mind off what she is about to do. Because it won't be easy. Eva will make sure of that. There's always a small part of her that hopes she is wrong; always a small part of her that wants to see the best in her errant friend. But she is also a pragmatist and knows this task is going to be a tricky one and it will take all her powers of persuasion to make Eva see that she is chasing a wish and that wishes are surreal and slippery. They are ethereal creatures that can't be transformed into reality no matter how hard you try. She should know. And when the scenario that Eva has in her head fails to properly materialise, Celia knows all too well how she will react.

She shivers and bats the thought away. They will cross that particular bridge when they come to it.

'Where are you staying?' Lizzie asks and Celia feels her heartbeat falter ever so slightly. She hasn't booked anywhere and now with the news that Whitby is hosting a festival as well as its usual throng of tourists, she is concerned that everywhere will be full.

'With my friend,' Celia replies with far more gaiety and conviction than she feels. Why did she not book a room? Such a stupid oversight. To think she has come this far and not given it a second thought.

She pulls out her phone and checks the dozens of text messages she has sent, hoping against hope that Eva has replied. She hasn't. Of course she hasn't. As erratic as Eva's behaviour is, when she is feeling vindictive or morose or just downright angry, she is infuriatingly predictable in as much as she will ignore all pleas put her way for her to be rational and logical.

Celia drums her fingers on her thigh and tries to push it out of her mind. She wants to enjoy this journey, to chat to these girls and not become overwrought about what may or may not happen when she gets there. And anyway, she has quite a few changes of trains to make before Whitby. She may as well kick back and relax for a few hours. Easier said than done when you have no idea whether or not there will be a room available or where you are going to spend the night in a strange town.

She does her best to ignore the small, still voice in her head that is telling her to get off at York and go home, forget about Eva, that her own safety and wellbeing is more important than Eva's. She turns off to its echo as it rolls around her brain. She has to. The lure of her warm bed waiting for her at home will prove too much if she listens to it and she would then be in danger of stepping off, leaving Eva to her own devices and heading back home. And where would that leave poor Eva? Celia would never forgive herself for abandoning her friend, leaving her to fend for herself when she is quite obviously in a tricky situation, Eva's mind absent as she does more damage to herself, trailing after people who discarded her.

Celia shuts off to it all, focusing on the two young females opposite, listening to their laughter, reminding herself that once, she and Eva were like these two. Except, of course, they weren't. She wishes it were so, but it isn't. They were nothing like these two carefree creatures.

Celia clenches and unclenches her fists. Enough. She has had enough of this constant going round in circles, revisiting the past, attributing present thoughts to past actions and situations. It's a vicious circle, like being stuck in a never-ending loop of bitterness and blame. She has to focus on the here and now, appreciating the present rather than constantly looking to the past.

She spreads her hands on the table and smiles. 'So, girls. How about you enlighten me as to what it is that interests you? Apart from being a Goth, that it?'

They spend the remainder of the time chatting, browsing reading material – a pile of teenage magazines that amuses Celia no end – and swapping anecdotes about seeing ghosts. Turns out the girls are experts and Celia struggles to keep her face straight as they count how many they have seen between them on their weekly visits to the local graveyard.

Their idle chat keeps her busy and before she knows it, the announcement is made that they're about to arrive in York. Celia stands up awkwardly as the train pulls in and they all struggle along the narrow aisle, their bodies bumping together as they wrestle with bags and coats and backpacks.

'We're catching the later train so we might see you in Whitby!' Tyler calls as they both step onto the platform and haul their bags up onto their shoulders. Celia watches as they tromp away, a mass of wild hair and bustling fabric disappearing into the distance, swallowed up by the crowds of waiting passengers.

She smiles wistfully and stares up at the burgeoning clouds overhead. The weather has suddenly changed from a clear, spring day to windy and overcast as she steps off the train and heads for the board that will tell her when her next train is due.

Temptation grips her as she strides across the platform. She could so easily make her way to the exit and head for home. She doesn't. She does the right thing and checks the time. With only minutes to spare, she runs to the next platform and boards the train. She has spent her life doing the right thing, and at times like this, it irks her. She has no doubts whatsoever that Eva will be far from appreciative when she gets there and if things were the other way around, Eva would put herself and her own needs well before Celia and any needs she may have. But that's not how Celia operates. She is who she is, and Eva is who she is and nothing will alter that fact. People don't really change, do they? Eva can't help being selfish. It's just part of her intrinsic self. It's one of her less attractive traits and nothing Celia says or does will ever change that. All she can do is to stick close by her friend and limit any damage that occurs along the way.

The journey from York is short before another change at Middlesbrough and then on to Whitby, where the weather shifts again. She is greeted with a blast of sunshine and a soft, warm breeze as she steps off the train and looks around at the small, quaint station where a handful of people are waiting on the platform, their faces turned up to the blazing azure sky.

'Reckon we've broken the back of winter now, eh? Nice to see a bit o' sunshine for a change, int' it?'

Celia spins around to see an elderly man, small and sprightly with a pearl-white dog sitting obediently at his side. He is wearing a beige fedora and a smart, blue blazer and has a smile a mile wide.

'It certainly is,' Celia says softly, her bones crying out for the promised warmth. 'It's been a long time coming.'

The old man smiles back and pulls at his hat. Out of nowhere, a rush of air tugs her backwards. She feels herself being propelled into reverse as a figure pushes past her: a sturdy, solid frame of a young man whose face is creased in anger and obvious frustration. Celia stops and steadies her breathing, watching as the tall figure turns to her and mouths a hurried apology before twisting back around and heading out of the station.

'You all right there, love?'

Celia blinks hard and stares at the man next to her, nodding at him that she is still in one piece before turning her surprised gaze to the rapidly disappearing individual who is already making his way out of the exit. Why does she feel as if she knows him? It was only a fleeting glance but in that few seconds, his features and tall, lumbering gait struck a chord with her, as if they have met somewhere before.

'Are you sure you don't need to sit down? You look a bit pale there, my dear.'

The small dog yaps and despite the man's kind words, all Celia can think about is getting away and following the strange character who almost knocked her off her feet and sent her tumbling onto the cold concrete.

'Honestly, I'm fine,' she says smiling, her jaw tight as she brushes herself down. Nothing damaged except her pride.

'If you're sure,' the old man says cautiously, one of his silver, bushy eyebrows hoisted up in mild consternation.

'Thank you for your concern. It's nice to know some people care.' She keeps her irritation under wraps. She's finally here, and apart from being almost knocked to the ground, it's been a fairly uneventful trip, enjoyable even, but worry is niggling at her and she just wants to find somewhere to stay. Her inner voice is telling her to move from here and find a room for the night before everywhere gets booked up. Finding a warm bed comes before everything, even slotting in ahead of finding Eva.

'Ah, here's my train,' the man declares as he bends down and scoops the little dog up under his arm and tucks it in, leaving a furry, bright-eyed face sticking out from under his jacket. It would be a comical sight were it not for the fact that she is under pressure to get going and make her way into town. Her skin prickles with exasperation and impatience.

'Well, I'll be off then. Nice to meet you, my dear,' he says as he holds his free hand out for her to shake. It takes a few seconds to register, for her limbs to work as they should. She reciprocates, his palm cool and dry against her hot, sticky skin.

The old man saunters away, his arthritic movements creaky and laboured, and already Celia's mind is elsewhere as he boards the train and vanishes out of sight.

Clinging onto her bag with hot hands, she makes her way outside, shielding her eyes against the glare of the sun. She scurries through the crowds, her eyes darting everywhere, suspicion eating at her.

She heads past the tacky shops and noisy amusement arcades where children congregate with candyfloss and ice creams, and up past the RNLI building. She remembers from her last visit that there are plenty of B&Bs up there. One of them is bound to have a *vacancies* sign in the window. And if they don't... She quashes the thought, refusing to even entertain the idea. No matter what, she will find a place to stay. Turning round and going back home isn't an option. Not when she has come this far.

Grabbing a coffee from the kiosk, Celia all but runs up the nearby steps that lead up to West Cliff. A group of Japanese visitors is standing next to a bronze statue and listening to a tour guide tell them all about the seafaring exploits of Captain Cook when she gets to the top. She passes through them, sipping at her coffee, her chest tight as she gulps down air and tries to catch her breath.

The sight of a large, cream-coloured building over the road makes her heart glad. A hotel. She swigs more coffee down, the instant hit of caffeine adding more potency to her already fluttering heart. The place is huge. It's bound to have a room free, even if it's a tiny single stuck at the back of the building, overlooking the rubbish bins. She really doesn't care. As long as it's warm and dry and has a bed.

Draining the remainder from the plastic cup, Celia throws the empty carton in the bin and strides over the road towards the reception area, a determined fire building in her belly. The sight of the haughty-looking woman behind the main desk doesn't stop her as she drops her bag on the floor and places her hands on the marble top just centimetres away from the receptionist, who quickly slides her fingers away like a wild animal retracting its claws.

'A room, please,' Celia says with as much authority as she can. 'I need a room for the night.'

14

EVA

I wake with a clear head, which is both a bonus and a novelty. I honestly can't remember the last time I went to bed without a drop of alcohol passing my lips, certainly not since I moved here, anyway. Last night was a turning point for me; getting into bed and falling into a sleep without the aid of wine and gin to help take the edge off it all, and then waking up without a mammoth headache and a tongue that feels as if it's been coated with ground glass.

I roll over and enjoy the sensation of the cool, clean sheets beneath my skin. Everything feels so much lighter: my body, my mind. Even the air in the room feels fresher and less oppressive.

In my peripheral vision, a small beam of light catches my attention. I lie for a while ignoring it until eventually the wink of red crawls under my skin, irritating me as it drags me further in a state of wakefulness.

I reach out and grab at my phone, rubbing at my eyes with my free hand to clear the morning coat of mist that clouds my view. A stream of missed calls and messages greet me, none of them from him. Of course, they're not. Disappointment grips me. They are from her. Each and every one of them. One after another after another. My stomach goes into an involuntary spasm. I had hoped she would have given up by now, got the message and left me alone, but it would appear that Celia is more determined than ever. She has never changed. Still hell-bent on trying to rekindle our childhood friendship, not fully comprehending that we have both moved on with our lives.

A small stab of anxiety pulses through me. I sit up in bed and stare at my phone. I could always block her but then it would probably make things worse. There is no telling how she would react to such a drastic move, and history tells me that whatever her reaction is, it most certainly would not be pleasant.

I fling my phone to one side and leap out of bed, determined I will not allow her the pleasure of ruining my day or any of my plans. She has no right to do this, to try to interfere and control my life, but then with everything that happened in the past, I guess I should have expected it, really. I should have cut all ties with her a long time ago but instead I took her calls, kept her up to speed with what was going on in my life, kept her sweet, and this is where it has got me.

She plagues me at least ten times a day with repeated calls and messages to get in touch with her, to let her know how and where I am and what I am up to, and whether or not I will be visiting her anytime soon, and it is draining. As if my move here and my attempts to find my parents isn't exhausting and stressful enough, I've also got Celia on my back, like a monkey clinging on for dear life. Shaking her off isn't proving easy. I need to find a better way. I just haven't quite worked out yet what that way is.

I know that we spent our teenage years together under the same roof but that's where our similarities end. Celia and I are nothing alike. In fact, we are poles apart, completely different, despite what she would have people think, despite what *she* thinks. There were so many times where bad things happened – terrible things – and I no longer want to remember those times. We have all moved on, or at least I have. Celia, it would appear, is desperate to hang onto the past, using it as a way of keeping us together when if anything, it should be the perfect reason why we should be apart.

I step into the shower and let it pummel my back. It feels good to be ever so slightly punished by the heat and ferocity of the water as it rains down on my skin.

* * *

By the time I am dressed, I have managed to push all thoughts of Celia out of my head. She isn't part of my plan and never will be. She is an irritant: no more, no less.

Breakfast consists of a toasted bagel and coffee, the healthiest I have eaten in a long while. I'm usually too hungover to face anything other than a sip of black coffee most mornings, but today, I enjoy the tranquillity of sitting in silence and eating. It's really quite therapeutic, giving me time to organise my thoughts and get my brain into gear. I'm used to stumbling into the day, blurry eyed and nauseous. This is progress, nibbling on buttered bagels and drinking a coffee that doesn't look as if you can stand your spoon up in it.

I finish eating and clear the pots away, keen to get outside and on the move. I want to get to their house before they have a chance to go off and do whatever it is they do most days. I have to catch them in or I think I might just go mad with the frustration of it all. At long last, I have a clear head and a sense of purpose, so much so, I feel as if electricity is running through my veins. I slept well, too. No nightmares, no paralysis, just a restful evening, which is why I am so full of energy this morning. I pass the hall mirror on my way out and give my hair one last ruffle, putting a few stray hairs back into place, then smile at my reflection. Today is going to be a good day.

The air is crisp and clear and the sky a wide stretch of blue. I allow myself a small smile. It feels good to be alive. I inhale deeply and make my way towards West Cliff through the back streets. There is no way I'm going to go past that hut again and get drawn into any sort of drama with the gypsy woman and that peculiar child. I pick up my pace, the click of my heels echoing through the empty street. I love the sound it makes as my feet hit the cobbles, relishing how quiet it is here, away from the harbour where the crowds all flock. Somewhere above me, a gull caws loudly and the smell of the sea air fills my nostrils. A thin smoke trail from a distant plane snakes its way overhead, cutting the blue expanse of sky in two. Everything is perfect.

And then I look up and my insides turn to liquid. I stop and half stagger into a nearby doorway, clinging onto a wrought-iron railing to keep me upright, my breath coming out in a ragged, staccato fashion. My head spins and I have to take one long, deep breath to stop myself from passing out.

This can't be happening. It just can't.

'You okay there, love?'

I turn to see a small gang of people behind me. My heart beats out an uncomfortable rhythm against my ribcage, tapping away like a heavy pendulum trapped in my chest as I stare at them. They are all dressed in black overcoats and top hats, one of them sporting a veil that hangs in front of her heavily made-up face. The man in front is staring at me with a perplexed expression. He is wearing the largest boots I have ever seen and his black, leather overcoat almost touches the floor. His hand is reaching out towards me.

I want to speak, to tell them I'm fine, but the words won't

come. They stick in my throat. My gullet is coated with sand, my fear making it impossible for me to say anything. Instead, I nod and wait patiently until my voice finally comes. When it does, it's deep and rasping as if I've spent the entire morning sucking on unfiltered cigarettes.

'I'm fine, thank you,' I mutter quietly, feeling anything but fine. 'Just a bit of a dizzy spell. I get them all the time. Low blood pressure.'

I say the first thing that comes into my mind. I do actually have low blood pressure and suffered dizzy spells many years back but that isn't what this is. Far from it. I wish it were.

'You sure you're okay?' He looks concerned and the rest of his gang are murmuring behind him, probably discussing how sickly I look and whether or not they should call an ambulance. Mild panic crowds my mind. I have to pull myself together before one of them turns into a good Samaritan and calls the emergency services. I can't let that happen. I have to start acting normally.

'Absolutely,' I say with a weak smile, 'feeling better already.' I rub my hands together briskly and try to relax, my insides a swirling mass of liquid. 'I just needed a minute to pull myself round.'

I try to straighten my stance but feel as if I am sinking in deep water, my body weighed down, the world around me distorted and blurry.

'As long as you're feeling better,' he says cautiously, looking me up and down as if I'm a fragile flower that might wilt and die at any given moment. My face grows hot under his scrutiny and my armpits prickle with sweat.

After what feels like an age, they turn and leave, their long, black coats and huge hats in sharp contrast against the bright, blue sky and bouncing horizon, a soft, wavering line in the distance. I stare at it, trying to use it as a focal point to pull myself round.

Only when they disappear around the corner do I make my move. My legs are still weak with shock, my innards still churning, but it won't stop me. I won't let it. I need to catch up. I have no idea whether or not I'll see him now but I have a pretty good idea of where he was headed. I have to get there before him. I have to stop him. I cannot even believe that he is here at all. It never occurred to me that he would make this visit and yet when I think about it, it's the obvious thing for him to do.

With my chest so tight it feels as if it's about to burst open, I break into a run and head towards the top of the street where I turn sharp left and bear towards North Terrace. I stop to catch my breath and stare into the distance, trying to focus properly, the glare of the sun causing me to squint and turn away.

I continue on. I've come too far to stop. This isn't how I planned it but if I don't go through with it now, I fear I never will. I have things that need to be said, questions that need to be asked. So many years of unspoken words brewing up inside me, I am in danger of it boiling over and spewing out uncontrolled; a cauldron of hate and fear and loneliness running free and I don't want that. I have worked too hard to make sure this whole thing goes the way I want it to. There is no way I am about to let it all slip away.

I pick up my pace once more and run as fast as I can before I stop, pain coursing through me, thousands of needles stabbing at my ribcage. Years of fast food and limited exercise have taken their toll. In no time at all, I am doubled over and breathless. I bring my hand up to shield my eyes from the sun and let out a small gasp. He is there, just yards ahead of me, and he is staring straight at me, his face filled with horror and rage.

Gareth.

My heart batters wildly as he turns and walks towards me. Pure terror creeps its way up my throat, choking me with its intensity. I have never seen him look so angry before. His features are distorted and his face is blood red as he runs towards me, his arms pumping at his sides, his hands formed into tight, hard fists that look capable of just about anything, including damaging me. I don't know this person; I don't recognise any of this anger. This is not the Gareth I remember, the gentle, carefree soul who held me in his arms; this is a man with a charred soul who will obviously do anything to get back at me. Anything.

Without a second thought, I turn and run as fast as I can. Unfit or not, the look on Gareth's face is enough to keep me going, to force me back to where I came from, through the side streets where hopefully I can lose him and stay safe. It doesn't work. I don't need to look behind me to see him gaining on me; I can hear his footsteps hard against the concrete, moving faster and faster. I visualise his face – that solid, handsome expression bent into something ugly by my deception, by what I did to him.

We weave through the back streets, my feet aching, my limbs burning. I don't slow down. I run onto Wellington Terrace and cut through Mount Square. I soon realise my mistake. It's a narrow alley and is completely isolated. He could do anything to me here and nobody would see a thing. With a small shriek, I tear my sweater off and throw it behind me. Perspiration courses down my back but without an added layer of clothing making me hot and uncomfortable, I feel more capable of running.

'Stop!'

Gareth's voice echoes behind me, bouncing off the walls, ricocheting around the confined space we are in. I ignore him. I cannot listen to anything he says now. He means me harm; I can just tell. I will not be persuaded by his charms or his soothing voice. I need to get back home before he catches me and something happens that we both regret.

I run even faster, flames licking up through my calves and into my thighs, continuing through my torso and punching into my chest, hot and vicious like churning, swirling lava. No time to stop. I have to keep going. I need to get to the bridge in order to get home. A thought comes to me in a great, sickening swell. What if the bridge has been raised to let a boat through? What then? How in God's name will I get home? There is no other way over the river on foot. Not unless I fancy making the trek to the main road which is over a mile away, and then I would have to walk back up into town, by which time I would be exhausted and Gareth would very probably have his big, strong hands wrapped around my neck. Despite the heat billowing out from my clothes and burning torso, I shiver at the thought of it. Were it not for the fact that it is happening to me, this would be rather droll – racing through the town, surrounded by tourists and Goths, and being followed by a man who I am certain wants to kill me. It isn't funny, however. This is deadly serious, and I have caused it.

All of this is my fault.

I barrel out of the alleyway and turn left and then sharp right. He is still behind me. I have no idea if he is getting any closer and am too terrified and exhausted to look. I just need to keep going. Drawing on reserves of strength I didn't realise I possessed, I run down Cliff Street towards Flowergate. It will be wider there with more people. I can immerse myself in the swarms of tourists. There is no way he can continue chasing me once we reach that part of town. There will be too much going on, too much noise and movement. A chase through such a busy area is unthinkable.

I hear his footsteps behind and feel my blood freeze as he roars at me once more.

'Eva!'

I don't slow down. His voice is losing its impetus. He is getting tired. The anger is still there, however, and I can't face his wrath. I no longer recognise who he is. I have done so much damage to him, instilled him with so much hatred towards me, that it terrifies me. I'm not surprised, really. There are days when I terrify myself with what I have done. Too late to change anything now. I did it and wish every single day that I hadn't, but I can't turn back time, can I? What's done is done and cannot be undone.

The road seems to go on for miles, every bone and muscle in my body screaming out in pain and threatening to seize up at any second. I pray for my own skin and blood to not let me down. Just this once – please keep me safe and let me get home in one piece.

'Stop!'

I don't, even though his voice is softer now. It's more of a beckoning than a command. Gareth is a charmer and will use all his powers of persuasion to make me turn around and face him. It's not going to happen. Instead, I move even faster, my muscles locked into position.

Only when I near the end of the tiny road do I slow down. There are people out there. I can see them through the thin gap at the end of the terrace. They will hide me, keep me safe. I will melt into them and disappear.

With as much delicacy as I can muster, I slow right down and turn into the wider road, my legs glad of the rest, my lungs still burning from the exertion. It's packed with people who will protect me. Even Gareth with his simmering hatred wouldn't risk doing anything rash out here. Or at least I hope not.

I turn left and slip through a gathering of tourists who are listening intently to a tour guide, nodding gleefully at the tales of the shipwrecks and smugglers and ne'er do wells that frequented the place many moons ago. If I can just keep on going, keep up a brisk pace that doesn't draw any attention to my plight, then I feel hopeful that I might just make it home safely.

Daring to glance behind me, I can see Gareth's head bobbing through the crowds, his tousled fringe flopping about in front of his eyes. His height makes him easy to spot. I watch as he runs his hand through his dark hair, dragging it back to push it into place. He stops, narrows his eyes and stares at me. I go cold. He is a good fifty feet away. Far enough for me to hide but close enough to make me frightened. I need to keep going. I have to lose him. I do not want him knowing where I live.

We emerge onto the main road next to the harbour and I almost weep as I see the bridge directly ahead of me. My apartment is so close, I can almost see it. So close, so very, very close.

I lean my body forward and gently push past the people standing, leaning on the railings and staring over at the water below. Got to keep moving. I have to keep moving. Every step I take gets me closer to home and that's where I want to be. That's where I will feel safe.

I grit my teeth and almost cry out loud for people to move, to get out of my way. I feel as if I'm pushing against the tide. Out of nowhere, a group of teenagers decked out in garish Goth attire steps out in front of me, almost knocking me to the floor.

'Sorry, missus!' one of them shouts, a streak of genuine remorse in his voice as he holds out his hand to steady me.

'I'm okay,' I say, the exasperation in my tone difficult to conceal. I pull away from them and see the shocked expressions on their faces as I gallop off, leaving them standing there in a whispering huddle. No time for social graces. Every second wasted puts Gareth a second closer to me, putting me in danger.

I turn up Church Street, my pace hindered by the cobbles underfoot. Damn. But then if I'm struggling to run, so is he. We'll be disadvantaged together. Except I know this street and I know the side alley that conceals my door. If I can vanish into it without him seeing me, he will continue straight ahead and end up wondering where I went. I feel flushed with excitement at having a slight lead over him.

With heavy legs, I forge on, the base of my back screaming at me to stop, my calves threatening to go into a spasm at any moment. Nearly there. Just a few more steps and I can do it.

It all happens before my brain has time to register what is going on. At the last minute, my exhausted body folds in on itself. Whether I slip on a loose stone or my legs simply give up on me, I don't know, but before I can stop it, I am down on the floor surrounded by a gaggle of people who are hovering over me. Their words are muffled by the screaming in my head as I look up to see Gareth behind them, waiting, smiling. My stomach leaps up and down, and for a second, I fear I might vomit. I wipe beads of sweat away from my brow and feel a pair of strong arms being placed under mine. Slowly, I am hoisted to my feet by two burly looking men who I guess are in their sixties. I'm not sure whether or not I feel terrified or elated by their presence. I mumble my thanks and assure them that nothing is broken. I find myself hoping that they hang around until I get to my turn off into the alleyway. I feel more protected with them here. They don't. Instead, they stroll off away from me and suddenly I feel very exposed. I can't bring myself to look again but feel sure that Gareth is so close, we could reach out and touch one another.

My movements are awkward and I feel as if I am submerged underwater as I walk home. My legs tremble and buckle under me and it seems to take forever to move the smallest of distances. I just know that somewhere behind me, Gareth is watching. He may even be directly behind me. I don't turn to see. I just keep hobbling along, weak with fear and self-pity. A thin trickle of blood runs down my trouser leg, the scarlet line a vivid reminder of my clumsiness. I've lost. Gareth is here and he is following me. The terrible mistake I made is about to crack right open, here outside my front door. The revenge he wants is here for the taking.

I swing round, ready to meet with his icy stare. It doesn't happen. Instead, I am met with an almost-empty street. A pulse thrums in my neck as my eyes dart about all around me. There is nothing. He has gone.

My already-weakened legs turn to jelly. I hang onto a nearby wall for balance and stagger to the exit of the alleyway that leads to my door. Ignoring the concerned and puzzled glances from a handful of pensioners that are making their way up the street, I rummage in my pocket for my keys, gripping them tightly to avoid having to bend down if I drop them. My hands are shaking violently and I am sure that if I were to bend over, I would never get back up again. I have never felt so tired.

I slot the key into the lock and turn it slowly, relishing the sensation of the blast of warmth that greets me as I push the door open and step inside. For a second, I am convinced somebody is behind me. Sucking in my breath, I crane my neck, my spine clicking with every infinitesimal movement. There is nobody. I quickly lock the door, shake my head and laugh so loudly, it echoes around the empty flat. It's a shrieking, hysterical giggle that turns into hot, uncontrollable tears. They pour down my face, dripping onto the floor in tiny, dark orbs.

I give the door a firm tug to make sure it's locked then gently pull myself upstairs using the handrail. I feel a hundred years old by the time I get to the top. Blood is smeared on my beige jeans, covering the front of my left leg, and I am beyond exhausted. I catch sight of my reflection in the mirror and what I see is a far cry from the well-groomed individual I was when I left the flat this morning. My hair hangs in rats' tails and sweat glistens on my face. A streak of oily, black mascara is running down under my right eye and to top it all, my nose is running, a stream of snot trailing down over my top lip. I am so hideous, I even scare myself.

Staggering over to the sofa, I make to slump down on it then think of the stain my bloody leg will leave on the fabric and opt for a sturdy dining chair instead.

Part of me cannot believe what has just happened. The whole thing was ludicrous, farcical even, and yet another part of me thinks that I should have expected it. If I had thought it through properly and not been so impulsive, I should have known that at some point, Gareth would make his way here. Bumping into him was unfortunate yet inevitable.

I bite hard on my lip to stop it trembling. I'm home now, no more tears are needed and yet they are hard to stop. They continue to roll, like a dam that has been building for a long time and has burst with such ferocity, it is almost impossible to hold back.

I rub at my face and place the heel of my hands over my eyes, pressing down firmly until I eventually regain some sort of control over the incessant weeping. I feel like a small child desperate for comfort from its mother.

Standing up, I decide to run a bath to clean my leg. I also need to put my jeans in to soak before the stain sets in as a permanent fixture on the fabric.

I lean down to pull them off then stop and walk towards the window. It's just as I'm about to close the blinds that it happens. A tiny flicker in the distance, the smallest of movements out there on the street, but I see it. My pulse races once more as I watch the dark-haired figure step out of the doorway opposite and look up at me. And there he is – Gareth – staring, his chiselled features set like stone, his eyes piercing through to my very soul.

I let out a small shriek and my hand flies up to my mouth as I watch his expression change to mild amusement.

He finds this funny?

I close my eyes and when I open them again, he has turned his back and is strolling down the street, his hands slung deep into his pockets as if he doesn't have a care in the world.

I lean against the wall and slide down onto the floor in an ungainly heap, my legs, hands, even my face shaking in fear. My skin feels slack and fragile, so loose it could melt away from my bones at any time. I hug my knees to stop the vibrating, my teeth chattering rhythmically as I rest my chin on my kneecaps.

I stay in that position for so long, my entire lower half goes numb.

Gareth.

He is all I can think about as I drag myself up and half walk, half crawl towards the bathroom. I no longer care about leaving bloodstains everywhere. There are worse things in life. Like Gareth and his untethered hatred.

Another sob rises and erupts out of me in a child-like hiccough. I try to stop it, but once it takes hold of me, there is no stopping it. I tried so hard to lose him, to wind my way through the backstreets, to disappear into the crowds, but it didn't happen. I lost my cool, staggered and fell, and that fall will cost me dearly because Gareth is here, in town, still furious, still ready to go to any lengths to get to me.

And now he knows where I live.

15

GARETH

He thought it was all over before it had even begun after that collision on the platform. He genuinely thought it was her – Eva. It was the long, red hair that fooled him: more than just the hair, actually. She had the same slim build, the same mannerisms. He saw her from a distance as he got off the train and it was only as he approached her that it became apparent it was somebody else and not Eva at all. It was too late at that point. He was already on the move, his body angled towards her like a hunter ready to trap its prey. It was all he had thought about on the journey there: meeting Eva and the look on her face when she realised he was in town. He wants to see that raw fear in her eyes, to see her tremble as he closes in on her. He wants her to feel the shame he now feels every day.

He should have known that it was somebody else, and with hindsight, he's pleased it was. What would he have done or said right there in the train station in full view of all the passengers? He had no plan, no real idea of how he was going to handle the situation, so instead he charged past her, mildly embarrassed by his mistake, and kept on going until he was out on the pavement where he slowed down and tried to regain some sort of semblance of normality, straightening his jacket and slowing his pace to a leisurely walk.

He had looked around the seafront once he was in the light, and it came as no surprise that nothing had changed since he had left. Why would it? Whitby has stayed the same for hundreds of years so it's not likely to alter that much in his absence. Apart from a smattering of shops that have sprung up, everything was pretty much as it was when he left well over a decade ago. Still as many tourists cluttering up the place. He had stared at the many Goths touring about the area in their weird get ups with their pale faces. He and his mates had found them entertaining as kids and followed them around town asking them all manner of daft questions, nearly all of which involved having sex with vampires. Had they ever done it with Dracula? What was it like to French kiss somebody who had elephant tusks as teeth? Stupid, childish, schoolboy stuff that never failed to entertain their unsophisticated minds and feed their insatiable curiosity about sex.

He had let his mind wander over old memories as he made his way through town towards his parents' house. After he left town in his late teens, he made the decision to cut all contact with everybody from his past and start life afresh in the big smoke. He didn't want to be remembered as the poor kid from the cursed family; the one who wore the ragged, second-hand clothes, the one whose father got into fights every weekend in the local pub, the one who spent his childhood avoiding the blows and punches that came his way almost every single day of his life. Who would want to spend the rest of their days saddled with such stories and memories? Anybody in their right mind would want to escape and start again, wouldn't they? Which is exactly what he did. He was lucky that he had a decent brain and a bit of ambition. It stood him in good stead, gave him something with which to build firm foundations for a more-than-decent career in the world of IT.

And now he has ended back up here, in the place he vowed he would never return to.

He couldn't quite believe it when he saw her in town. Of all the people to see, why her? That's when he snapped. It had all came rushing back to him – that argument, that night at her flat. That hideous fucking disclosure...

He had been blinded by fury, blood filling his head, stars popping behind his eyes. She had been behind him and something had made him turn around and there she was, looking as radiant as ever, her long, auburn hair bouncing around in the breeze. He had to admit, she looked amazing and had needed to remind himself how furious he was with her.

It didn't take him long to shake off those feelings. They were superficial anyway: fleeting and shallow. Within seconds, he remembered what she had done. And then the hatred had come flowing back, washing over him, drenching him. In no time at all, he was ablaze with anger.

She had turned and run away from him. He hadn't expected that. As silly as it sounds, he had expected her to walk right up to him with a huge smile and act as if none of it had ever happened. He's not sure how he would have reacted had she done just that. As it turned out, he dealt much better with the latter scenario where Eva turned and fled. It fuelled his anger, pumped him full of adrenalin, and by the time he reached her, he had wanted to kill her, to wring her tiny neck with his bare hands and hear the delicate bones in her throat crack one by one.

He had no idea how fast she could be on her pins. He had been ready to drop, his muscles burning and throbbing by the time he finally reached her. At one point, he genuinely thought she was going to get away from him, that she was going to slip away somewhere and his marathon through the town would all have been in vain.

And then it happened; she fell. Down she went like a sack of shit onto the street, sprawled out over the road, her dignity rapidly disappearing into the ether. But even at that point, she still managed to pull it out of the bag and was up and on the move again as fast as she could despite the fact that she was obviously hurt. Her leg was damaged and bloody and she looked a complete mess, her hair matted and all over the place and her face bright red and dripping with sweat.

That's when he made the decision to hide. He had got too close and needed to disappear. If he had stayed that near to her, within her line of sight, then there was a strong chance she wouldn't have gone home and he would be clueless as to where she was living. So he had slipped into a doorway; a dart under a nearby awning, nothing too elaborate or mind stretching. Eva had been frazzled, too exhausted and in too much pain to give his sudden disappearance any great deal of thought. He could tell by the look on her face she wasn't prepared to put much effort into locating him. Her expression said it all – she was just relieved that he was gone.

So he waited and watched to see where she went. She made it all so easy for him.

He didn't have to stand and look up at her window once she had gone inside. That was just for effect, to unnerve her. To let her know who was boss. For once in their relationship, he was in charge. And it felt good. It gave him a surge of power to see her frightened. No more than she deserved after what she did to him. At long last, Eva Tweedie was getting what was coming to her.

* * *

Gareth sits in the café, his hands clasped around a mug of hot coffee. The chase after Eva has just about done him in. His sedentary occupation and too long spent in the pub instead of the gym has resulted in him being in the worst shape physically that he's been in for many years. He chews on a bacon sandwich and takes a long gulp of the steaming coffee, screwing his eyes up as the scalding liquid coats his mouth and travels down his throat. He still needs to find somewhere to stay the night. He also needs to buy a few items of clothing and some toothpaste and other toiletries to see him through until at least tomorrow. He has to finish up here and head to the shops then make that visit to his mother's house.

Wiping his mouth with the back of his hand, he finishes the sandwich and leaves the coffee. It was the texture of syrup anyway and had about as much flavour as watered-down mud. Living in London has spoilt him when it comes to decent beverages with its array of cafés and coffee shops that serve every type of drink you can think of.

He stands up, his chair scraping hard against the tiled flooring. A group of nearby children eyes him cautiously, sipping at their juice through multi-coloured straws, as he gives them a weak smile and brushes past, their silence and lowered eyes an indication that he is still giving off the vibes of a deeply agitated man. This is what it has come to – he is so rattled, so on edge, that even the local school kids are scared of him.

Shaking his head in exasperation, Gareth heads outside, briefly tempted to go back in and let them know that this isn't him; he is usually a nice guy, a warm and friendly sort of man despite the fact that life has been pretty shit to him over the years, always making him work twice as hard as anybody else to make a go of things.

He doesn't go back in. Of course he doesn't. They're just kids.

What would they know, anyway? They would end up terrified of the crazy man who is desperately trying to convince them that he is an upstanding citizen and not the monster they think he is. So instead, he keeps on walking, heading into the centre of town to do a bit of shopping before going to see his mother. That's the bit he's reluctant to do. It's a duty, something he has to do to settle the demons currently dancing about in his mind, to ask all the questions that need answering. She has the information he needs and he won't leave until he gets it. She owes him that much.

* * *

The house is empty when he eventually gets there. He still has his key. He won't use it. He doesn't want to use it. This isn't his home now. If he is being honest, it never felt like home. Home should be a safe place, a haven from the outside world. Gareth's home was a prison. School was his sanctuary, somewhere he could feel wanted and valued. And safe. Other kids developed tummy aches on a Sunday evening at the thought of school the following morning. Gareth developed tummy aches on a Friday afternoon at the thought of spending a whole weekend at home.

He knocks and rattles at the handle one last time in case she's left the key in on the other side and fallen asleep in the chair. No reply. He knows where she'll be and he's not prepared to go there. The thought of it makes his skin flush with humiliation. He would sooner sever one of his own limbs than visit her at that place. He has no idea why she even does it. It's pathetic, a woman of her age engaging in those sorts of antics. She is making a complete fool of herself and has done for many years. It's about time she realised how stupid it makes her look.

He turns and heads off in the opposite direction. He'll get a bed at The Royal down the road. A hotel that size is bound to have a couple of spare rooms. It's way too conventional for any of the visiting Goths to consider stopping there. They'll have vacancies for sure.

He keeps his head down, hoping he doesn't bump into any old neighbours or school friends. He's lost touch with all of them and that's just the way he likes it. Memories of this place aren't pleasant ones and he doesn't think he has it in him to feign the social niceties required to engage in polite conversation. He's way beyond that. Time has done nothing to erase the horror of his childhood. He has simply learnt how to keep it well hidden, pressing it firmly down whenever it threatens to bubble up.

The walk to The Royal doesn't take long and it doesn't look overly busy as he heads into the main reception area. It hasn't changed that much from the days when he worked here behind the bar before he upped and left for London as a teenager, starry eyed and desperate to get away.

He is about to check in when he feels himself being knocked sideways by somebody in a hurry. Scrambling about to keep his balance, he leans on a nearby wall, his hand spread across the flock wallpaper, his feet struggling to find purchase on the highly polished floor. He spins around to see a slim figure bound past him towards the main entrance, muttering apologies in her wake. All Gareth can see is a trail of wispy, red hair billowing out behind the mystery figure as she runs across the large vestibule, her feet a sharp tap against the ceramic tiles. He shrugs his shoulders and turns back to the desk, a wry smile touching the corners of his mouth. Retribution is swift. After all, he did the very same thing only hours earlier to some poor, unsuspecting female at the train station.

Keen to appear casual after his ungainly collision with a complete stranger, he waits while the lady behind the counter checks for rooms; her tiny, manicured hands tapping away at the keyboard, her heavily made-up eyes lowered in concentration. She allocates him to a small double with a side sea view and smiles as if she has just done him the biggest favour ever. He feels like telling her he would sleep in the cupboard under the stairs if that was all that was available, but instead stands quietly while she locates the key and talks him through the usual tourist-style spiel about the magnificent views and the Goth weekend taking place. He smiles politely, his patience waning as time drags on, his teeth gritted slightly while she checks him in, in the most fastidious and meticulous way possible before eventually locating the key and handing it over. Gareth all but snatches it out of her hand and thanks her profusely. By the time he turns around, the main door is empty, the mysterious redhead gone and he isn't sure whether to feel embarrassed or mystified by what has just taken place.

He takes the stairs, two at a time, forgetting the ache that has set in his legs after the run through town.

By the time he reaches the top, his calves are burning and threatening to seize up. What he needs is a hot shower to rinse off the grime of the mad gallop earlier. Once he's sorted, he'll give some serious thought as to what his next move is going to be. Firstly, he needs to speak to his mother. She should be home in a couple of hours. He wonders if she's still on the gin or whether she's changed her preferred tipple to something different since he last spoke to her. When he was a kid, it was anything she could get her hands on, but time has taken its toll on her and nowadays, her ageing body can no longer tolerate the undiluted shots she used to knock back with gay abandon. He hopes she is sober when he goes to see her but very much doubts it. People don't change, do they? She is too set in her ways and, quite frankly, too addicted to suddenly give it all up, to turn over a new leaf and become a half-decent human being.

Throwing the bags of cheap clothes he bought in town onto the bed, Gareth stretches and yawns. Exhaustion has suddenly decided to show its face which is hardly surprising given the couple of days he has had. He tries to fight it, marching into the bathroom and splashing cold water on his face, even brushing his teeth and drinking a glass of cold water, feeling its trajectory as it travels down his throat to his stomach, a cold spike darting through his intestines. Nothing works. The tiredness is overwhelming, as if he has been hit with a huge tranquillising gun.

With eyes so heavy he struggles to keep them open, Gareth sweeps the bags off the bed and onto the floor, then drops heavily onto the taut, white sheets and within minutes, slips into a deep slumber.

16

CELIA

Celia rubs her shoulder, an ache already setting in where she accidentally bashed into that chap in the hotel reception. She had spotted him as she came down the stairs and knew he was there, but somehow managed to crash into him, almost knocking him to his feet. She was too embarrassed to stop and apologise. Too embarrassed and worried about Eva.

She tries to shake off this feeling she has that something isn't quite right with this whole Eva situation. It's silly, really. She has no hard evidence to go on that things aren't as they seem, but all her life she has gone with her gut instincts and thus far, her feelings have served her well.

She takes a deep breath, the sharp air coating her lungs as she sucks in as much oxygen as she can. She had forgotten how blustery the wind is here; how it rushes in from the sea, catching you unawares and dragging the warmth right out of you. Such a beautiful view though, so she can forgive the gusts of wind that slap at her skin and whip her hair into her face, leaving it a tangled, frizzy mess.

Stopping to stare out to sea for a brief moment, Celia recalls the time she and Eva had stood further up the road, hoping to see Eva's family. How they waited and waited, Eva plunging deeper and deeper into despair, until at last, even Eva herself could see it was a pointless exercise.

Celia shivers and makes her way into town, knowing exactly where she is headed. The address that Marie gave her is tucked deep into Celia's jacket pocket. She dips her hand in and gently fingers the soft, curled edges of the small, dog-eared card.

It's only as she is walking towards the steps that will take her down to the main route into town that she realises how long it is since she has actually seen Eva. They speak on the phone regularly and text one another, and sometimes even use email, but it has been an age since they last met up and chatted face-to-face. They both have busy lives and even busier jobs so she supposes it's to be expected. And of course, there's the distance between them. With over two hundred miles separating them, meeting up for a coffee is out of the question. For months, she has had to make do with texts and emails and the briefest of calls, but now the time has come for them to speak in person. She has had enough of being brushed off with excuses and given reasons why they cannot get together. It is all about to come to an end. Today, she will see Eva, whether Eva likes it or not.

Hurrying past the cluster of schoolchildren who are busy sketching views of the Whalebone Arch and statue of Captain James Cook, Celia smiles sadly. It only feels like yesterday that she and Eva were young and struggling to find their feet in a terrifying new world, and now here they are – here she is – still looking out for her long-time friend, protecting her, trying to keep her out of harm's way.

Saving her from herself.

Celia pulls her coat tighter around her body and shivers, goosebumps prickling her scalp as she reaches the bottom of the steps. Winding her way around the curved road, she pulls her phone out of her back pocket and checks for any new messages and missed calls. Nothing. Exactly what she expected really but she always lives in hope. Feeling determined, she decides to give it one last try. It might not work but it's better than doing nothing at all. She holds the phone to her ear, listens to the ringtone and then lets out a heavy sigh as the all too familiar answer machine kicks in, telling her to leave a message after the beep.

Perching on a nearby bench, Celia holds her mobile tightly in her hands and stares straight ahead, wondering how much longer Eva will go on ignoring her. It's all so pointless really as they both know deep down that she needs Celia, and that Eva's life will empty and devoid of guidance without Celia by her side.

Her fingers ache as she grasps the phone, her knuckles shiny and taut with the effort. She has to get Eva back into her way of thinking. She absolutely cannot allow her best friend, the person she grew up with, the person she is closest to in the whole, wide world, to slip away.

With freezing fingers she presses the keys, her jaw grinding painfully as she searches for the elusive words that will catch her friend's attention and finally penetrate her steely resolve and get her to start answering the messages.

Eva, please answer my calls.

She clicks the arrow and watches her sentence float away into the ether. She already knows that a reply won't be forthcoming. The message is too bland, too repetitious of the others she has already sent over the past few weeks. She needs to change her tone, be more ambitious with her words. She needs to let Eva know that she has had enough of her little games and to tell her that she is being selfish. Or she can just go and knock on her door and take her by surprise.

Standing up, Celia sends one last message, suddenly infuriated at being constantly stonewalled. She thought their friendship was stronger than this. It's exhausting having to always be on the lookout for her, to watch the vulnerable friend who it would seem is hell-bent on going her own sweet way without a thought for anybody but herself.

On my way to your new flat. Why are you ignoring me?

Driven on by anger and frustration, and carried along by the tide of people, Celia is over the bridge and almost at Eva's door before she knows it. Dragging out the card, she checks the address one more time, even though she knows it off by heart and has Googled it at least ten times.

Wandering along the side street, she counts the numbers on the doors, wanting to be certain she gets the right one. She purses her lips. The numbers don't run consecutively and many of them have annexes round the back and holiday lets attached. Jesus, all these tiny winding streets and higgledy-piggledy houses piled on top of one another. Why is this place so fucking confusing?

Feeling her anger building, she steps back and mentally counts them again, her eyes dancing along the rows of doors and windows, some modern, many refurbished, all of them exasperating and bloody confusing with their hidden numbers and unfathomable, concealed entrances.

The noise catches her by surprise. She is so unaccustomed to its ringtone that at first, she is convinced that it's music from one of the arcades over the river or a child's nearby toy, or anything at all, but not her phone. It's the vibration in her pocket that finally alerts her to the fact that it's ringing. Her palms are slick with sweat as she grapples with it and sees the name that is there right in front of her, flashing up on the screen. Eva.

Blood drains from Celia's head and she wishes there was somewhere nearby so she could sit down – a bench, even a doorstep would do right now.

Eva is finally calling her. At long last. After all this time, with the worry and heartache Celia has endured, all the running around and endless messages, Eva is about to break her silence. And not before time.

Celia's heart practically crawls up her throat as she drags her fingers across the screen and tentatively answers the call, her voice weak and scratchy with shock.

'Eva?'

She is greeted with a drawn-out silence, then a barely audible sigh.

'Celia, what *exactly* do you want?' The ice in Eva's voice catches Celia unawares. It takes her a couple of seconds to reply. Her eyes are wide with shock and the words when she says them feel disjointed and disconnected, as if they're coming from somebody else.

'Why didn't you tell me you'd moved? I went to London looking for you.' She doesn't want to plead with her but can't seem to help herself. She is feeling desperate. This is her chance to break through Eva's armour, to penetrate the steel bars she has surrounded herself with. It's now or never. She has to get this right.

'Look, Celia, I can't keep doing this with you. Not any more. You know this. We both know it.'

Celia feels a sickness take hold in the pit of her stomach. She needs to take back control. This is typical Eva. This is what she does. She commandeers situations and twists them around to suit her own ends. She doesn't even realise she is doing it. It's a self-preservation thing that she has mastered over the years to keep her secrets safe and her sanity intact.

'Eva, I'm outside your flat. Please let me in and we can talk about what's going on.' Her breath puffs out in front of her as she inhales and exhales rapidly, a tiny element of fear setting in. Celia is losing her. She can sense it.

'You're lying,' Eva whispers. 'You don't have my new address. Ask yourself why I didn't tell you I had moved, Celia. Ask yourself that question.'

'I know exactly why you didn't tell me that. And we both know why you came here as well, don't we?' Celia is panting slightly, her nerves getting the better of her. She needs to calm down. She has to be composed and unruffled if she is to help Eva. Charging in there like a whimpering wreck will solve nothing. Celia has to be the strong one, strong enough for the both of them. Eva needs her. She just doesn't realise it. She never has.

'I'm looking outside my window and I can tell you're lying. There's nobody there.'

Celia moves along the street again, counting the doors, mentally trying to work out where the door to Eva's flat is. She stops in front of number thirteen, scans the nearby area and rapidly spots it. She has no idea how she missed it earlier. It's so obvious – the narrow alleyway. She can see the sage-green door with its grey slate number sitting above the letterbox from here: 13a, right there next to her. Bingo.

The gasp down the phone is so slight, so whisper-like that at first, she doesn't even detect it. Celia lets her gaze roam over the front of the house. White painted shutters cover the inside of the windows. It looks empty, as if the place is shut up even though it's coming up to peak season. Perhaps Eva is the one who is lying and she isn't even here. She could be anywhere right now, wandering through the town, on the beach, in her parents' house.

Celia isn't sure what makes her do it but she looks up to the bay window directly above the shuttered window and there she is – Eva – phone to her ear, staring down at Celia, her eyes dark and unforgiving. Celia lifts her hand to wave, unsure of what her movements should be. Even from here, she can see the look of horror and anger on Eva's face.

This is all wrong. Why does she suddenly feel as if she is a nuisance when all she is doing is trying to help her?

'I've found your door,' Celia says as she attempts to inject an air of authority into her voice without sounding too bombastic and controlling. She needs to be firm but kind, and gain entry into her flat without doing or saying something that will tip Eva over the edge. 'I'm coming up to see you. This is really important. We need to talk. Please let me in. I'm not leaving till you do. And if you don't let me in, then I'll find my own way in. I'm really concerned about you, Eva. Please…'

There is a moment's hesitation on the other end of the line, and for one awful moment, Celia thinks she has blown it, broken the spell and lost her forever. She has no idea how she would cope if that were to happen. Their relationship, if she is being honest with herself, is a symbiotic one and she needs Eva as much as Eva needs her. They are a team and always will be. They have a shared history, too much to lose if they drift apart. Too many secrets.

'It's locked. Look, I haven't got long. If you insist on talking then wait there and I'll come down and let you in but I'm really busy today and only have a few minutes to spare.'

Celia puffs out her cheeks in relief. She's done it. Once she's inside, she feels sure she'll be able to talk Eva round, to make her see sense. This time tomorrow, she will be wondering what all the worry and fuss was about. This time tomorrow, things will be back to how they were, how they should always be.

She heads into the dark alleyway, raps her knuckles gently on the door and waits.

17

EVA

My heart hammers out a horrible, dull beat as I listen to her knocking on the door downstairs. For fuck's sake! How the hell did she find me? This whole scenario is surreal. After the carry on with Gareth earlier, I feel as if I am being stalked. What the fuck is going on here? I make a decision that I've been pondering over for years, to come and see my parents, and all of a sudden the world and his wife are here spying on me, tracking me down. Trying to ruin all of my plans.

I consider closing the curtains, ignoring her, even sending a message telling her to leave me alone, but I know what sort of reaction that will provoke. I need to be cautious here, to step carefully around her. This is a delicate situation. She is mad at me for moving away without telling her. I understand that, I really do, but she left me with no choice. Surely even *she* can see that? My options were so limited, I felt as if I was choking on the intensity of it all.

I thought I had everything tied down tightly when I left London, that I had managed to slip away into the night with no forwarding address, but with Celia outside my flat, it would appear not. I may as well have a tracking device plastered across my forehead for all the good it did. My stealth-like plans have amounted to nothing and now I'm at the mercy of the two people I have tried to escape from. It was all in vain. It would seem that I can't even disappear successfully.

I trudge down the stairs, dreading opening the door to her. I have no idea what I'm going to say, anyway. I will leave the talking to Celia. She can ramble on and on about why I have come here and I will remain silent and nod in the right places to appease her. Always the best way. I will do whatever I can to keep her at bay, which won't be easy but it's all I can manage right now. I don't mind admitting she has caught me unawares and I don't have any tricks up my sleeve to solve this. I'd like nothing better than to send her packing, but knowing how she is, how capricious and unstable she can be, it's highly unlikely that that will happen. Instead, I will do what I've always had to do: soothe and cajole her, agree with everything she says and then hope that she buggers off back to where she has come from.

My fingers are like pieces of wood as I fiddle with the ancient lock and slide the chain back off its catch. I pull the door open slightly and do my best to look confident. She smiles at me and her appearance takes my breath away. I try to not show my shock and step back to let her in. A waft of cold air breezes in behind her and I shiver and slam the door closed, leaving the chain off. I have no idea why. I somehow feel safer that way; just that little bit closer to the outside world should things take an unpleasant turn.

'You look different,' I say quietly as I head back up the stairs. Fear surfaces at the thought of her behind me. I had hoped my move would sever our relationship but it would appear that Celia thinks differently, although to be honest, most of the time, I have no idea how Celia thinks. Her current appearance tells me she is way off balance at the minute, perilously close to another breakdown.

'Do I?' Her voice is light, slightly contrived, designed to keep me sweet, no doubt, after she trailed halfway around the country, stalking my every move under the misguided belief that we are close friends.

'Yes,' I say with more anger than I intend, 'you look very different, Celia. Very different indeed. You know you do.'

I feel her footsteps falter behind me and hold my breath in anticipation of her reply. Instead, she lets out a small giggle and I am flooded with relief. I don't want to upset her. Knowing Celia's capabilities, that's the last thing I want to do. I'm just furious at being found. I was hoping for some peace and solitude, and the last few days have been anything but that. All I want is to be left alone.

'A change is as good as rest sometimes, isn't it? Plus, I wanted to look my best for you.'

I know this is a lie but I say nothing. Instead, I fill the silence with a low, tuneless whistle as I show Celia into the living area and beckon for her to take a seat on one of the cream, leather couches. She slumps into it and the creak of the leather under her body unnerves me more than it should. Today, everything about Celia unnerves me more than it should.

I watch as her eyes rove around the room, taking in every minute detail, her mouth tightened in concentration while she looks for pieces of me in the ornaments and knick-knacks that are placed strategically on the surfaces in every corner of the living space. She won't see anything of me in them because none of them are mine. My things are still in storage and will stay there until I find my own place. This entire area is neutral, devoid of me. None of my personal touches have been applied and now she is here, I am glad of it. I want to keep myself back from her. If I could, I would remove myself completely, but it's highly unlikely that is ever going to happen. God knows I've tried.

'Coffee?' I ask and am surprised by the forcefulness of her reply.

'Tea. You know I prefer tea, Eva!'

I clench my teeth and furl my fists into tight little balls of fury.

'Tea it is,' I say softly as I head into the kitchen, hoping she hasn't detected the slight shift in my mood. Neutrality is the key when dealing with Celia. She is like a mirror, reflecting the moods of those around her. On the odd occasion when I have dared to stand up to her, she has erupted with such magnitude, I have been forced to apologise immediately, retracting everything I have said to avoid her spiralling into some sort of demonic state. However, today I am feeling slightly frail and less able to put up with one of her moods. Today, she may well get short shrift from me if she tries to manipulate me or use any of the devious techniques she often applies when she wants to get her own way.

I leave her sitting there while I watch the kettle boil, the steam billowing out in small curling clouds. I open a packet of biscuits and arrange them neatly on the plate then pour the tea and head back in, taking my time, putting off having to sit opposite her and discuss why I made the choice to leave London without telling her.

I place the tray on the coffee table in the centre of the room and hand Celia her cup. She takes it from me and puts it on the floor at her feet. I am mesmerised by how measured and precise her movements are. While I am sweating and wondering what to say next, she is sitting up straight and taking in every aspect of the room, scrutinising my clothing, staring directly into my eyes. I shift my gaze elsewhere, her stern expression making me hot and uncomfortable.

'What's going on, Eva? Why have you come here? This is a bad idea. You know it is. Sometimes, I despair at your decisions. I really, really do.'

She sounds like a Victorian school ma'am. My head pounds and I want to scream at her to leave me alone, to get out of my flat and to keep her feeble, unwanted opinions and probing questions to herself. But I don't. Of course I don't. I know all too well what the repercussions of such a move would be. So instead, I sit down in an armchair opposite her and think long and hard before giving my reply. I can feel my nostrils flaring as I try to stay calm and keep a level head.

'Celia. I'm fine here. I am managing perfectly well. It's good of you to think of me and I understand you've travelled a long way to come here, but you didn't need to. You really didn't.'

I hope I've pulled it off, said just enough to convey what it is I want to say without sounding too callous or dismissive. It's all about getting the balance right, you see.

She continues to watch me closely, her eyes concealing her thoughts perfectly. She has never changed. She looks positively regal, sitting there, passing judgement on me. Celia always did prefer having the upper hand, making up ludicrous stories about her family, telling people they were wealthy and that pretty soon she would be returning to them. It was nonsense, of course. We all knew it. I told the odd lie about my family and background simply because I was embarrassed by it all. I felt as if people knew about my parents just by looking at me. But Celia... her stories were so outlandish and embellished upon, it was laughable. And, of course, she never wanted me to find mine. She was convinced I would form a bond with them and it would drive us apart. What she doesn't realise is, Celia and I were never together to begin with.

'You told me you were happy living in London,' she says sullenly. 'You said everything was going great for you and that you were settled there. So why would you just suddenly up and leave?'

I don't know what to say, how to reply to make her understand. She thinks she knows me and can fathom what goes through my head. She doesn't know me, not at all, and in reality, she never has. Celia is the last person on earth I would confide in and bare my soul to. She sees our friendship as something deep and long-lasting. She is deluded, and she is most definitely not a person I would turn to in times of need. I have other friends in both York and London that I would call should I need to. Celia does not even register in my head as a friend. She slipped off my radar many moons ago. I just wish she had stayed there.

'It's all a bit complicated,' I whisper, hoping against hope that this will be enough to put her off. It won't. I know her better than that but I try it anyway. I desperately try to think of some fabricated story to tell her while she watches me.

'Enlighten me then,' she says, and I'm not sure if I am imagining it, but I swear I detect a hint of menace in her voice.

I don't reply and grasp at my wrist, tugging at my sleeve, feeling a sheen of sweat form on my upper lip as I struggle to find the right words.

'I'm all ears, Eva,' she whispers softly, making me even more nervous. 'You know I'm only concerned about your welfare. Always have been.'

I wince at her words and watch her eyes travel down to my arm then back up to my face and see the flicker of recognition. My bracelet. She has spotted my bracelet: the only thing we have in common. I put it on after my shower. Silly, really. After finding it earlier, I thought I would wear it as I haven't had it out of its container for some time, but now Celia's here it feels wrong: a reminder of the past. Just another thing to fuel her anger. She tries to hide her expression at seeing it, but it's too late. I take a deep breath and try to suppress the sickness I feel at her unexpected presence in my new flat. I don't want her here. If I had wanted her to follow me, I would have given her my new address. Surely she can see that? Even Celia, with her warped ideas of what constitutes normal behaviour, can see I didn't want her to know where I am now living.

'I broke up with my boyfriend and decided I needed a change.'

'Your soul partner?' She raises her eyebrows in a disapproving arc and clicks her tongue. My face burns. I want to slap her. 'So why here? I mean of all the places to come to, why would you pick this town, Eva, with all its horrid memories?' Her voice is gaining in momentum, and I don't like it. Not one little bit. I need to find a way to get her out of here. I think I've put up with quite enough of her nonsense over the years. I am an adult and can live my life however I choose. I most certainly don't need her approval. I am now beyond mollifying her. This is my home; she is a visitor. I control what goes on in here. I surprise myself at how authoritative my words sound as they race across my mind. So why do I feel so scared?

'Look, Celia,' I say briskly as I stand up and smooth the creases out of the fresh trousers I put on earlier. 'I know you've come a fair way and I appreciate your concern, I really do, but I have an appointment that I need to get to so if you wouldn't mind...?'

She doesn't move and for one horrible minute, I have a vision in my head of dragging her out of her seat and practically throwing her out of the flat. When she gets in this stubborn state of mind, I know all too well what she is capable of. And it really does frighten me. She can be angry outside on the street if she so chooses but I won't have any of her volatile behaviour or outbursts here in my home. I need to get her to leave.

'This is silly,' she says softly, a sudden smile cracking her cool demeanour. 'We haven't seen one another for, ooh how long has it been?' she says brightly, tapping her chin lightly with her index finger, 'It must be over a year!' she exclaims loudly, her tone contrived and too hearty for my liking. Something is amiss. My skin crawls with dread as I try to work out what her next move will be.

'Two,' I reply frostily.

'Really?' she shrieks. 'I think that calls for a celebration, don't you?'

I suck in my breath, wondering what she has in mind, what sort of warped activity she wants me to participate in. The last time we were together, she insisted on calling her ex-boyfriend in the middle of the night and telling him exactly what she thought of him whilst she was drunk. I had sat, paralysed with horror as it unfolded, watching her sob and scream at him down the phone, knowing he was with a new partner who was four months pregnant. I tried to stop her but when it comes to dealing with Celia, there are boundaries that simply cannot be crossed. Not if you know Celia like I do. And I know her very well indeed. I had only gone to see her that time because she was beside herself with grief after their break-up. She had bombarded me with calls until I eventually relented and made the journey to York. I had initially feared she would do something stupid; something final. It was only when I got there that I realised she was actually consumed with anger, not sadness. She spent the entire weekend raging about how she was going to kill them both with her bare hands.

'Like I said, I'm sorry but I have to be somewhere and—'

'Where?' she barks at me, her eyes like dark slits in her face. 'Where *exactly* is it you're in such a hurry to get to?'

I don't answer her. I want to tell her that it's none of her fucking business and to get out of my home but I opt for silence, knowing what she might do if I tell her how I really feel.

'Come on, Eva. We both know why you came here and where you're planning on going so why don't you just spit it out and stop playing these ridiculous games.'

I still say nothing. There is a heavy pause. The only thing I can hear is the sound of my own blood as it pulses around my head. My chest is tight with rising panic and a slow, augmenting anger, and my feet are rooted to the floor.

'Okay, I'll say it for you since you've decided to remain mute.' Celia crosses and uncrosses her legs and leans towards me as if we're carrying out a business transaction. 'You came here on a wild goose chase, looking for a family that didn't want you way back when, and still don't. That's what binds us together, Eva, you and I, the fact that we're not wanted. Adult orphans, that's what we are. Yet you still cling on to this mistaken belief that you can just slide back into a family who forgot to ask you back. It's about time you got real and accepted your life for what it is – a black hole devoid of anybody who really cares about you. Except me, Eva. You seem to have forgotten that. *I* care about you. *I* want you, and yet you ran away and didn't even tell me. What kind of a friend *are* you?'

She leans back in her chair, her face flushed, her eyes dancing with enjoyment. It's evident by her expression she thinks she is in charge here. This woman, this unbalanced, crazy woman thinks she can actually control me and tell me how to live my fucking life.

Suddenly, I am furious. Not scared any more, not even mildly apprehensive. Just bloody furious. How dare she? How dare Celia march in here and tell me what I can and can't do? Who the hell does she think she is? I don't waste any time in telling her exactly what I think of her interference in my private life. Standing up, I point towards the stairs behind us with trembling fingers.

'Out!' I bellow at her. 'You need to leave right now, Celia,' I bark, my voice rattling around the room. 'What I do is my business and nothing to do with you. I want you to leave here right now.'

I watch for any sudden change in her demeanour but she is scarily serene, as if I have just asked her if she wants sugar in her tea.

'Eva, Eva,' she says in a sing song-voice that sends my pulse soaring. 'You need to stay calm. You know what happens if you get all riled up. Remember the incident at Greta's house all those years ago when you lost your temper, threw a vase at her and broke her nose?' She smiles, picks her cup up and slowly and deliberately sips at her tea, her lips pursed so severely, thin, crepe-paper lines appear around her mouth.

I go dizzy at the memory. It's as if somebody has poured a jug of cold water over me as her words sink in.

'I'm sorry?' I manage to say through gritted teeth. 'What did you just say?'

A low, droning sound fills my head and my skull feels as if it's in a vice. I can't quite believe what I'm hearing. My face grows hot and I listen incredulously as she speaks again, each word like a physical blow to my body, her words alien and detached.

'Eva, don't tell me you don't remember? And what about the time you spat in your food and told her that she should eat it instead of you? It was such a torrid time for you, though so I understand why you acted the way you did. Greta understood too. She always forgave you as well, didn't she? We all did. It wasn't your fault.'

My throat is like sand and my eyes bulge. I need to stop her. I have to get her out of my apartment before something awful happens, before I do or say something terrible to her. I can feel it in the air; the crackle of danger is everywhere, emanating from us, leaking out of our pores like hot oil. She has overstepped every boundary, broken every single rule and from this moment on, there will be no going back. Our friendship has gone beyond the point of no return.

'But those incidents pale into insignificance compared to the day you picked up that knife, don't they? Gosh, that was such a frightening time for everybody involved. You were so lucky that the other girl's injuries were superficial and her parents didn't get the police involved. Such awful times.' Her eyes cloud over as if we are reminiscing about a day at the beach.

I can hardly breathe. Air forces its way out of my chest in short bursts. I absolutely have to do something – *anything* – to get her out of here, to remove her from my home.

I lunge at her and grab her arm, dragging her across the room. She is limp and much to my relief and surprise, puts up no resistance. Only when we are near the stairs does she spring to life, like an animal unfurling itself after a deep sleep. Her nails claw at my face and a sharp, stinging sensation rips across my cheek. A slender line of blood runs down my face and gently drips onto my sweater, a tiny glob of scarlet soaking into the wool.

We are equally matched when it comes to physical strength and I fear I won't win until luck plays its part. As I drag her further along the room, she trips and loses her footing on a nearby rug. I seize the opportunity and twist her arm up her back, ignoring her howls of pain as I haul her to the top of the stairs. A sob explodes out of my chest. With our feet locked together, I drag her down, over each and every step, my legs buckling under me, her legs twisting and bending. She is heavier than she looks, and in no time at all I am sweating and panting for breath.

Part of me knew this was going to happen when I first spotted her standing outside on the pavement. That was why I left the chain off. Deep down, I just knew it was always going to end like this. Some things are just meant to be.

'Eva, please stop! This is *exactly* the point I was trying to prove. You're doing it again!'

I feel my throat practically close up at her words. Keeping her arm forced upwards, I twist her around and push my face so close to hers I can almost taste her breath: sweet and sickly like rotting lavender.

'What *the fuck* are you talking about?' I snarl, no longer caring whether anybody outside can hear me shouting or even if they are alerted by Celia's cries of pain as I grip her arm even tighter. I just need to get her out of here. I need her gone.

'Your temper,' she says softly, her voice so delicate and artificial it makes me want to rip all her hair out until it falls to the floor in great, dyed-red clumps.

'*My* temper?' I almost drop her arm in shock. 'Celia, what the hell are you talking about?'

Her eyes roam over my face and it's only then that I notice she is wearing the same shade of eyeshadow that I usually wear. The same shade of lipstick too. I feel horribly sick. Celia thinks she is me.

'Oh come on, Eva, we both know exactly what I'm talking about. The terrible meltdowns you had when we lived with Greta, all the commotion you caused that time you daubed the walls and our bedroom furniture with red lipstick. And what about that incident with the knife? You were lucky that poor girl didn't die, let alone not have any serious injuries. All she did was try to befriend me and when that happened, you turned into a complete maniac, screaming at her to get away from me and that I belonged to you.' She stares into my eyes and smiles. '*Now* can you remember? Now do you understand why I'm so protective of you and why I came here to find you?'

Blood squirts through my body, thick and fast. The floor

threatens to swallow me up whole as I shake my head over and over, the cold tiles tilting and swaying under my feet.

'You need to see somebody, Celia. You're not well,' I say breathlessly. I can't think what else I should say. I suddenly feel ill from her words and need to sit down.

'See somebody?' she says so calmly that I wonder if she actually understands what it is that I am implying.

'Yes, I think you need to see somebody, a doctor perhaps. Somebody who can help you with your mental health issues.'

I glance down at her clothes – so similar to the style I used to wear years back – at her hair, dyed red to resemble my hair, and only then do I realise how far she has fallen, how vulnerable and potentially dangerous she is. And I thought I was the needy one.

'Why are you saying these things about me, Eva? Why?'

'Because all of those things you said about me back there... it wasn't me at all, was it? It was you. You were the one who broke Greta's nose. You were the one who ruined the bedroom. You were the one who tried to stab somebody.' I'm panting hard now, stars bursting behind my eyes as I gasp to catch my breath. 'It was you, Celia. All those awful things you mentioned. You did them all, not me.'

I know I should help her, get her to see some sort of counsellor or specialist, but I am scared of her. I know *exactly* what she is capable of so, instead, I push her out of the door into the alleyway where she falls onto her knees with a sharp crack.

Slamming the door shut, I double lock it and put on the chain. It suddenly seems like a weak barrier between my aching body and Celia's ravaged mind, but it's all I have.

For years, I have dreaded this day. I had hoped that in the intervening years since we last met, she had found the help she needed, but events today have proved me wrong. She is as damaged as ever. Even more so than me.

I trudge back upstairs, raw fear tugging at my insides. I will jam a chair up against the door handle, make sure she cannot get back in. It's unlikely she will try, but then I would have thought it unlikely she would turn up here looking like me and that's exactly what she has just done. Her madness, it would appear, knows no bounds. It has grown and multiplied since I last saw her, turned into something ugly and unmanageable. Her teenage tantrums after being passed from one set of foster parents to another were one thing, but this...? This is way out of my comfort zone. Her anger hasn't subsided over the years and, having seen her in action, I dread to think what she is truly capable of.

For years, she has tried to stop me seeing my parents, telling me it would disrupt my life and ruin everything I've worked hard to achieve, but it's not that at all. She has another reason to stop me seeing them. She doesn't want me finding them because then she will be left on her own. That's the only thing Celia and I have in common – the years we both spent in foster care, the fact that we both came from deeply damaged families – and if I change that, then she will have nobody. She once told somebody that we were like twins. We are far from having such a strong bond. We are polar opposites, and if I forge a reunion with my parents, that will alienate Celia even further. For so many years, I have tried to not hurt her, humoured her, kept her at bay. She has been intense, overpowering, unable to see things from my perspective and now I have to make a clean break. I can no longer put up with her demands.

I grab a hefty dining chair and drag it down the stairs, pushing it hard against the metal handle. I try to drag the handle down but the back of the wooden chair stops it from moving. I attempt it a couple of times until I'm satisfied that her entry back in is well and truly blocked. There is no other way in. This door is it, the only means of entry, and she would have to develop superhuman strength to get past this barrier.

Lots of questions race through my brain as I head back up, like how did she find me? I have done my best to avoid her over the past few years once it became apparent that her obsession with me was out of control. I tolerated the countless messages and calls and emails, fearing what she might do to herself if I blocked her or refused to reply. I did what I could to keep her at bay and for a while, it seemed to work. The distance between us helped.

And our careers. Whenever Celia suggested meeting up, I would throw a business meeting into the conversation, tell her I was working that weekend and could we do it another time? She always seemed to fall for it, never questioning why I was being sent on so many training courses and working so many weekends. Her job was very different, of course. Celia is a receptionist in the hospital and our commitments are totally different. I think she imagined me in the city, surrounded by financial geniuses who controlled the stock market. I am an accountant, not a stockbroker but then again, Celia only knows what I have chosen to tell her, which is actually very little indeed. I figured the less she knew about me, the better.

But in Celia's mind, we are still best friends, those young girls from broken homes, dented and bruised by their histories. I have moved on. Celia has remained static, stuck in the past, trapped and damaged by the upheaval in her life prior to living with Greta. I know she had moved about a lot and suffered a lot of abuse in some of the care homes she lived in. So many people and places, so little love. And now look at her; look at what it has done to her. I'm not sure she will ever be able to move on from this.

She was always fixated on me, ever since we were first introduced all those years ago, and I tolerated it, pitied her and took her under my wing even though I had my own fair share of issues.

I was the lesser injured of the two. A pair of fragile creatures in a torrid, tumultuous world. We had Greta, obviously. Greta was my saviour and I loved her dearly. Celia, however, did not. She did all she could to make poor Greta's life a misery, doing the things already mentioned and plenty more. It seemed as if she loathed everything and everyone, especially her mother, constantly telling me how she would love to see her rotting in the ground. Hatred and anger were her *modus operandi*.

As the years passed and I forged out a life for myself, it became apparent that Celia wasn't prepared to let me go that easily. She wasn't the reason I moved to London but I don't mind admitting that I felt more than a little relieved to be leaving her behind. I half expected her to up sticks and move with me and wanted to cry with happiness when she wished me luck, saying her heart was firmly in the north and always would be.

With so much distance between us, I could easily put up with the calls and messages that she bombarded me with on a daily basis. I tolerated her, kept her sweet for fear of what she might do if I cut her off completely. I even gave her titbits of what was going on in my life. She has no idea that all I was doing was keeping her at arm's length. And I had Gareth too. My eyes mist over and I blink back unexpected tears.

I had Gareth. And then I didn't. My fault entirely.

A hard lump sticks in my throat at the thought of him. I flop onto the chair, my chin trembling. It's all such a mess. I have ruined everything. Visiting my parents' house is all I have left. I hope to God I get to meet them, otherwise all of this will have been for nothing.

I stand up and peer out of the window at the street below, not daring to breathe in case Celia is down there, staring up at me, waiting for me to crack. She isn't. The street is jam packed with Goths and pensioners, and school children stuffing their faces

with ice creams and sticks of rock but thankfully, there is no sign
of Celia.

I half smile, feeling a sudden need for a glass of cold, white
wine. I suppress the craving. The answer to my problems doesn't
lie at the bottom of a bottle. I've been down that unpleasant route
and have no desire to return there. All I want is to meet my
parents and have my questions answered. A reunion with Gareth
is out of the question. I know that now. Once I have my answers, I
can get on with the rest of my life instead of being suspended in a
hiatus. I have no idea what the future holds but I do know that it
doesn't include Gareth or Celia. From this moment on, I plan on
being a damn sight more selfish and if that means being on my
own in this rollercoaster we call life, then so be it.

18

GARETH

It's almost dark when Gareth eventually rouses himself. He sits up on the bed, disorientated and groggy, initially unsure of his surroundings. The room is out of focus as he rubs at his eyes like a small child, his hair sticking out at divergent angles, his clothes crumpled and askew.

The window affords him a view of a darkening, grey sky with a gathering of heavy clouds across it. The moon is slightly visible behind them, shimmering and watery. It silvers the room, glazing everything with a thin trail of light.

He has no idea how long he has been asleep for or what time it is. He looks around, suddenly remembering where he is and rapidly wishing he was back in London, in his tiny house where it's comfortable and close to everything he cares about: his friends, his job, his security.

The dull light in the room gives it an eerie glow and fills the corners full of dark shadows that look vaguely threatening. He blinks again and switches the lamp on, killing the darkness and highlighting the slightly dated decor. Still, at least it's warm.

When he worked here as a young lad, the place was like one huge fridge.

He swings his legs off the bed and yawns, stretching his arms out and shaking himself vigorously, attempting to throw off the shackles of sleep that still envelop him. He strides into the bathroom and turns on the shower, hoping it will help wake him up. He is also ravenous. A meagre bacon sandwich wasn't enough to fill his belly and stave off the hunger that is clawing at his stomach. Once he's showered and has had a shave, he will head off down to the restaurant and see what's on offer. Hopefully they'll have some decent seafood on the menu. And a beer. He could really, really do with a drink. His body feels empty, devoid of any sustenance after a jog through town and a long sleep.

The shower is thankfully hot and once he's shaved and changed, he enters the restaurant feeling half human, his body still trying to catch up with the time he lost while slumbering.

He is seated at a table near the window away from the large party of pensioners and the family with the screeching kids. He watches, both fascinated and mildly disgusted, as the two grimy-looking children gorge themselves with chicken nuggets and slurp at large glasses of bright-blue juice that have a radioactive glow to them. The parents are oblivious to the noise and act is if they are the only two people in the room, refilling their glasses and chatting and laughing while their offspring fire food at one another and spill drinks on the starched, white tablecloth.

Gareth orders a craft beer and chooses the calamari starter followed by the surf 'n' turf with an extra portion of chips. The beer arrives almost immediately and he takes a long swig, smacking his lips together appreciatively. He finds himself smiling at the taste of it, something he hasn't done for some time. He was beginning to think he'd forgotten how to be happy. It feels good, as if he has somehow grown a couple of inches or is floating on air. Looking at the carnage on the other table with the noisy kids, he's delighted he isn't a father, especially to those two little bruisers.

He turns to catch the waiter's eye to order another beer. He is standing in the corner of the room speaking to a lady and pointing to the menu. She nods as he talks, thanks him and walks in Gareth's direction. Gareth watches as she strides over and seats herself directly next to his table, then turns around, sees him and smiles.

He is unsure how to react. He came here for food and a quiet beer. Of all the vacant tables in the place, she decides to sit right next to him? He returns the smile and watches as her face colours: a flush creeping up her neck and spreading over her face in a pink web. On a whim, he stands up and changes his chair, moving closer to her as he leans forward and holds out his hand.

'Hi, I'm Gareth. Tell me to leave you alone if I'm bothering you. I know this sounds like the worst chat up line ever, but have we met somewhere before?'

This is very unlike him. He is usually reserved to the point of being aloof but something about her has grabbed his attention. And she did smile at him. Technically, she made the first move. He has no idea how she'll respond to his words but continues to smile at her with his hand still outstretched. What's the worst that can happen? She could ignore him, turn her back on him, in which case he will finish his beer and eat his meal then go to up to his room where he will watch some TV and post on social media about how drunk he is and how cold it is in the north. He will then drink some more beer and watch more rubbish TV before falling asleep, probably fully clothed.

She doesn't ignore him. She leans forward, shakes his hand in return and speaks in a soft voice that is so quiet, he has to tune out the clatter of crockery behind him to hear what she is saying.

'Perhaps. Actually, not perhaps. We have met before. I owe you an apology for bumping into you earlier in the hotel lobby. I'm Celia, by the way.'

There is an awkward silence as they watch one other, his eyes travelling the length of her slim frame, his gaze admiring her legs that seem to go on and on. He can't help staring at them, locked provocatively together as she sits tilted to one side, slightly away from him. He should have noticed the copper-coloured hair; the same shade on the figure that knocked him sideways earlier. There is something about her that pulls at him, something deeply familiar even though he knows for sure they've never met before.

'Do you want to pull up a chair here?' she says, catching Gareth off guard. He had planned on eating on his own tonight but sitting with her suddenly seems very appealing. Infinitely preferable to dining alone and besides, sitting with her will help distract him from the appalling display from the monster children and their neglectful parents.

'I've got some food coming. Do you want to join me here instead?' he says, gesturing towards his table that's set for only one.

Her hesitancy is a momentary flicker and he's relieved when she nods and picks up her bag to join him.

It's her hair: the way it shines dark auburn under the low lights. That's what makes her seem so familiar.

She orders a gammon steak and a glass of Chardonnay and they eat heartily, making small talk about the music festival taking place at the weekend and which is superior: the Steampunk phenomenon or the Goths currently roaming around the town.

'You're not from round here then?' Gareth says casually as he pours himself a glass of wine from the bottle he ordered once the beers became too filling.

'Not Whitby, no, but not too far away. I live in York,' Celia replies dreamily.

He watches the wine take hold, increasing the flush on her neck and slurring her speech slightly.

'Ah. I knew you were a Yorkshire lass by your accent. A lovely city. What brings you here? The festival?'

She laughs and shakes her head. 'God, no. Although I did get chatting to a couple of lovely young girls on the train journey who were going. I've come to visit a friend. What brings you here?'

'My mother lives locally. I've come for a fleeting visit.' Gareth feels his body tense up at the mention of his family.

'And yet you're staying at a hotel?' She brings her hand up to her mouth and reaches out to touch his arm briefly. 'Sorry, none of my business. Sometimes, I just open my mouth and out it comes!'

He feels the electricity course through his body at her touch and smiles. 'It's absolutely fine. I prefer my own space and my mother's choice of decor is stuck firmly in the 1970s. The rooms here are just fine for me.'

She nods and removes her hand. He wants to tell her to leave it where it is. He wants to ask her to press her mouth onto his and to go up to his room with him. Instead, he refills her glass and they talk some more about the weather and what a lovely city York is and lots of mundane topics until their wine is gone and they have nothing left to say to one another. The conversation may have dried up but his desire hasn't.

'Would you like another one in the bar?' He expects to receive a firm 'no' but to his surprise and pleasure, she agrees and they head off, her arm so close to his it makes it skin tingle with anticipation.

'Why don't we take them up to your room?' Celia is standing facing him, her eyes alluring pools of warmth and seduction.

By the time they reach the first floor, his hands are firmly placed around the back of her head, pulling her closer to him and his tongue is sliding between her teeth. They stumble along to the door at the far end of the corridor, impervious to the stares of the couple leaving their room next door.

Gareth stops and fumbles with the handle; he feels her breath close to his, escaping in short bursts as they fall in through the open doorframe, a tangle of arms and legs locked firmly together, their glasses clinking, wine spilling in small spots on the carpet.

His sweater is pulled roughly over his head and her hands pull at his belt. He stops her by sliding his hand under her blouse and unhooking her bra. She pushes him back and unbuttons her blouse, letting it fall to the floor in a tantalising, silken heap.

They are both undressed within seconds and slump onto the bed, Gareth on top of her, her legs wrapped tightly around his. Her hair is fanned out over the pillow and she lets out a soft moan as he presses himself into her.

It's over barely before it has begun, and Gareth rolls off her and hooks his arm under her neck, pulling her into his chest where she lays, her fingers softly stroking his stomach, circling his navel with her long, painted fingernails. He had no idea such a simple action could be so erotic.

'You remind me of someone,' he says quietly. 'I get the feeling we've met before. I know we haven't, but you are the absolute double of my—' He has no idea why he says it and as soon as the words are out of his mouth he wishes them back in again. Too late. He feels her entire body stiffen beside him. Her soft curves are suddenly sharp and unwelcoming.

He tries to stave off her obvious departure by running his

fingers through her long auburn hair and kissing her neck and shoulders but the damage is done. Her defences are up.

'I really should get going,' she says, her tone still soft and gentle, a stark contrast against her body which is now pointed and tense.

'Stay,' he says, 'please. You don't need to dash off.'

He thinks he's persuaded her as she lets out a barely audible sigh and shifts slightly beside him, but before he can protest, she is up off the bed and striding into the bathroom, closing the door behind her.

He waits, hoping she comes out and slides back in beside him but when the door finally opens again, she emerges with wet hair and is wrapped in a towel.

'I took a quick shower. Hope you don't mind.'

He shakes his head and murmurs that it's fine, wishing she would drop the towel so he can see her naked just one more time.

She perches on the edge of the bed and leans forward as she slips into her clothes, and pushes her feet into her suede boots.

'So who was it, then?' she asks as she turns to watch him. Gareth sits up, feeling vulnerable and slightly ill at ease at being the only one who is now nude.

'Sorry,' he says, knowing exactly what it is she is about to ask, 'who was what?'

'Who was it I remind you of? That's what you said a few moments ago, wasn't it? That I remind you of somebody. I was just wondering who it was. Not an ex-girlfriend, I hope!'

She lets out a forced giggle and tries to look composed but Gareth can see that she is rattled by his words. He has no idea why as they barely know each other but he regrets saying them all the same. It was crass and thoughtless but there's no taking them back now.

'Just a friend of a friend from a few years back,' he says,

hoping it's enough to appease her. If there's one thing that pisses him off, it's women who throw tantrums at the mention of another female. It's childish and puerile, and if women could understand men and how they think, they would know that it's unnecessary because despite what women think and what the media would have them believe, not all men want to leer at any passing female and haul them into bed. They want to commit to relationships as well. Why do women think they have the monopoly on feelings and sentimentality? He *loved* Eva and look what she did to him, what she told him. That bitch broke his fucking heart.

'Right,' she replies sounding unconvinced, 'well anyway, must dash. It's been great, Gareth. I'm here for a couple more days, if you fancy a meet-up?'

He nods, unsure if he really wants that now. Just a few seconds ago, he would have given his right arm to see her naked again and now he is working out ways in which he can avoid bumping into her in the hotel. How quickly things can change. A few subtle movements, a couple of throwaway comments and before you know it, everything changes beyond recognition.

He listens to her pad off down the hallway and lies back on the pillow, thinking that yet again, without him even realising it, Eva has penetrated his thoughts and caused another fucking great rip in his life. He opened his mouth and the first thing that came out was Eva related. It's as if she has crawled right under his skin and is fucking well controlling everything he says and does. She is an itch that refuses to be scratched: a gaping, festering sore that simply will not heal.

Tomorrow, he will finally get the answers he craves and put an end to all of this and then maybe, just maybe, he won't have to creep around the hotel, hoping to avoid Celia. Perhaps once he sorts it, he can be on the next train back to London and settle into the original rhythm of his former life. A life before Eva. A life when he was content.

He flicks the light off and turns on his side, the soporific effects of sex already taking effect. The last thing he sees before sleep takes him is the face of Celia slowly morphing into Eva's, her long hair knotting together in an unruly, red mess, her teeth bared in anger, screaming his name and clawing at her face until her features are a pulpy mass of bloody, raw flesh.

* * *

When he wakes a few hours later, the silence is all pervading. After a series of horrific nightmares, his body is coated in sweat, and he feels grubby and greasy, but his mind is clear, his thoughts ordered and precise. He knows then what it is he must do. It's all so obvious, embedded in his brain like a permanent fixture.

He craves a drink, the need for it so great, it obliterates everything.

He crawls out of bed – his limbs heavy with sleep, his anger at an all-time high – and pulls on his underwear and jeans and a warm sweater he bought as a windcheater while he is here. He leans into the mini bar and grabs at a miniature bottle of wine, twisting open the cap and glugging from it greedily. He stops and wipes his lips with the back of his hand, the acrid aftertaste flooding his mouth with a slightly acidic kick.

He finishes it and opens another one, drinking it like it's water until it is all gone. At the back of the tiny fridge, he spots a bottle of Bacardi and a can of Coke. A smile spreads over his face as he lifts them out and cracks them both open. He pours them into a plastic cup that is sitting on the dressing table and drinks it in one whole gulp, the alcohol taking effect almost immediately.

He smiles. This is all he needs for what he's about to do. This and the white-hot fury that is eating away inside him. It will help see him through his next task. And then he will pay a visit to his mother's house to tell her exactly what he thinks of her. After that, he will board the train and never return here.

He slams the cup down on the walnut top and zips up the sweater to his neck. No time to waste.

He grabs his key, shoves it in his back pocket, closes the hotel door behind him and heads out into the night.

19

CELIA

She is furious, her heart pumping against her ribcage as she makes her way back to her room. What's wrong with these people? Why can they not just accept her for who she actually is? First Eva accuses her of lying and emulating her looks and then this Gareth guy has the gall to fuck her while he was obviously thinking of somebody else. Celia did her best to remain calm, to not appear flustered or perturbed in any way by his words, but it was so damn hard. What he said hurt her. It was stupid and insensitive and yet again, she was the one who had to mask her real feelings, to plaster a smile on her face and be pleasant, when what she actually wanted to do was walk right over to him and shove something sharp deep into his ribs and twist it till he curled up and cried and shrieked like an animal stuck in a trap.

Celia pads along the corridor and lets herself into her room, shame and anger consuming her. Is this what happens to decent people who spend their lives looking out for others? Because that is all she is doing; being a concerned friend and always trying to keep the peace. The decent folk, it would appear, get trodden underfoot by the egotistical and thoughtless people of the world

who don't seem to care about anybody but themselves. They have
no idea how their selfish actions squeeze every last drop of energy
out of those around them. If she could only be one of those
people, then perhaps her life would have been a whole lot easier
and she definitely wouldn't spend her days worrying about somebody who obviously doesn't give a shit about her.

Pulling off her clothes, she climbs into bed, her arms wrapped
tightly around her torso, her skin still tingling from the hot
shower in his room where she did her best to rid herself of the
scent of him. She felt dirty, contaminated by his touch and
scrubbed herself until every last trace of his DNA had been
removed from her body.

She should have known better, really. He was too upfront, too
charming by far. Men like Gareth always have a hidden agenda.
They prowl and pounce, unconcerned about how others feel.
Predators: that's what they are. Her last boyfriend was the same:
slick, smooth talking, keen to get her into bed. Her feelings mean
nothing to them. She is just another notch on their bedposts.

She rests her head back against the wrought-iron bedstead,
her eyes sore and gritty, a solid lump lodged in her throat, and
assesses her life. She is in her mid-thirties, single, living in a
rented flat above a bakery and has only one real friend worth
speaking of. Or at least *had* only one real friend. After today, it
seems that even Eva has turned her back on her, accusing her of
some terrible things, shouting at her that she has made up all
sorts of tall tales. It's not true. It's Eva who is the deceitful one, the
one who acts as if she doesn't have a care in the world when they
both know she is nothing but a conniving, dreadful liar.

A lone tear spills out of Celia's eye and rolls down her cheek.
She leaves it there, not bothering to wipe it away. What's the
point? She had travelled here in the hope of helping somebody
and in return has been used and abused. A small howl escapes

from the back of her throat, raw and feral. What is the fucking point of it all?

Celia sniffs and fiddles with a long strand of hair, twirling it around her finger, trying to decide what she should do next. She can't leave without seeing Eva again. It's out of the question, not when she has put in all this effort and travelled this far. And anyway, Celia is the civilised one; the courteous companion who does actually give a shit, and she will not leave until she sees Eva one last time. If nothing else, she at least has to make sure her weak and vulnerable friend is happy and safe, but at the same time, Celia cannot risk another re-run of today. She has to find another way, a more subtle way of accessing her without being denied entry into her life. The one thing she still does have is her dignity, although even that is slowly but surely being stripped away bit by bit by bit: an erosion of her decorum until she is a husk of her former self.

The idea doesn't come to her straight away but when it does, she all but shrieks out loud into the surrounding silence. Of course. It's suddenly all so clear. She can't believe she didn't think of it earlier. After all the effort she has put in, all the planning and scheming, this is an obvious move. She knows exactly where Eva's parents live. She could turn up there and enlighten them, tell them what their estranged daughter is really like, let them know what Eva is truly capable of. She will be their protector. She will stop the worst from happening and in the long run, they will all thank her for it, Eva included. She needs Celia to look out for her before she does something stupid, something permanent. Something that once done, cannot be taken back.

Excitement balloons in her belly, warming her through. She presses her face into the pillow to stifle her near hysterical laughter. At least now she will be able to sleep knowing she is back in control. Fuck Eva and her denials, lies and downright selfish behaviour. Fuck Gareth and his careless words and the way he used Celia for sex and then discarded her like a worn-out piece of old rag. She will show Eva just how clever she is and how her friend cannot possibly function without her. Celia has her own schemes and plans, her own way of getting out of this stalemate situation that she has suddenly found herself in.

She lets out a contented sigh and stretches, wiping away the tears and running her hands through her hair in a smooth, rhythmic fashion. This is better. This is how it was always supposed to be. Everything is settling back into place, and pretty soon, it will be damn near perfect. She will have the only person she has ever truly loved or cared about back in her life. Eva will soon be hers again. They will spend time together and become even closer than they were before Eva left for London. Eva will look up to her and respect her and be the friend Celia has always wanted her to be. And that is all she has ever wanted.

20

EVA

I consider leaving the chair there overnight but then years of health and safety training taps at my brain, telling me it's dangerous to be locked in. What if there's a fire and I'm trapped upstairs and the door is jammed solid downstairs? I visualise the fire service struggling to force their way into the only entrance into the flat while smoke and fumes fill my lungs on the upper floor. I would be dead before they could break the door down and rescue me. Reluctantly, I remove the chair, the only barrier between my safety and Celia and her ever-growing displays of insanity, and fling it to one side.

Telling myself she would have come back by now if she was going to do anything untoward, I trudge back upstairs, engulfed by fatigue. Today hasn't been the best of days – far from it – and I'm in desperate need of my bed.

I wander around the flat, checking the windows are shut properly and curtains and blinds are closed. The last thing I want is to wake in the middle of the night and wander into the bathroom for a pee while Gareth or Celia are downstairs staring in at me.

My stomach plummets at the thought of Gareth. Never seeing

Celia again is something I can definitely handle – in fact, I would welcome it – but the idea that I will never see Gareth again causes me actual, physical pain. Look at what my life has already become without him by my side. The thought of going another thirty or forty years without having him around makes me go cold. That's not to say I don't feel utter shame at what I did. Of course I do. I'm not a monster. I never meant to hurt him. I simply got carried away and my outpouring of love for him was so great, I crossed a line and I don't blame him one little bit for hating me. Every time I think of it, I hate myself.

It's after 11 p.m. by the time I feel settled enough to get into bed. A headache is already setting in behind my eyes and I am dizzy with exhaustion.

I slide down between the sheets and soon feel myself sinking into oblivion, a comfortable blackness so deep I couldn't claw my way out of it even if I wanted to. The air around me is light, all the noise from outside slowly dissipating, leaving me cocooned in a cloud of nothingness.

I dream of being weightless. I am flying through a vast, cloudless sky, my body soaring above the ground. I look down to see people below me milling about and wonder if they can see me flying above them like a bird, swooping and diving, my body streamlined into a graceful arc.

I slow and, for a minute, I fear I might fall from the sky, but I only have to kick my legs to speed up again, moving swiftly over the hills and the sea, watching as the waves below thrash around and crash into the rocks with a bang, beating into the cliff face before retreating again. There is no breeze, no chill factor at all, just warmth and movement, smooth and effortless.

I fly away from the water and move back over the land. In the distance, I hear the sound of the chatter from below, the banging and clattering of movements from the people down there. There is the slamming of a car door beneath me as I fly overhead. I smile. I'm as invisible as the wind. A ghostly being spying on the world below me.

It's an amazing sensation. It feels fabulous, relaxing, soothing. I don't want it to end.

But it does.

Suddenly, everything changes. I'm heavy and feel myself sinking into the darkness, my body weight returning to normal. My head throbs and terror slithers over my flesh. I know what this is; I know all too well what is coming next. I try to stop it but I'm too tired to put up any sort of resistance.

Everything closes in on me. I am no longer free as a bird. I'm trapped in a confined space and I feel a pressing sensation on my limbs, a slow pressure that locks me into position. A familiar fear creeps in as I try to move, my entire body rocking with the force of attempting to free myself out of the paralysis that now has me in its grip. My breath catches in my throat and my skull pounds, blood roaring through my ears as the heavy feeling on my chest and abdomen increases.

I tell myself to relax, to just go with it, be carried along with it until my body is able to free itself, but the usual, all-consuming feelings of terror at being trapped always win over any rational thought, and in no time at all, I am panting and gasping for breath as the paralysis grows. I feel as if I can hardly breathe. A gurgling noise fills my head and I want to scream out but I am powerless, everywhere solid and immobile. My face burns, and from somewhere nearby, I hear a grunting noise. It sounds as if it's coming from over my head and yet I know there is nobody here but me.

Again, I try to move my head, but there is such an enormous pressure bearing down on me, I feel sure I'll never be able to free myself. The rattling, gurgling sound is there again and my mouth and tongue feel swollen, my thoughts distorted as I struggle for breath.

This is it. This is the time that sleep paralysis will win. I will never wake up and will be stuck forever in a terrifying limbo, a hellish nightmare where I can't move or breathe. Left in the darkness forever more.

The weight on my entire upper body grows heavier and heavier until my face and neck feel as if they are about to burst. I gasp and judder, a thick pulse hammering away in my neck.

That's when I realise. Something has changed. This is all wrong, different. It doesn't feel like the other times. The heaviness on me is greater and my head is pounding like my skull is about to crack open.

I push all my force into my left hand and feel my fingers form into a claw. My upper arm feels as if it's made out of iron as I try to lift it up to alleviate the horrible intense pressure on my ribs and throat. I want to scream, my mouth slowly forming an O shape. Nothing comes out, just a rush of hot air that circles in front of me, pungent and acrid.

I can no longer stand this. I have to free myself. I give one last mighty push and suddenly snap awake.

The nightmare, however, continues. I can't move or breathe. A shadow looms over me, hot and heavy, its breath sickly and stale. The reek of alcohol wafts into my mouth. I retch and gasp and scratch at the shadow. Except it's not a shadow. My hand hits something firm as I flail about, striking fabric with solidity underneath it. I want to let out a terrified shriek but something is pressing on my throat. Constricting, squeezing. Crushing the very life out of me.

I feel my eyes bulge. My heart thrashes out a horrible, erratic thud and I just know that if I don't do something to shake this presence off and do it soon, to free myself of this thing, then I will die.

I bring my legs up and thrash them about, wriggling my backside and hips in the process. Something shifts, only slightly, an almost imperceptible reallocation of weight, releasing the pressure and pain on my throat. Not too much, but enough to allow me a couple of seconds to gather some more strength – strength I didn't know I possessed – where I rock to one side and throw the shadow away from me. It's short lived.

In no time at all, they are back on top of me, their hands scrabbling about for purchase, pushing my head back, trying to grab at my throat. I roll and buck about, making myself as slippery and unmanageable as possible, gasping and choking, trying to suck as much air into my oxygen-deprived lungs as I can.

I claw, spit, gasp, kick my legs around, thrash my exhausted body about in the hope of dislodging the entity that is on top of me, pinning me down, trying to kill me.

Once again, hot, heavy fingers find my throat and clasp around my windpipe but I am fast to respond. I feel skin close to my face and without a moment to spare, I crane my head slightly and sink my teeth into the warm flesh, deep and hard, ripping and tearing, clenching my teeth together around the skin, pulling, grinding, doing all I can to save myself. I feel a layer of flesh come away slightly, and gag as fresh, warm blood soaks into my mouth.

There is a roar of pain and a light smack to the side of my face. But more than that, there is a release of pressure from my chest and throat. I can breathe again. I am free.

Still thrashing about to defend myself against any incoming blows, I roll off the bed and land on the floor in an inelegant heap, my bones rattled by the sheer force of the fall onto the floorboards. No matter. Not enough time to nurse any possible broken bones, bruises or swellings. I need to get away, to call the police, to save my life.

I crawl away, my hands clasped at my neck, my throat burning, my lungs still struggling to get enough air in. I need to breathe properly. I have to get some oxygen into my bloodstream if I'm to do this, if I am to get away from this person who wants me dead.

I spit out flecks of skin and blood, gagging and gasping for air. My neck feels as if it could snap at any moment and my tongue is too big for my mouth. I have no time for nursing my ailments. Creeping along the floor, my hands pad up the side of the bedside cabinet. My phone. I need to locate my phone.

Out of the darkness, hot fingers grab at my ankle, pulling me hard onto the floor with a thump, my chin hitting the wooden slats as I land. My teeth crack together and there is an explosion of pain behind my eyes. All I can think about is the gap that will be where my two front teeth should be and worry that they have flown out of my mouth and are scattered all over the floor. No time to check. I bring my free foot back and kick out as hard as I can. There is a satisfying crack as I connect with something. I feel skin and bone beneath my heel and a shriek ensues.

The hand gripping my ankle goes slack and I scramble up off the floor, running my tongue clumsily over my teeth. All present and correct. I would smile but everything is too painful, my tongue thick and heavy, my mouth too swollen and sore.

I stagger to the far wall and switch on the light, ready to grab the heavy lamp that's sitting on the chest of drawers next to me. I may be injured but I have enough strength to swing it hard and connect with bone; to do enough damage to save my own skin. My fingers are trembling and slick with sweat and my legs so weak, they feel as if they are made of liquid, but I will do what is required to save myself; to stay alive and find out who it is that is doing this thing to me.

I don't notice the blood dripping from my chin onto the beige rug, nor do I care about the ripped bed sheets that are slowly staining crimson, a dark hue spreading and blooming over the entire mattress. I don't even register the pain any more that is ripping through my body.

Because all I can focus on is him.

Gareth.

He is curled up there on the floor, nursing a bleeding arm and what appears to be a broken nose. His uninjured arm is held up to his face and his hand is cupped around it, catching the blood as it runs from his nostrils in thick, snotty lumps.

I let out a ragged breath, my thoughts racing, trying to process it all. I attempt to speak but words fail me. Gareth. I know he hates me but never thought him capable of this. He has tried to kill me. A pain shoots over my head making me woozy and nauseous.

I stare at the shrivelled figure before me and shake my head. I am hurt, upset, terrified. This person, this *mess* curled up on the floor, has just tried to murder me. I can't quite believe it. How far reaching is his loathing for me? I knew he was angry. There was no denying that, but this? When I thought him capable of hurting me, I didn't actually think he would go through with it. I visualised him following me, making idle threats, crying, even. But not this.

'Why?' I manage to say weakly, my tongue feeling as if it has been hit with a mallet.

He doesn't answer, just sits there moaning and rocking back and forth, blood spilling from his hands and running through his fingers, a pool of red slowly spreading around him.

'Why?' I shout, more force in my tone than I thought possible given how battered and sore I feel.

'Because I'm so fucking angry with you! That's why!' he splutters, snot and spit and blood mixing and merging in a frothing, sticky mess on his face. 'I am just so fucking furious with you that I wanted to kill you with my bare hands!'

'Kill me?' I half howl. 'Kill me?'

'Yes!' he roars from behind his wet, bloodied palm. 'Yes, I wanted to kill you. I've thought about nothing else since that night!'

I slump on the edge of the bed; a trickle of blood on the satin quilt snakes its way through a bundle of bunched-up fabric and heads towards my leg. I don't move. I should feel repulsed and squirm about to escape it but I don't. I just sit there. My heart is still thudding and a line of static curls over my skull, threatening to split it in two. I close my eyes and rub at my forehead.

'But you can't kill me,' I say with more conviction than I feel.

'Why?' he moans, his voice guttural and charged with menace. 'Give me one good reason why I shouldn't take a knife and plunge it into your fucking neck!'

'One good reason?' I wail at him. 'I'll give you one *very* good reason why you shouldn't kill me. Because I'm your sister!' I scream, tears streaming, snot bubbling. I drag a hand across my face to wipe it away. 'I'm your sister,' I repeat, my words a whisper in the near silence of the room.

It takes him a few seconds to reply. His voice is stone and laced with such coldness it makes me shudder.

'That's *exactly* why I want to kill you. What kind of a sick fuck are you? For God's sake, Eva, we *slept* together. Have you any idea how fucking wrong this all is?' His eyes are blazing and the stream of blood from his nose has now thinned out to a small line. It trails out of his nose and merges with the sticky, rapidly coagulating blood on his face.

'How did you get in here?' If Gareth can get in then so can Celia. For all I know, there could be a line of people outside my door waiting to hurt me. After tonight, anything seems possible.

'You think an ancient lock can't be picked, Eva?' he replies from behind his hand.

I shrug and stare helplessly at the floor, words deserting me when I need them the most. I genuinely don't know what else to say, how to make any of this any better. Deep down, I should have known how angry he was, but never in a million years did I think he was capable of this. Then again, a few years back I wouldn't have thought myself capable of incest but it happened, didn't it? I wish I could pinpoint the time when my feelings changed towards him. It was a slow process of connection. I had gone to live in London to be near him after finding out he existed. Keeping tabs on my family was all I could focus on once I was adult enough to know how. Gareth had been born after I was taken into care. In fact, if my dates are correct, our mother was probably pregnant with him when the only family photograph I have of me with my parents was taken: me sitting on her knee, Gareth safely lodged in her uterus, away from all the harm and distress. I don't mind admitting that after I discovered he was out there, I became obsessed with him. Who wouldn't develop the same feelings after spending their entire life thinking they were an only child? Apart from Nancy, who brought me up after I was removed and helped me through the worst of times when the contact for my parents set up by social services failed to materialise, and Greta, who stepped in when Nancy became too old and ill to continue, I had nobody else.

Time after time, my parents had let me down, not turning up to see me or giving feeble excuses, until in the end it was decided that no contact at all was better for my well-being rather than sporadic half-hearted attempts from parents who couldn't care less about their daughter. I was alone in the world. Greta was amazing and I loved her, but she wasn't my family – not my biological family. I crave being wanted; it's all I think about day in, day out.

It had been decided by a team of social workers that Gareth's existence should be kept secret from me. My mother had refused to have me back, and as for my father – as far as I am aware, he was too drunk or too absent to care. I was nobody's child. They felt that a clean break would be better for all concerned. And just look what it's done to me. I am a needy, grasping individual who will stoop to any level to feel wanted and loved. Even sleeping with my own brother.

My relationship with Gareth didn't start that way. It's not as if I sought him out with the sole intention of making him my boyfriend. I may be damaged but I'm not a complete psychopath. Once I was aware of his existence, I tracked him down and visited him with some cock and bull story about setting up my own business and needing software advice. We spent a couple of weeks messaging each other, my excitement at discovering I had a sibling at an all-time high.

We were about four weeks into our friendship when I noticed it: the way Gareth used to look at me. It wasn't the way friends should conduct themselves. He used to gaze at me for long periods of time when he thought I wasn't looking. At first, I wondered if I had been rumbled, and that perhaps he was looking for similarities in our features, trying to see if I had his eyes and working out which parent I looked like. But of course, that wasn't the case at all. He was slowly but surely falling in love with me.

It soon became obvious that my business queries would come to nothing. I told him I had decided to ditch the idea of going self-employed as a financial consultant and would continue my job at the accountants where I worked. Whether or not he saw through my tissue of lies at the time is anybody's guess. Everything was too far down the line at that point to even matter. We were firm friends and I knew Gareth had visions of it going even further.

After a while, he'd asked me out for dinner as opposed to getting together in the pub after work. Then came the gifts. First it was chocolates and flowers. Then the necklace: a gold chain with a tiny ruby heart at the centre. At that point I should have come clean and told him who I really was – I know that now – but I was so desperate and in need of affection that I let him continue. I don't mind admitting that I was flattered. The most I had ever been given by any of my previous boyfriends was the occasional birthday card, and flowers from one particular guy, bought from a petrol station forecourt after an argument. He hadn't even bothered to remove the price. Gareth was in a different league to any of them. They were just boys, whereas Gareth was a perfect gentleman.

I had drunk far too much the first time it happened. I know I should have told him. I *know* that now. But it's all too late. I was attracted to him for sure, but I knew that he was head over heels in love with me. I held his heart in my hands and eventually I broke it.

It was a Wednesday evening after work when I finally came clean. The burden of guilt had become too much to bear. I wasn't sleeping and had spent night after night trying to work out ways to break it to him. He had to know sooner or later. It wasn't fair on either of us. I had done this terrible thing and I couldn't go on any longer with the deceit.

I had hoped that he would be forgiving about the whole thing and lenient towards me, given the circumstances of my upbringing. A small part of me actually hoped he already knew and would save me the heartache of having to tell him. I should have just lied and said nothing about who I was, just walked away, citing other reasons for our break-up, but the whole thing was making me insane. He was my brother and I still wanted to have contact with him. He was all I had. I had waited my entire life to see my family and I didn't want to lose him. As it turned out, that was exactly what happened.

We were in my house, the place we spent most of our time since our relationship had taken off, and I had sat him down with a glass of wine and told him, as gently and as sensitively as I could, who I really was.

I told him how I had kept check on my parents, looking them up on the electoral roll every few months to make sure they still lived at the same address. I had been doing it for years. The fact that they still lived in the same house somehow soothed me. It was the only bit of stability I had in my life. They were my comfort blanket. It gave me such happiness, seeing their names in the same place year after year.

And then Gareth's name appeared alongside theirs once he was old enough to be registered as an adult living at that address. So I did a bit of digging, researching birth certificates, and that's when I discovered I had a brother. I kept checks on him too, noticing he had moved to London as soon as he was old enough. I didn't go there straight away. I needed a job, somewhere to live. London is a big, expensive city and although I am needy, I wasn't stupid enough to think I'd go there and find a job and somewhere to live immediately. It took a good few years to make the move. It was a risk, but it was one I was prepared to take. I had a brother. Somebody just like me. That's when I set out to find him.

I watched as he initially laughed, thinking I had gone mad, then felt my legs go weak as his face turned a sickly shade of grey, all colour leaching out of it. I knew then that I should have found another way. He adored me. It was an indisputable truth, evident to all who knew us, and whatever I did to end our relationship, and go back to the amicable people we once were, would have left him shattered. He deserved to know the truth. At least that's what I told myself. I convinced myself I was doing the decent thing – the right thing by him. I wasn't. If I had wanted to do the right thing by him, I would have walked away before it all began, but I didn't because I needed him. Not as a lover but as a brother. I needed him to be the family I never had.

And now look what I have done to him.

He sits opposite me, a complete wreck of a man, barely recognisable and covered in blood. I am a cursed individual, ruining people, even myself.

'I'm sorry,' I mutter, aware of how feeble my apology sounds. It's all I have to give.

I expect a backlash from him, a torrent of abuse and blame which I will accept, but there is nothing. He sits, slumped, his energy spent on attacking me while I slept. No more than I deserve.

There's no way out of this. I know that now. The damage is done and no amount of time will ever repair it.

'I have to go,' he says suddenly, wiping his face. His skin is stained bright red with blood and his arm is in an awful mess where I sank my teeth into it.

'Here, let me clean you up,' I say as softly as I can, while getting up to my feet.

He shakes his head like a frightened child and scrambles back away from me. 'No! I'll be fine. I just need to go.'

I don't try to stop him. That would simply fuel his anger, and I fear things are bad enough without exacerbating them any further.

'I suppose you'll be going to the police?' he says. I watch him as he limps towards the stairs, his eyes dead, his tone weary.

'No. Of course I'm not,' I whisper, too afraid to say that I deserved everything he did to me. That and more besides.

He nods, and for a brief time I pray that he will turn around and tell me that he forgives me. He doesn't. I don't really expect him to but I live in hope. Hope. That's all I have. I've destroyed everything else, haven't I?

He drags himself down the stairs with the gait of an elderly man. I have really injured his arm and face. Guilt rips through me. I want to shout him back, to return to how we were when we were just friends. Instead, I follow behind him at an acceptable distance and watch as my brother, the only family I know, disappears into the darkness of the street.

The door closes with a click. I survey the damage to the lock. I can call a locksmith in the morning and get it fixed. The landlord need never know. If anything, I will be doing him a favour by replacing it with a more substantial lock than the flimsy, old one that was previously on there.

I go upstairs and drag a chair back down, jamming it up under the handle once more. My earlier efforts at staying safe in a possible fire left me wide open to Gareth's anger. I shrug and sigh heavily then head back in the bedroom to begin the clean-up process.

Who would have thought one person could lose so much blood and still live? It's everywhere, tiny splashes up the walls and smeared over the floor.

I spend the next hour scrubbing and rinsing, stripping off bed sheets and washing floors and walls. The metallic, pungent scent of blood is everywhere. I keep at it, refusing to stop until every mark, every splash of blood, every single microscopic trace of Gareth's presence here in my flat has been removed.

* * *

It's 3 a.m. by the time I finish. My hands are raw and my throat feels as if Gareth's hands are still clasped around it. I don't go back to bed. I am awake. Instead, I sit by the window with a cup of cocoa. I have no idea how I am going to move on from this juncture in my life but I have to find a way. I resist the urge to top my cup up with alcohol. That isn't the answer.

I do know what I am going to do next, however. I may as well get on with it while I'm up and there is nobody around to see me. I gather together what I need and wrap up warm, making sure it is tucked away in my pocket. I can't lose it. It's the only connection I have to them. I just hope they know how it got there and that they don't destroy it. If they do... well, if they do then there's nothing I can do about it. I'm taking a chance on them and hoping that just for once, they won't let me down.

The walk there doesn't take long. I slide easily through empty streets, shadows making me jump, strange noises making the hairs on the back of my neck stand on end. Even in the early hours of the morning, Whitby seems to have its own secret little world going on with the sound of the sea in the distance and the echo of dripping water as it hits the cobbled alleyways.

I am there before I know it. Everywhere is in darkness. This is good. I don't want to be seen. Not at the minute when I am a complete mess. I also want to give them some time to adjust to the idea of me being here: to break them in gently, so to speak. I'm being kind and showing them the generosity of spirit they never once showed me, but then I am not my parents, am I? I am me, and despite my issues and mistakes, I will always try to do the right thing. As tonight will show, I don't always make the right decision but kindness is never far from my mind.

Once I've posted it, I head straight back. Although I don't feel unsafe or threatened in the town at this time of the morning, I would rather get back as quickly as I can.

At home, I make myself another hot drink and resume my position by the window, my eyes fixed on the horizon. I sit for what feels like forever, waiting for the sun to make its ascent, then finish my drink and stand up.

In another bid to put some demons to rest, I seek out every bottle of wine and Bacardi and gin I can find and empty them all down the sink, then slump onto the freshly made bed and let the tears come.

I have no idea if I am tired or not. I no longer know my own body. My senses have been dulled by what happened earlier. If sleep comes then it comes, and if it doesn't, then that's fine as well. What will be, will be. Last night, my ex-lover, my brother, the person I almost destroyed with my careless, thoughtless behaviour, attacked me. I am done with questioning everything, planning my life with military style precision. I will take life as it comes.

I'm not complaining. I deserved his anger. The only question I have now is, what am I going to do? My life is a disaster area and I no longer have the energy or inclination to do anything about it. I could go back to London. There are more jobs for me in the city for sure, but then I will leave here no wiser than when I came. They kept Gareth and abandoned me. Why? Why would anybody do that? Is there something about me that is inherently bad? I would rather not have the answer to that one, actually. Not after what has just taken place.

My eyes get heavy and my body finally succumbs to sleep.

By the time I wake a few hours later, I am rested and ready to what needs to be done. I deserve Gareth's anger and more, but I also deserve to find out who I really am and why I was discarded and forgotten about. And today, I will get my answers no matter what.

21

GARETH

They're not half as bad as he first thought. Once he washed all the blood off, the scar on his hand is no more than a superficial wound and his nose is swollen and sore but it doesn't look as if she has done any permanent damage. He's pretty sure it's not broken, though only time will tell. He had no idea the bitch had it in her. He had no idea he had it in himself.

Maybe it's genetic. After all these years of hating his father, what if it turns out he is just like him? Violence breeds violence. That's what they always say, don't they? All the psychologists and therapists would have a field day if they were to study his family, to see what he and his sister have done, what they have put each other through. They would think them half insane. And that's without taking a good look at his parents who *are* actually mad. Gareth shakes his head and puffs his cheeks out. This entire thing is one huge fucking farce.

He stares in the gilt-framed mirror that is sitting on the dresser and studies his face. How did he not see it before? The fact that he and Eva resemble each other. Is that what attracted him to her in the first place? He once read somewhere that people are drawn to other people with features similar to their own. Was that what he saw in Eva, perhaps? Were their similarities so great that his attraction to her was like a great, big magnet and he was powerless to its lure? He'd like to think he has more self-restraint than that, more control over his impulses and that it was Eva who caused it all, but he has done much soul searching in the past few weeks, and loathe though he is to admit it, he was totally captivated by her and made a huge effort to get to know her better.

In fact, if he is being honest, he pursued her relentlessly, sending her gifts and calling her ten times a day until in the end, she capitulated to his demands and requests for dinner and more. That doesn't excuse what she did. She knew from the beginning they were siblings and made no attempt to tell him. She'd had plenty of opportunities to let him know. They were friends long before they were lovers. He feels like throwing up at the very idea of using that word when it is associated with Eva.

He looks again at his reflection. He no longer wants to study his own features. Every time he looks at his own face, all he can see is Eva. Only her hair is different. His is dark brown like his mother's whereas Eva's is a deep copper colour. Just like their dad.

He'll go and see his mother later. Not that he wants to, but there are things he needs to know – like why didn't she tell him he had a sister? And why was she left in care? Although he can't help but feel that she was better off there. He doubts very much that she suffered the beatings and abuse that was meted out to him on a regular basis. He should envy her, really. She got off lightly, not having to be part of the Tweedie family that stayed put and had to endure the wrath of Russ the drunkard who once told Gareth he would rather spend his life in prison for murder than spend it with his son. That's when Gareth knew it was time to leave. He was almost as big as his father at that point and had fought back, to defend himself against his useless brute of a dad.

Gareth rests his head back on the chair and closes his eyes. He also wants to ask his mother why she did nothing about his father's violent ways. Not only did she do nothing about it; she went to great lengths to actually hide it. In many ways, that is as bad as what his father did. She enabled him; she gave him permission to use their only son as a punch bag. He feels his temperature begin to rise and drums his fingers on the edge of the chair to curb his agitation. He's had enough stress for one night and needs to get some sleep.

He steps over his clothes which are in a bloody, crumpled heap on the floor and lies down on the bed. Soon, he will visit his mother and he will ask her all those things, then once he has his answers, he will return to London, where he will remain. Never again will he come back here. Not as long as his mother is alive, anyway. Once she shuffles off this mortal coil, he may reconsider but until then, he will stay well away. He will return to London, to his secure job and circle of friends and carve out another life for himself. One without Eva. He's done with her.

Gareth closes his eyes and brings his hand up to nurse the swelling on his face. He won't miss her. Not after this. There will be no void in his life once she is gone. He turns onto his side and lets out a small groan as a wave of pain tears through his face. Eva is toxic: a reminder of a family he would sooner forget. She may well be his sister, but she will never, ever be his friend.

22

CELIA

She is up and out of the hotel shortly after 8 a.m. She will have breakfast in a nearby café. The last thing she wants is to be in the hotel restaurant and look up to see *him* walk in. It would take all of her resolve to not launch herself at him and stab him with her cutlery or hurl a hot drink over him.

The temperature outside is chilly but bearable. She pulls her scarf tighter around her throat and tugs at her gloves, flexing her fingers in a repeated fashion until she is satisfied that they are on properly, and then sets off towards the town. There will be a plethora of cafés serving hearty breakfasts there. She has a deep craving for a full English and a large latte.

Sleep evaded her but she isn't tired. Energy is pulsing through her veins setting her senses alight. A solid breakfast will add more fuel to the already raging fire that is burning deep in her belly.

* * *

The town is relatively empty and she finds a seat tucked away in the corner of the first place she passes. She is too hungry to be selective about eateries and their levels of hygiene, something that is normally high on her agenda. It's not too far from the pier and is equidistant between Eva's flat and her parents' house which is just perfect. She doesn't want to get too close to Eva at the minute. She needs to give her some time to cool down, which she will. Of course she will. She and Eva have known one another for too long to let a silly spat like the one they had yesterday be the ending of them. They are stronger than that. They've had to be.

Besides, isn't that why she is here? To help Eva come to terms with her upbringing and convince her that meeting her mum and dad is most definitely the wrong thing to do. It will be the undoing of her. They didn't want her when she was a cute little toddler so they're not going to want her now, are they? Plus, Eva is teetering on the brink at the minute. Yesterday's carry on proved that. She is in complete denial over how she was as a younger person, making out as if it was Celia who did those dreadful things. It's nonsense, but poor Eva with her addled brain and warped sense of reality has gotten everything backside first.

'Are you ready to order?'

A slim woman barely out of her teens is standing at Celia's table, notepad and pen in hand. Her hair is scraped back into a tight ponytail and her eyes are sparkling with the vitality of youth.

Celia affords her a tight smile and points to the menu. 'Full English, please, and a latte.'

'No lattes, sorry,' the waitress says with a sigh and taps the pencil on the notepad irritably. 'Machine's broken. We can do instant, though.'

Celia feels a smattering of anger edge its way up her throat. She has been thinking about this latte since dawn. She really needs it. She can do without the breakfast but the latte is a must.

'Can you not make one by hand?' She tries to smile but her features feel constricted, as if she is wearing a tight mask over her face that is pressing down on her and stopping her from breathing properly.

'Not really,' the girl continues, 'we need the machine for the steam, you see. The kettle doesn't get hot enough to make a proper latte. And the milk has to be boiling for the froth. And besides, there's only me and the chef here at the minute and I'm not really sure how—'

'Fuck's sake! All I want is a fucking cup of coffee! You can manage that, can't you? You are a fucking café, after all! What sort of cheap restaurant doesn't serve their customers a fucking coffee, eh?'

It's out before she can stop it. The words ring around the empty room, echoing off the tiled walls and bare furniture. Celia's chair scrapes sharply across the stone floor as she stands up and arches her body towards the waitress. Celia's head has a tight ribbon of pain around it and her breath comes out in short gasps. She brings her hand up to her mouth and is horrified to see that the waitress is now crying.

Where in God's name did that outburst come from? Her skin is prickling and behind her she hears a roar emanate from the kitchen area.

'Oi!'

The waitress is standing wide eyed, her notepad clutched tightly in her tiny hand. Fat, perfectly formed tears drop from her eyes and run down her face in perfect symmetry.

Celia turns around to see a large, middle-aged man making his way towards her. He is wearing a white apron and his eyes are wide as he stalks over to where she is standing. He jabs a finger in her direction and spits out the words, his face flushed with fury.

'We will *not* tolerate anybody abusing our staff! You need to leave this establishment right now!'

'I... I'm not sure what—'

But before she can say anything else, he takes her by the elbow and marches her over to the door.

'Out! And if you try to come back, I'll call the police.'

She feels a hand pushing her in the small of her back, propelling her forwards, and in just a few seconds, she's out in the cold. The door is slammed in her face and she listens to a lock being turned, a shutter rolling down, and the distant murmuring of voices from the other side of the door.

She staggers over to a nearby bench where she sits and tries to work out what has just taken place. This has never happened to her before. Never. She feels humiliated and can't bring herself to turn around in case anybody saw it all. Her face burns with shame as she stuffs her hands deep into her pockets to still the tremble that has taken hold of them.

Did that man in the café really just throw her out? She widens her eyes and shakes her head in disbelief. She is a grown woman and she has just been ejected from a restaurant. And for what? All because she refused to accept shoddy service and requested a cup of proper coffee. Her mind feels fuzzy, full of cotton wool. She is disorientated and can't seem to think straight. That *was* what just happened in there, wasn't it? Sometimes, her memory gets a little frayed around the edges and her thinking gets a bit disjointed, but she is pretty sure her request wasn't so bad that she deserved to be ejected into the street. He actually manhandled her, grabbing her arm with force. It should be *she* who reports him. She has a mind to rap on the door and tell him exactly what she thinks of him and his dim-witted little waitress but has more important things to do. He isn't worth the effort.

Sitting up straight, Celia readjusts her jacket and tightens her clothing. Why is this place so bloody cold all the time? Her eyes water as the breeze picks up and bites at her exposed skin. She sniffs and looks at her watch. Now would be as good a time as any to go and see Eva's parents. Celia has no appetite for coffee or any damn thing at all. Her stomach is in knots. The walk back up to West Cliff will do her good, help her clear her head and get her thinking straight again. That man has pushed her off balance with his wild accusations and forceful manner and now her mind is in a whirl.

She stands up, her legs still weak with shock, and heads back up to the steps. The noise of the gulls overhead suddenly seems deeply invasive, their screeches blocking out all other sounds nearby. She brings her hands up to her head and stops for a second. This is silly. She has to pull herself together. Is she really going to let one bombastic man spoil her day and ruin her plans? She is better than that, stronger and a damn sight more capable than that silly little waitress back there. She was a waste of space. No wonder the economy of this county is in the state it's in if the nation is relying on the likes of her to keep it turning over.

Celia carries on up the steps, her energy waning after being wrongly accused like that. She gets to the top and stops to catch her breath and checks her watch again. It's only just after 8.30 a.m. She is almost certain that Eva's parents are either retired or unemployed. Celia is bound to catch them in. It doesn't even matter whether Eva has already made the visit there or not. Celia will soon set them both straight and let them know who the sane one is out of the pair of them and who is delusional. It will become apparent anyway, once she gets talking to them. Celia is good with people. They warm to her. She may not have many friends but those she does have, remain so for life.

The noise of the gulls above her continues, rattling her thoughts and putting her on edge. For the love of God, what is it about that noise that is so unsettling? It makes her want to gnash her teeth and scream out into the open air for them to stop. It's all-pervading and an assault on her ears.

The beach below her is empty apart from one dog walker. She watches as a man braves the elements to throw sticks for his golden retriever. The dog responds by running off in the other direction and chasing its tail round and round like a whirling dervish, sand and water spraying far and wide.

Celia looks up again at the huge, white birds swooping and diving overhead, their hooked beaks and beady eyes making her feel quite sick. One of them lets out an almighty screech directly above her head, causing her to bring her hands up to cover her ears. The whole thing makes her giddy and unsettled.

Another sound in the distance draws her eyes away from the birds. It's coming from behind her. Somebody shouting, calling her name. Her blood thickens in her head. The people from the restaurant – could it be them? She shivers as a strong gust of wind takes her by surprise. Of course it's not them. How silly of her. They don't know who she is so how on earth could they be calling her name? The whole episode has made her paranoid.

She listens again. Is it somebody calling her or is the sound of the sea and the circling gulls above her playing tricks on her over-anxious brain?

There it is. Definitely somebody shouting her name.

Oh God. Please don't let it be him. That awful Gareth man from last night. She doesn't think she could bear to even look at him, let alone have a conversation with him. Perhaps he's calling her to apologise? She hopes not because she won't accept it. It may be prissy of her to get so uptight about something so small, but she refuses to be second best to anybody, especially some-body's ex-girlfriend. He can take his apology and shove it up his arse.

Her ears become attuned to the cry from behind her. It's not him. This voice belongs to a female. It's not Eva either. She would recognise her voice anywhere. This one has a distinct timbre and a completely different accent. Eva has a slightly northern accent whereas the one that is currently calling her is lacking in any sort of local brogue. It's coming from somebody who enunciates every sound, each and every syllable coming out clearly and ringing through the crisp, morning air.

Celia feels herself sigh out loud, suddenly realising who this person is. Not now. Of all the times to spot her, it has to be when she is on her way to do something very important. Why can't they just let her be so she can get on with seeing Eva's family? Of all the times for the girls to bump into her, why does it have to be now? Celia can practically see the house from here.

She hears the clatter of feet pounding up behind her and turns to give them her best smile, the force of it making her face ache.

'Hey, lovely lady, Celia! We've been calling you from back there. Did you not hear us?'

Lizzie and Tyler, the Goth girls from the train, stand opposite her, their attire and make-up even more severe and outlandish than on the journey here.

'Girls!' Celia cries with her arm outstretched towards them. 'Sorry, I couldn't hear a thing with these bloody awful things whining and whirling around up above me. How are you? Enjoying the festival, I hope?'

'Oh, it's ace!' Lizzie says with a slight squeal of excitement. 'We're already looking at booking for next year, aren't we, Tyler?

The other girl nods, her pale face and long hair shimmering in the early-morning light.

'That's great,' Celia says, happy that they are having a good time but desperately anxious to get away.

'So where are you off to so early?' Tyler asks softly as she pulls at her fingerless gloves to straighten them.

'Me?' Celia asks as she flaps her hand dismissively. 'Oh just out for a stroll in the quiet.'

'On your own?' Lizzie looks genuinely concerned as she speaks, 'Why isn't your friend with you? We go everywhere together, don't we, Tyle?'

Tyler nods enthusiastically and they link arms as if to prove their point.

'Oh, don't worry about me being on my own, girls,' Celia says quickly. 'I'm an early riser but Eva prefers a sleep in. I'll be just fine.'

'Is that the name of your friend? Eva?' Tyler says in a squeaky voice that is almost childlike in its innocence.

Celia could kick herself. She wishes she hadn't told them Eva's name. She has no idea why. It just feels safer that way, more secure. When it comes to dealing with Eva, Celia would much rather keep it all to herself and not share any details with strangers. Eva is her problem. Hers and hers alone.

Celia smiles and nods, hoping this will be enough to tide them over. Why are people always so curious about what she is up to and who she is seeing? Like the time Jade, her ex-boyfriend's sister, kept asking her where she and Liam were going to and why Celia had stopped Liam from seeing his family. Sometimes people just don't get it. She told Jade as much and a whole lot more which included some home truths about what Liam actually thought of his family. Jade obviously got straight on to her beloved brother and told him a pack of lies about what Celia had said. He broke it off with her a few days later, choosing to believe his sister over his girlfriend.

Celia bites her lip. All she had done was say what he was really thinking. He didn't need to say it out loud. It had been evident by his expressions and body language what he thought of them all every time they were mentioned.

Celia smiles. Jade got what was coming to her afterwards, however. Nobody could prove that the dog shit posted through Jade's door was linked to Celia, or the threatening letters. They tried to pin it on her by getting the police involved but they got nowhere with their wild accusations. The whole family was sent packing. Sometimes karma is very sweet and swift indeed.

'Anyway, girls, it's been lovely seeing you. Enjoy the rest of your holiday and don't do anything too untoward!' She gives them a hearty smile and quickly backs away as Lizzie tries to hug her.

There is a flicker of shock in Lizzie's face at being rebuffed. She hides it with a sudden smile.

'Oh, we most definitely will!' Tyler cries.

Celia scrutinises Tyler's wide-eyed expression. She is clearly unaware of the fleeting awkward moment that has just passed between Celia and her friend. Such naivety and innocence. Such complete stupidity. Some people see nothing. They're too wrapped up in their own hedonistic lifestyles to notice or care about the plight of others.

Celia smiles at them one last time and watches as they head off into the distance, relieved to see the back of them. She is a busy woman and has things she needs to do. And as for the hug? She has never been particularly tactile and doesn't have any plans to start cuddling near-strangers in the street. Her mind is honed in on one thing and one thing only: seeing Eva's parents and informing them of how deranged and unstable their daughter is; telling them how she will try to warp their minds and convince them of many untruths about her life. Nobody knows the real Eva like she does. They're inseparable. Eva doesn't see it like that at the moment, but it will soon become apparent to her that they are practically the same person.

Celia turns once again towards the house and feels her heart leap up into her throat. She squints and blinks hard and deliberately, as if it's an apparition and closing her eyes will make it all go away. Her pulse quickens at the sight of the figure over the road. She watches it closely. There is something deeply voyeuristic about being able to observe people who don't know they are being watched. You see them in their true form; see them for what they really are. They are stripped bare of any pretensions and artificial mannerisms. What you see is the very essence of their being, their inner core. The real them.

Celia stares hard. It looks so much like him, *Gareth*. She needs to get closer to see properly. The powers that be are really putting her patience to the test today. It feels like she is taking one step forward and two steps back. She quickens her pace, focusing on the individual ahead. Her breath stops as the figure turns around. Celia lets out a sharp bark of a laugh. It's not Gareth. Of course it's not. She can see that now. This person is much older, stockier around the midriff. She has no idea why she even considered it. Anybody would think she was obsessed with him, the way she's going on. She hardly knows the man and that's exactly how she wants it to stay.

Shaking her head, she continues walking. The road is almost clear of cars. All she has to do is cross it. The house is almost within striking distance, so close she can almost feel its warmth emanating from within.

The sudden clatter causes her to stop. A small, shrill scream pierces the air, rising above the sound of scraping metal. Celia turns around and behind her is a cyclist lying on the side of the road, the handlebars of her bike twisted at an awkward angle, her legs jammed under the frame. The cyclist's face is pressed into the asphalt and a gathering of fruit from the basket on the front of the bike rolls around the road, scattering in all directions and circling in the gutter next to Celia's feet. Frustration grips her. Something else put in place to stop her. Reaching down, she gets on her haunches and puts her face next to the cyclist's head. A lone apple rolls to and fro in the gulley at the side of the tarmac, a chunk of its skin missing, revealing the creamy moist flesh inside.

'I'm fine.' The strength of the voice takes Celia by surprise. 'But if you wouldn't mind helping me up, it would be much appreciated.'

Placing her hands under the woman's armpits, Celia manages to hoist her to her feet, the cyclist's legs half dragging the bike off the edge of the road and onto the pavement.

'Damned stone on the road,' the woman says as she stands up and brushes herself down with mottled, gnarled hands. She taps her arms and legs and smiles at Celia, offering her hand to shake. 'Nothing broken. I'm Frances, by the way. Thanks for helping me up. I'm not quite a supple as I used to be.'

Celia nods, annoyance beginning to grate at her. It's obvious this lady is fine, no injuries and as she just said, nothing broken, and yet she wants to hang around and have formal introductions when all Celia wants to do is get moving and get inside that house. So many hindrances and obstacles and this cyclist is just another one: somebody who is getting in her way and impeding her progress.

'Well, anyway,' the woman says as she retracts her hand in mild embarrassment and leans down to salvage what she can of the fruit. She places two apples and an orange back in the basket and pulls her bike upright then straddles it again, a fleeting look of confusion crossing her features. 'Best be off. Thanks again for helping me out.'

And with that, she is gone, a speck in the distance, her long cape fluttering out behind her as she picks up speed and rounds the corner, quickly disappearing out of sight.

Celia turns back to look at the house and feels her stomach plummet. She is just in time to catch a brief glimpse of a young-looking person step over the threshold and close the door behind them. It was all too fast to see who it was but what she can say is that it wasn't either of Eva's parents. Celia digs her nails into her palms, enjoying the mild pain that bites at her skin. *Shit!*

She turns her back to the house and stares out to sea. Could it be Eva in there right now? If it is, she should take this opportunity to knock on the door and settle this once and for all, tell Eva to leave it be, that her parents abandoned her and that it's Celia she should be with, not the cruel, callous people who left her behind. But what if it isn't her? What if it's a neighbour or a friend? This is a delicate situation and she may only get one chance to speak with them, to persuade them to let her in so she can put her side of the story across. She has to get it right first time.

Celia looks around for a seat. She can sit and wait. She has no other pressing engagements, nowhere she needs to be. She drops down on a nearby bench and sighs heavily. The one thing she does have in her empty life is time.

The bench is exposed to the elements and within minutes, she is freezing, her skin numb to the touch. She huddles down under her collar and digs her hands deep into her pockets for extra warmth. It wouldn't be so bad if she had a flask of something hot or even if she'd had something to eat or drink this morning, but her stomach is empty, her throat is dry and she is freezing.

The time seems to go on and on. She sits and waits, her patience stretched to capacity, her face growing colder by the second. It's like a form of torture, having to sit here in these freezing temperatures with no endpoint in sight. She stares at her watch. The visitor has been in there for over half an hour. What if they don't come out for hours? Is she really prepared to sit here and freeze her backside off all morning?

Right on cue, her stomach lets out a howl. A headache is setting in behind her eyes. Whether she likes it or not, she needs to eat. She can find a decent café, one that actually serves lattes and doesn't abuse their customers, and then come back here once she has eaten.

She is too cold and hungry to sit around waiting.

Her legs are like jelly and she is light-headed with hunger as she walks back into town. This whole visit has turned out to be somewhat livelier than she ever anticipated. It will be worth it in the end, though, once she has Eva back on her side. Things will seem brighter then. Things will be back to how they were when she and Eva were teenagers. That's all she wants really: to have her best friend back in her life with some sort of tangible relationship that will make her feel secure again. It's all she's ever wanted.

There is a light tinkling sound at her feet as she stands up. She stops and looks down, her eyes drawn to the sparkle of the tiny pile of jewellery on the floor next to her. She reaches down and scoops it up, threads of silver hanging between her frozen fingers. It's her bracelet, the one Greta gave her. It must have come loose at some point. She isn't sure how it has happened but thanks whichever deity drew her attention to it. She could so easily have marched ahead and lost it completely, leaving it for some stranger to find. It would have broken her heart when she realised it was gone.

Lifting it up to the light, she counts the charms, making sure they're all there and securely fastened on. With a quick nod, satisfied that everything that should be there is there, Celia shoves it into her pocket, zips it up and marches back into town.

23

GARETH

He wakes up earlier than he thought he would, considering last night. The room is blanketed in grey and it's silent outside save for the weak and distant roar of the sea.

He makes a point of not looking in the mirror as he passes. He's not sure he can face seeing himself all battered and bruised. His arm feels as if it's been hit by a mallet and his nose is so stuffed and choked up, he can barely breathe. But he's alive at least. And so is Eva. It could all have gone so horribly wrong, turned out very differently. He'd had too much to drink; that's what spurred him on. Fortunately, that's also what made him less able to kill her. He was clumsy, awkward and disorientated, unable to control his limbs properly, unable to *think* properly. Just as well, really. Today could have been very grim indeed.

Stumbling through to the bathroom, he showers and cleans himself up, feeling the damage to his face as he traces his fingers over it. His nose is swollen and a purple bruise is blooming on his cheek. As for his hand – well, she had a good bite at him and it hurts like hell, but he'll live. No stitches needed which is always a bonus. He couldn't face having to sit in a hospital waiting room surrounded by last night's drunkards and druggies who, after a skinful and a good fight, would all look like him – injured and covered in blood. He'll manage on his own. He did in the past so why should now be any different?

Hunger gnaws at him, his empty belly growling and contracting, screaming out for food. Breakfast is a croissant and coffee. It's all he has time for. He has stuff to do, a person to see, unfinished business to attend to.

He doesn't notice the sharp breeze that whips in from the sea. And he certainly doesn't see the lady in the distance talking to the two young women. Nothing else is on his radar except his mother. His guts twist in anticipation of what he is about to do.

She's in the house for a change, which is a positive. That means she's not in town doing that ridiculous nonsense she actually calls work.

He doesn't say anything. He wants to, but the words just won't come. He sees her looking at his bashed-up face and clocks her trying to hide her shock. He doesn't know why. She should be used to seeing him covered in bruises. She became a past master at hiding them for so many years, she's almost an expert; putting him in long-sleeved sweaters until the bruises faded, changing his hairstyles to cover the bumps and scars on his head. She should be beyond being shocked by this sort of stuff.

She steps aside to let him in and they sit opposite each other in the living room, the atmosphere so charged and heavy it practically crackles, until eventually she breaks the silence with her words.

'So,' she says softly, 'at long last, you've decided to come home.'

He knows exactly what she's getting at – the fact he didn't

come back for the old man's funeral. What the fuck did she expect? Did she really think he was going to turn up decked out in his best suit and pay tribute to an old soak who regularly beat the shit out of him? If so, she is clearly delusional and needs her head looking at. There was no way Gareth was going to take part in the sham that was his dad's funeral. His father's friends from the pub will have been there as well as a handful of neighbours who thought of him as no more than a working-class guy who liked a drink every now and then and the sort of man who occasionally gave his boy a clout to keep him in line.

None of them have any idea. Not a fucking clue.

'I'm not staying for long,' Gareth says stiffly, trying his hardest to keep the anger out of his voice. He has to remain calm, to get his words out properly so he can get his point across and hear her answers.

'You never do,' she replies, staring hard at his face.

'No,' he says quietly, 'I never do, do I.' He wants to ask her why she thinks that is, but opts for silence instead. If he speaks now, it will be an explosion of fury that pours out him: years and years of pent-up anger and resentment and frustration. He has to stay cool and not rise to her remarks.

'So what brings you back then? Not very often I get to see my son. Be nice to see you here more often.'

He grits his teeth and brings his knees together, gripping them with his hands to stop them from knocking. He is so hot and furious he feels he could combust at any moment.

'I want to ask you something.'

Her eyes flicker slightly and a tiny pulse hammers in her jaw. She blinks slowly and deliberately, then turns her gaze to the floor.

'Okay. I can't guarantee I'll give you an answer, or at least the answer you're looking for, but I'll do my best.' Her voice is tight and croaky and Gareth couldn't be sure but her skin looks shiny and damp, as if she is breaking out in a sweat.

He sits for a second trying to work out how to phrase it but eventually decides that blunt force is the only way. No matter how many times he has worded it in his head over the past few weeks, he has never found a way of doing it that seems fitting, each and every sentence feeling clunky and contrived. His eyes fill up as he speaks. He can't seem to help it. So many weeks of anger and upset locked up inside. And now it is all slowly leaking out of him.

'Why didn't you tell me I had a sister?'

She looks as if she has been shot. Her head wobbles slightly and she brings her hands up to her abdomen, gripping onto her stomach with bony, wrinkled fingers. He waits for her to reply and watches as her mouth moves. Nothing comes out. Her features go slack and she slumps back in the chair, her eyes distant and uncomprehending.

'I deserve an answer, Mother!' He promised himself he wouldn't lose his temper. He's had enough outbursts in the past few weeks to last him a lifetime and he is tired of them. He no longer likes who he has become. Who he has become makes him sick to his stomach. He has turned into the person he hated and feared the most with his violent ways and uncontrollable temper.

Her head lolls about as if she is having some sort of seizure. Gareth doesn't move. He refuses to be drawn into her stupid little game. Because that's what this is. She is pretending to have one of her funny turns, hoping it will stop him. It won't. He will not leave until she tells him why. He won't let his temper get the better of him, not any more, but he won't move until she opens her mouth and starts telling the truth.

'I've got all day, Mother. Take your time,' he says dryly, and watches, fascinated, as she suddenly perks up and lifts her head up as if nothing has just taken place.

She drums her fingers lightly on the edge of the chair. Her nails are yellowed and ridged, her skin splattered with liver spots. Time hasn't been kind to her, but then, she hasn't been particularly kind to herself over the years. As the old saying goes – you get the face you deserve.

Gareth scans the room, looking for empty bottles stashed away in hidden corners or down the back of the sofa. No need to hide them now she lives on her own. There was no need to do it when his father was alive. It's not as if he disapproved. She stashed and hid them because all these years, she has been lying to herself, pretending she was a good mother and that there wasn't a problem when all the time this house, this *family*, was breathtakingly deceitful, carrying on in the most insidious way possible.

'You didn't need to know. They took her away and she never came back. Why would you need to know?'

His anger is at boiling point. He has to keep himself in check. After last night, his capabilities scare him. He doesn't want to lose control again. Not like that. Not ever.

'Why would I need to know? Because I have a sister out there and *you* should have told me!' His chest feels tight and for a brief second, he feels sure he is having a heart attack. He had forgotten how obtuse and stubborn his mother could be, burying her head in the sand, pretending everything is just fine when it is anything but.

She shrugs and half turns away from him. He wants to launch himself at her but sits, his eyes boring into her, until she turns back and sighs loudly. 'This place would have been no good for her. You know that.'

Gareth almost chokes on his own spittle. His eyes are fixed on her as she continues.

'He hated her. I have no idea why.'

Gareth wants to add that he hated everyone but lets her go on, afraid she will stop.

'He broke her arm.'

There is a prolonged silence. He doesn't need to ask who and she doesn't need to say. The silence says it all.

'That doesn't answer my question. Why didn't you tell me?'

She slumps, and Gareth can see the tears as they pour down her face. He has never seen his mother cry. Through all the arguments, the drunken battles, the beatings, the screaming and hollering, never once did he ever see her break down.

He lets her cry herself out. This could just be another way of stalling, yet another of his mother's strategies to deny him what he wants to hear. He will not leave here until she explains it to him.

'I don't know!' she suddenly splutters through a river of tears. 'I don't know why I never told you! At first, you were too young to understand and then as time went on, it all seemed to be so far in the past, it was pointless bringing it up. What good would it have done?'

Gareth remains mute. There are so many things he could say to her in return, but he knows she would never be able to comprehend any of his words. She knows nothing of his life, of his contact with Eva. She has never truly known or understood her own son.

'I've met her,' he says and watches his mother for some sort of reaction. She hides it well, he'll grant her that much, but it's there. A stiffening of her spine, a vein that protrudes slightly on her neck, all signs that she is under stress. That and yet more tears. At long last, Trish Tweedie is starting to crack. Not before time.

She sniffs and glares at him. 'When? And how?'

He decides that it's none of her business. She doesn't need to know that part. She doesn't deserve to know. 'I just did. We met up. She was in London and so was I.'

She nods and wipes her eyes with the back of her hand. 'If you want me to say sorry, then I'm sorry. I don't know what else you want me to say, son.'

He grits his teeth at her use of the word 'son'. She has never been a proper mother to him. He remembers the blows from her fists when he was a small boy as well as those from his father. His mother didn't hold back once the gin started flowing.

'She's here at the minute, in town. She lives here.'

He sees his mother wince at his words and is glad.

'I know she is. I've seen her. She posted this through my door recently.' She produces a small photograph from the side of her chair and hands it over to him. Gareth takes it and stares at it, waiting for the blurry images to come into focus. 'It's your dad and me. And her, before it all happened. Before she was taken.'

It's hard to understand how this picture can paint such a happy scene knowing what he knows about the people in it. He can barely bring himself to look at his father's face without spitting on it. It doesn't look like his parents. They are younger, slimmer, less ravaged by alcohol and the passing of time. If she hadn't told him who it was, he would never have known. Funny thing is, he recognises this picture but can't think where from.

He continues to stare at it, his mind in overdrive, trying to work out why it strikes a chord with him. It looks so damn familiar. Then it dawns on him. Eva's house. It was in her house in a frame. He never really looked at it closely when he visited. She had so many paintings and wall hangings dotted about, it was lost in the plethora of colour and design surrounding it. God, he feels like such a fool. All the time, her connection to him was right in front of his nose and he didn't realise.

He hands the photo back, his face rigid with disbelief. 'So, are you going to meet her?'

She shrugs and juts out her bottom lip. 'Up to her, I suppose. If she calls, she calls and if she doesn't then life'll go on as it always did.'

He doesn't know what to say. If he is being honest, he hates them both equally. Why should he try to mediate some sort of reconciliation? How they handle their relationship is down to them. All he came here for is answers. He isn't sure if he got them but he doesn't think he's going to get much more out of his mother. He got to see her rattled and upset and that satisfied him. It doesn't exonerate her in any way for the unspeakable things that she did to him as a child. It just makes him feel better. 'I'm leaving now and I doubt you will ever see me again.'

He wonders if she will cry once more or protest or try to stop him. She doesn't do any of those things and he isn't altogether surprised. He turns up at her door with a battered face and she can't even be bothered asking him how it happened. That's the level of her compassion. If this is the best she can do, he doesn't want it. They are better off apart. His only regret is the fact that Eva was taken and he stayed. They have both been damaged by this woman. She deserves to be alone.

He hears a muffled sob as he gets up and makes his way to the hallway. He stops, hoping she will call him back so he can gain a little happiness by refusing. There is nothing but the sound of crying from behind him. Stifled sobs from a woman who didn't care enough.

He opens the door, steps outside and closes it behind him for the final time.

24

TRISH

Trish Tweedie listens to the sound of her son leaving her. He means what he says. He won't be back. She knows it. It was obvious by the look on his face, by the way he kept his simmering fury pushed down inside him. It frightened her, made her realise how serious he was. She's never seen him like that before. And his face... she has no idea what has gone on and didn't ask. Her first instinct was to reach out and touch him but she knew better and held back. Their relationship is too damaged to make such a bold move.

Her eyes fill up again. He was always such a sweet boy, such a gentle soul. She drags her hand across her face to wipe away the tears. She should have done more to help him: stopped drinking and took him away from it all. She knows that, but it was so diffi-cult at the time. And now it's all too late.

She has no idea how he met his sister. She doesn't want to know. The girl probably sought him out, the way she has sought Trish out. She's surprised it's taken her this long. What her daughter doesn't realise is, her life will be a hell of a lot sweeter if she remains in ignorance. She should take herself back off to where she came from. Easier for them all that way.

She bites at her nails until they are ragged and torn and then looks around the room. She still can't quite believe that Russ has gone. He was such a presence, such a big and vocal man and so full of life that the house has a vacuum where he used to be. Instead of him filling it up, the place is suddenly full of shadows and memories, few of them pleasant. That's why she spends so long out of it. She had planned on retiring soon but then if she does that, what else is she going to do with her time? Sit around this place waiting for God? Best to keep herself busy, keep working. At least that way, she gets out and meets people. It keeps her mind off everything, like her son just walking out on her for the final time. She knew it would happen. He's a good man and she has been a less than decent parent. And as for Russ? Well, the less said about him the better. She should have left him years ago, but then where would she have gone? And what if the life she made for herself was worse than the one she had walked away from? Sometimes it's better the devil you know.

Gareth didn't ask if she was still drinking. Would it have made any difference to his decision if she told him she hasn't touched a drop in over six months? Probably not. His mind was made up. She could tell by his stance and the way he looked at her. She disgusts him and it hurts knowing that. But it's all too late. Everything is way, way too late.

A shape shifts and moves behind her. Her spine stiffens in response. This house is cursed. They should have moved years ago. She wanted to but Russ wouldn't hear of it. Said there was no reason to go anywhere else. He couldn't see it – all the damage he had caused. He had a selective memory, sifting out all the bad things, pretending none of it ever happened. He was far less aggressive in the latter part of his life and seemed to have forgotten what had gone before. In her mind, it all grew, morphed into a monster of a memory, especially since giving up the drink. It gave her a modicum of clarity, which wasn't always a good thing. Some things are best left tucked away in the recesses of your brain, kept as unremembered images which only wreak havoc if toyed with and set free.

Another movement followed by a rustle behind her causes her to shuffle her body round. From behind the curtains there is the sound of something vibrating. All of a sudden, a cat leaps out from behind the fabric and lands on her lap with a thud.

'Sybil! For God's sake. You almost gave me a heart attack, you stupid beast!'

She runs her fingers through the cat's thick, silky fur.

'I thought you were outside. Are you wanting to go out? Is that it?'

She picks up the animal and walks to the front door. She opens it and scans the nearby area before depositing the cat outside. Gareth is no longer around. He has gone, nowhere to be seen.

'Go on, you silly old cat. Go and find your real owners and stop bothering me.'

She closes the door, knowing it will be back when it's hungry. It's been hanging around her for a few weeks since she started feeding it. She has no idea what its real name is. She named it Sybil after a close friend who died last year. Her long-time friend, Sybil, was a feline fiend, keeping dozens of cats until her house was practically overrun with the little blighters. They were all taken away by the council when she died, and her house given a deep clean by a group of men in white overalls. A young couple live there now. They've laid a patio and had new windows put in. Most of the houses around here have young families in them or are being run as B&Bs. There's only Trish left out of all the original people who moved onto the road back in the day. She's surrounded by youngsters, people who are too busy to even notice her. She doesn't mind it too much. She would rather be left alone than have people pushing their noses into her business. They're not her sort of people anyway – all too liberal and flowery with their showy, ostentatious houses that reek of money. Give her a good, solid family who all know their place any day, not these namby-pamby do-gooders who think it's their God-given right to tell others how to live their lives.

There's one sweet young thing – a single parent who works at the local off licence and lives three doors down. Things are tight for her money wise, and she continually works extra hours to make ends meet. She's always worth the time. Trish will do anything to help her out, but the others – brisk, efficient youngsters with high-minded ideologies and few manners – she has no time for them and she is pretty sure the feeling is mutual. That's up to them. She has made her mistakes along the way – lots of them – but she has never judged others. Not once.

These people, however, have a completely different mindset; she sees them gathered in their gardens together, knocking back their homemade, organic wine, and can hear them putting the world to rights, clicking their tongues at those who dare to be different to them, slating those beneath them who barely have two farthings to rub together. They have no idea what it feels like to have to struggle through life, to have to put up with your lot or get caught up in the drink to try to forget it. Not a bloody clue. None of them would survive if a hard time presented itself to them gift wrapped. They're all so used to being carried through life with no real stresses or strains to bother them that they would all fall flat on their faces if their worlds were turned upside down by a sudden tragedy. She sees them watching her, possibly even pitying her after the death of Russ. One of them even sent a condolence card on the day of his funeral. She tore it up and put it in the bin. She doesn't need their pity or sympathy. She'll manage just fine on her own.

She doesn't hear the door at first. Her thoughts are elsewhere – Russ, Gareth, past times... Eva. It pierces her brain like shrapnel as it comes again: a deep thudding that echoes throughout the room, puncturing her thoughts, jolting her back to the present.

Her muscles ache as she forces her body out of the chair. She feels far older than she actually is, her limbs aching and throbbing with every movement. The top of her neck is in permanent pain and her hips feel as if she is being repeatedly prodded with sharp pins. Still, at least she's here. Not like some of her friends who went at a very young age. 'Lifestyle-related deaths' they call them nowadays, don't they? Brought on by drinking and smoking and a piss-poor diet. She will go the same way no doubt, although hopefully not for a good few years yet.

She yanks open the door, her thoughts too full of other things to register who it is that is standing there, staring at her. It takes a few seconds. And then she realises. Trish feels herself go faint. It's her. Eva. Trish's head spins, the floor sways under her feet. She grasps the doorjamb to steady herself and swallows hard, hoping she has managed to cover up her shock. She should have expected this. She just didn't expect it this soon after Gareth's rapid departure. Everything seems to be happening at once with no time in between to catch her breath or mentally prepare herself.

She stares at the fragile-looking creature before her. The wind buffets Eva's hair, fanning the long, auburn locks into a peacock's tail. Her skin is pale and her eyes are a striking shade of green. She is a real beauty. Her features are all Russ's. He may have had his faults but there was no way of avoiding the fact that Russ was a handsome man, and Eva, this tall, winsome woman standing on her doorstep, is his double. That was the first thing she noticed when she saw her in town.

Eva sees her and lets out a small shriek.

'You!' Is all Eva can say to her. She lifts her finger and points in Trish's face, her fist shaking, her skin freezing as Trish reaches out to take her hand. She snatches it away, her features contorting as fury envelops her, changing her face into something starkly different to the delicate beauty she was just a few moments before.

Trish steps back, her heart thumping wildly in her chest. This isn't how she wanted it to be. She had always hoped that if Eva ever did find her, their reunion would be in a neutral environment, somewhere that didn't remind her of what had gone before. But it isn't. It's here and it's happening right now and she has to find a way round it all, a way of dealing with it and making the best of a bad job.

'Come in and we'll talk,' is all she can say as Eva stalks past her, pushing her hard against the wall. Trish rubs the base of her spine where she connects with the plaster. Her alcohol-soaked, post-menopausal bones don't take well to meeting with a hard surface. She'll have a huge bruise there later but it doesn't matter. This is Eva's payback, her chance to get even. Trish follows her into the living room and observes the deep scowl on her estranged daughter's face. And judging by the hatred exuding from her, this is just the beginning...

25

GARETH

He can leave here now and go back London. Meeting his mother didn't answer all of his questions but he got as much out of her as he could. She has never been one for quiet reflection or soul baring. He picks up his pace and heads back to his hotel. He can finally step away from it all and go back to London knowing he did what he could. The old woman will die at some point and the relevant authorities will contact him to sort out her estate, but that's something he will deal with when it occurs. For now, he can concentrate on the rest of his life while she lives hers. He cares not a jot what she does with it. She can drink herself into a stupor if that's how she wants it. It's not his problem any more.

He stops by the swing bridge, briefly considering going to see Eva. Just one last visit to tell her exactly what he thinks of her. If he really felt like it, he could force her back here, to his mother's house, and have it out with the both of them. He could tell the old woman exactly what her maniac daughter did, just to see their faces, to gain some pleasure from seeing their horror and misery. But he's better than that. He is better than the pair of them put together, and he will emerge from the wreckage of this whole thing stronger and more resilient than ever. He has no idea what Eva will do with the rest of her life and right now, he really doesn't give a shit. There will be no contact from him and he hopes she at least has the good grace to do the same in return.

A group of tourists bustles its way up the steps, forcing Gareth back out of the way. One of them smiles at him and offers her apologies. He smiles back and turns away. He has no anger left in him. It has evaporated and he hopes it never returns. Anger is for the weak and the hopeless. They are furious at their lot in life and lash out to blame others. He doesn't want to be one of those people. He has done more than his fair share of blaming over the past few weeks and it's time to move on.

He decides against a visit into town and instead goes back to his hotel. There is no sign of Celia, and Gareth finds himself grateful for the smallest of mercies as he trudges up the stairs to his room. He can be packed and out of this place in no time at all. Another overnight stop to catch a connecting train back to London doesn't faze him in the slightest. He contacted work when he arrived and spun a tale about a family emergency and that he would be back as soon as he could.

Sitting on the edge of the bed, he picks up his phone and messages his boss telling him he'll be back in a day or two. He will breeze into work as if nothing has happened even though everything has. His life has once again been through the wringer and he has survived. Nobody will know anything about it and things will go on as they always have, which is exactly what he wants. This is a chapter of his life he wants to shut and never re-open.

Using his phone, he books a ticket back to London, back to the place he belongs. He will leave here later once he's packed and has eaten and had a coffee to help rejuvenate him. His train doesn't depart until later in the afternoon which leaves him plenty of time.

Gareth glances around the room at the clothes scattered. He needs to buy some sort of overnight bag to carry his things back in. A last visit back to town means he can get some food, return to his hotel and pack before checking out. He will have to hang around Whitby for a few hours before his train leaves, which is a real pain, but that's just how it is. At least he's going home today. That's all he needs to think about. Everything and everyone else can go to hell.

26

CELIA

Celia bustles behind the queue of people, her tray clasped tightly between her fingers. Why are people so slow? Can she not even get a coffee in this town without it becoming some sort of major ordeal? She shuffles along behind an elderly man who looks and smells like he has slept in his clothes. An odour emanates from him that makes Celia want to gag. If she doesn't get something to eat and drink pretty soon and move away from this man, she feels sure she will scream.

The couple serving behind the counter suddenly sense the growing air of discontentment from the escalating line of disgruntled customers, and decide to pick up their pace, quickly filling up trays with plates of food and handing out cups of steaming tea and coffee.

Celia snatches hers, hands over her money and slinks off to sit in the corner. The last thing she wants to do is strike up a conversation with anybody close by. She fears she will descend into a near meltdown if she doesn't get some caffeine and food into her system in the next five minutes.

She watches everybody bustle past as she launches into her

breakfast. They troop in, red-faced and reeking of the cold air from outside.

It doesn't take her long to demolish the food on her plate and drain her cup. She sits back, finally replete and ready to undertake anything. The fog in her head has cleared and she is thinking straight again. Last night knocked her off balance. She has spent the morning wandering around feeling dazed and unable to function properly but now she is back on form, her thoughts clear, her mind razor sharp.

She pushes her chair back, pulls her collar up and strides through the centre aisle of the café out into the brightness of the daylight.

It's still relatively early and there are only a handful of people about. She thinks about what she will say when she sees Eva's parents at the door. She doesn't know these people and has to get them to see things from her point of view. It may get a bit heated and if it does, she will have to watch herself. She has a tendency to lose her self-control. Like the time she had the argument with a former colleague about something Celia was purported to have said about her. On that occasion, Celia's charm was in short supply and she lashed out and caught the woman in the face with her hand as she was trying to walk away. It was a silly accident but none of the other staff or the manager seemed to see it that way and Celia was asked to leave. It was a low paid job in a small shop but the stigma of it still stung.

Since working at the hospital, she has managed to get along with everybody. No problems at all. She did hear on the grapevine that shortly after the altercation with the other lady, the woman in question was given her marching orders for having her hand in the till. Just goes to show that it wasn't all Celia's fault and other people also have their failings and defects. That always makes her feel better. So often, she has been blamed for things that simply weren't her doing. It seems that people are always keen to drag her down and point the finger. But not any more. She has had enough of being trodden underfoot by everyone around her. From now on she is going to be more assertive and make sure people listen to what she has to say instead of casting her aside like a worn-out old sock.

The walk there takes just a few minutes. She feels an unexpected heart flutter as she knocks on the old, oak door, hoping the earlier visitor has left. Her chest tightens and she finds herself gasping slightly to get enough oxygen into her lungs. This isn't like her. She is normally a lot tougher than this, but then again, this is a fairly important event that she is about to commit herself to. What she is about to say will determine whether or not Eva's parents decide to take their daughter back into the fold. She is about to make sure they don't. She can't let that happen. She simply cannot lose Eva all over again. Eva's move to London was bad enough but at least they kept in touch. If Eva gets her feet tucked under this particular table, Celia fears she will never see her again and that is something she could not cope with. She simply will not allow it.

Celia knocks again and holds her breath as a murmur and a shuffling noise comes from the other side of the door. This is it. She has to be prepared. She has no script rehearsed in her head, no idea of what she will say or how she will greet the person who opens it to her. She curls her hands into tight fists and stuffs them into her pocket, her nails digging into her hot, creased palms.

Her face burns as the door opens with a dramatic creak. Celia holds her breath and doesn't exhale again until she sees who is behind the door. The heat escapes from her in a hot rush of relief as she stares at the person standing there staring back at her.

She moves forward, her left foot placed on the step, her hand outstretched as she speaks. Her voice feels detached from her body, as if the words she is saying belong to somebody else. Except of course, they don't. She is here now, and she has to convince this person that letting her in their home is a good idea. She is a stranger to them so she is going to have to use all her powers of persuasion to get them on her side. This is it. This is why she is here. She is doing this for Eva, for her, for the future of their friendship and she has to get it right. No room for errors or slip ups. Every word counts.

'Hi there,' Celia says softly, careful not to project her voice or make it too powerful. 'I was just wondering if I could speak to you about a personal matter regarding your daughter? I won't keep you for too long.'

Celia holds her breath. Her hand remains outstretched. Sometimes she surprises herself with the things she says and does. There is a pause as she waits for a response. She runs the risk of being ejected, of having a door slammed in her face for the second time this morning. But then the strangest thing happens. The person stands to one side and sweeps behind her to beckon Celia inside.

As tentatively as she can, Celia steps inside into the shadows and takes a deep and prolonged breath, heat wafting around her, highlighting the slightly stale odour of tobacco and unwashed clothes that hangs heavily in the air.

No room for error, she repeats to herself in a mantra fashion as she follows the older woman into the living room. Got to get this right if she is to get Eva back and keep her. That's what she wants. It's all she's ever wanted. Just Eva and Celia back how they were years ago, before life and other people dragged them apart. Celia knows it now; she will go to any lengths to restore things to how they were. All these years and she has put her moods and unhappiness down to the fact that her boyfriends were useless or her job was unfulfilling or a myriad of other reasons, but in actual fact, it's

Eva. It has always been Eva. And now she has found her, Celia will make damn sure she doesn't lose her.

Celia's legs almost fail her as she walks into the living room and sees her sitting there. She quickly recovers. A slight pulse visible through her sweater is the only tell-tale sign that anything is amiss. Other than that, she is every inch the composed, calm individual.

'Morning, Eva,' she says as she sits down opposite her friend and takes off her jacket, placing it carefully over the back of the chair. 'I think it's time to talk now, don't you?'

27

EVA

Things didn't go as planned, but then they never do, do they? Man makes plans and God smiles. That's what Greta used to always say to me when I was younger. If things ever went awry and I got upset, she would stroke my hair and say it to me, soothing me with her calm, solid words that always made sense. She had an idiom for every occasion.

The journey to my parents' house had my stomach in knots. By the time I reached it, my entire intestinal system was doing somersaults while my heart did a fine job of trying to escape out of my body, bouncing around my ribcage and clawing its way up my throat.

At one point, I even considered turning around and leaving but knew how pointless and silly such a move would be. After putting this much effort into finding them, after all these years, it would have been ridiculous. I was nervous; that's all it was, and it's understandable when you consider the circumstances. The fact I made it thus far is a feat in itself. Or at least that was what I kept telling myself as I marched up to the door with my heart in my mouth and knocked as hard as I could, so hard my knuckles burned and throbbed with the effort. I stood for a while, my tongue glued to the roof of my mouth, my shoulders so tense and rigid I had to rotate them to alleviate the pain that was setting in at the top of my spine.

When it eventually opened, I thought I was going to pass out. Blood rushed to my head and I had to hold onto the doorpost to steady myself. It took a few seconds for it all to sink in. It was her standing there – the lady from the cabin in town. My mother, the fortune teller. I can't even recall what my first words to her were. I'm pretty sure I shrieked and took a couple of steps back in shock.

She led me inside, or I barged past her. I can't quite remember how it all happened, but regardless, I ended up sitting in the living room trying to keep my anger in check. My initial shock quickly changed to fury. Those times she spoke to me – did she know who I was? And if she did, what did she think I was – some sort of doll she could tinker with? Somebody whose feelings didn't count for anything? So many things rushed through my head while I waited for her to sit down and speak to me. This woman held the key to both my future and my past and didn't seem to realise the damage she had done by just being who she was. I had already met her without realising it, and I felt stupid and deceived.

The silence in the house was the first thing I noticed once she had placed her backside down on one of the chairs after pacing around the room nervously. It was eerily quiet. No ticking clocks, no creaking floorboards. Just a deathly silence. I broke it with my words.

'You!' Was all I could say over and over. 'All this time and it was you!'

She had nodded and at least had the good grace to look shamefaced. My voice was shrill and echoed around us. I didn't care. I was furious and wanted her to know it. All my life, I had waited for this moment, planned it, dreaded it, dreamt about it, and she ruined it by being somebody I didn't want her to be.

'So where's your pathetic little familiar then? Gone into hiding, has she?'

My stomach went into a spasm at the thought of seeing that child again. I didn't think I could bear to hear her voice, to listen to the near truths that she comes out with.

'Bella?' my mother said sharply. 'She's one of the kids from up the road. I look after her sometimes when her mum goes to work. Got the gift, she has,' my mother said, tapping the side of her head conspiratorially. 'She can read people better that any spiritualist I've ever met. And I've met a few in my time.'

'Or you tell her!' I had shouted, thinking that she probably already knew it was me and had fed the child information. I was right all along; the pair of them were mocking me from the word go.

'I tell her nothing,' she replied frostily. 'Like I said, she has a gift. Got a good little intuitive brain on her she has. She'll go far in life.'

I shook my head dismissively and turned away from her to indicate how idiotic her words sounded. 'Anyway, forget about your stupid fortune telling nonsense. Where is he?' I had added, my eyes scanning the room for my father. I wanted them both to hear what I had to say. Things get distorted and changed when there are no witnesses to hand. I didn't want either of them twisting my words or trying to catch me out. They had the information I desperately craved and I had nothing. They were both one step ahead of me and I felt exposed, like a defenceless child again, discarded and unloved, standing on the outside looking in.

She had stared at me, her eyes rheumy and puzzled.

'My father!' I had shouted, tears spilling over. 'Where is he?'

She had shaken her head and looked away while I waited for

her response. I didn't initially understand what she had meant and it had taken a couple of seconds to click. She just sat there shaking her head over and over. I watched as she bit at her lip and dipped her head as if in prayer.

'When?' My mind had been in near collapse at this point. How had I missed his death? All these years I had kept a close eye on them to make sure they didn't move house and yet my own dad had died and I hadn't even picked up on it.

'A few months ago,' she had said quietly and looked away from me.

A few months ago, when my relationship with Gareth was coming to a head. I had been preoccupied and had taken my eye off the ball. So thoughtless of me, so stupid and negligent. I had put so much effort into chasing a phoney fortune teller and a dead man. All that energy, all those years of waiting, wasted on this... this pathetic creature in her horrid little house.

'How?'

I have no idea why I asked. I don't remember him and don't even feel any sort of connection to him but it seemed like the right thing to say at the time. I just wanted information and was prepared to grasp at anything.

She had sighed and rubbed at her eyes with her pale fingers. 'Heart attack.'

After that we had sat in silence for what felt like ages. It gave me time to gather my thoughts. I still had plenty to say, lots of questions that needed answering, and I wasn't prepared to go until I had the information I needed.

'Do you know who I am?' I asked tightly. 'You haven't asked me anything at all.'

She had nodded and I took this as a yes.

'I've seen you out there a few times, standing looking in. I didn't realise who you were the first time I saw you in town but then you've hung around here quite a bit and I just put two and two together, and then of course you look so much like Russ...'

She was right. I had stood out there a few times trying to drum up enough courage to go in but never quite managed it. One time, shortly after I moved here, I had drunk a full bottle of wine and almost got to the door before turning round and leaving. I was a mess, close to some sort of breakdown, so with hindsight I'm relieved I never managed to go through with it.

'Okay,' I had said after a while, my chest tight with anxiety. 'I'm going to come right out with this. I've spent all of my adult life with so many questions and now I would like some answers.'

I had watched as she slumped ever so slightly, her shoulders hunched and uneven. She looked different from the times I had seen her in town; older, less manicured. Tired and weary.

'Why didn't you come for me? I was taken into care and you made no attempts to get me back. Why?'

My mouth was desert dry as I spoke, the words ragged and misshapen as they tumbled out of me. Thirty-odd years they had been stuck in there, waiting to emerge, waiting to see the light of day.

She had nibbled at her nails and stared down at her feet, at the stupid, bright-pink slippers she was wearing, before answering. 'You were better off where you were, believe me.'

And that had been it. After all these years, all the waiting, all the feeling of rejection and that was her stock answer. That was the best she could come up with. A rock-sized lump rose in my throat.

It was all I could do to stop myself from shaking her. Did she have any idea of how lonely I had been over the years? Did she know or even care how much effort I had put into finding them and how insulted and unwanted I felt when I discovered I had a brother that they had decided to keep when I was left in care?

'Better off?' I had spluttered, my face rigid with disbelief and anger. 'Better off? How the hell do you know that? You have no idea about me or my life! For all you know, I could have been subjected to all kinds of abuse over the years.'

'And were you?' she said with a voice that betrayed no emotion whatsoever. 'Were you subjected to any sort of abuse? Because if you had stayed here, I can give you a cast-iron guarantee that you would have been abused enough for a hundred people.'

I had felt myself go cold at that point, my skin prickling with horror at what I was about to hear. I had known making this visit would be opening a can of worms and listening to her voice, I could tell they were about to come slithering out.

I had remained mute and watched her, willing her to continue. I wanted to hear it, every little bit of it, warts and all, no matter how indelicate or upsetting. I wanted every ghastly little detail.

She didn't disappoint.

'I should have left him but... things get in the way, and we were... we were both good drinkers. Not something I'm proud of, but that's how it was. Once I found out I was pregnant with you, I hoped the violence would stop, but once you were born, it actually got worse. It was you, you see...' She had turned to me and I saw then that tears were coursing down her face. I felt buoyed up. At least she cared enough to cry. It was better than hollow words thrown around the room with little or no feeling. 'He had always wanted a lad and when you were born, it gave him another reason to hate me. But he hated you more, I'm afraid, and nothing I could do would have ever changed that.'

I had felt myself gasp at that point. All this time, I had wondered if they missed me and thought about me. It had never once occurred to me that my own father might despise me. I had no words. She had plenty. It seemed that once she had started talking, she couldn't stop.

'Then one night it got really bad. He'd had too much. We both liked a drink but he'd gone right over the top. Been out drinking all day he had, and he had carried on into the early hours, knocking them back like there was no tomorrow. Still don't know how he didn't collapse or how his liver or kidneys didn't give out. I think they became hardened to it over the years. Anyway, he had come home full of hell, shouting about how I should have given him a son and how a girl would just be a burden on him, having to constantly fork out for clothes and other unnecessary stuff for you, and about how there would be no money for your wedding when you got older and that all girls did was whine and cry and cost money. He just went on and on and wouldn't give up saying you were a drain on him and had ruined his life.'

She had stared at me and I didn't dare breathe in case she stopped speaking. I needed to hear it, regardless of how bad it was. It was my early life, the formative years I have no memory of. This was it, in all its grit and glory. I had wanted the truth and by God, I was getting it.

'So I tried to get away. I was scared that night. Really scared. Not like the other times when I gave as good as I got. He was particularly vicious that night, threatening to throw you out of the window while we slept.'

I had tried to hide my shock. It melted back into me, mixing in with the rest of the horrors I store deep inside my body, mingling in with the misery and confusion that runs through my veins, making me who I am.

'He caught me trying to get away in the middle of the night. I had you in front of me as he dragged me back. He pulled at you and I heard your arm crack...' She had stopped at that point and closed her eyes, breathing hard and placing her hand over her chest before going on. 'I remember your screams. He was telling me to shut you up but of course, I couldn't. Your arm was broken.

He gave me a good few whacks for not being able to quieten you down. I ran upstairs with you in my arms and looked for places to hide you. Then fortunately, he fell asleep in a drunken heap on the floor. I dread to think what might have happened if he hadn't, if he'd stayed awake and found you...'

She had stopped then. It was enough. We both knew it. Nothing more needed to be said. I had felt myself thanking God that he was actually dead or at that point, I may have ended up killing him myself. I had visions of rushing into the kitchen, grabbing a sharp knife and plunging it deep into his mean, hateful body. But then, that would make me as bad as him, wouldn't it? Maybe I am. Who knows, maybe deep down, there is a part of me that will always be evil, tainted by what has happened. Or it could be that it's genetic and trying to escape it is futile. After all, look what I did to Gareth. So many unforgivable, atrocious acts, such a terrible, dysfunctional family. Perhaps we are all doomed and will never move on from this.

We had sat for what seemed like forever, each of us locked in our own enclave of misery, me thinking that I didn't feel particularly fulfilled by her revelation but at least I now knew why I was abandoned, and my mother... I'm not entirely sure what was going through her head. I'm not sure I *wanted* to know. Her face was flushed and I could practically feel the heat as it had pulsed from her agitated body.

I had heard it first. My mother was too immersed in her own thoughts. For such a big, old door, it made very little noise. I initially thought it was coming from somewhere out the back. I had heard children earlier and thought that it was just youngsters playing and being unruly. Until I heard it again. The hush in the house seemed to absorb the noise rather than accentuate it.

I had reached over and poked my mother in the leg, rousing

her from her trance-like state. 'I think there's somebody at your door.'

She had sprung into action, like somebody who had spent their entire life on edge. The thought that it might be Gareth crossed my mind, but I was too upset and still in shock to think about it too deeply.

What I didn't expect was for it to be Celia.

And now here she is, standing there, no trace of emotion in her expression, dressed like me, in my mother's house. She must have followed me. Either that, or she has an amazing memory. I showed her where my parents lived once, many years back. She had insisted we stand and watch to see if anybody went in or out, which they didn't. We ended up frozen half to death until eventually, I suggested we leave. Celia threw a major tantrum on the way home, refusing to speak to me. To this day, I still have no idea why she did that. If anybody should have been upset at not seeing them, it should have been me. I knew then that I had to start distancing myself from her. Her behaviour was too erratic, too unpredictable and quite frankly, too bloody scary for me to put up with. I'd had enough upset in my life and craved stability, not the impulsive sort of antics that Celia displayed time and time again.

'Morning, Eva,' she says calmly as she places her jacket over the back of the chair and sits down directly in front of me. 'I think it's time to talk now, don't you?'

I can hardly believe what I'm hearing. How dare she? I'm in awe of her confidence. She exudes power and authority out of every pore, marching in here, taking over and speaking to me in that accusatory tone like I am a small child about to be reprimanded for some terrible misdemeanour. Who the hell does she think she is? And more to the point, why is she even here?

'And you are?' my mother says in a tone that belies the weak woman she was just a few moments ago. She has regained her strength and is now a fair match for Celia and her false bravado. I wish I felt the same way. I feel sapped of all strength. This whole fucking thing has been a trauma. My throat is still sore as hell after Gareth almost choked me to death and the very sight of Celia makes me sick to the pit of my stomach. I have no idea why she is here but I do know that I want her to leave. Except I don't think I have the strength to do it. I pray my mother will tell her to get out, to tell her to leave here and never return.

But she doesn't.

'I'm a close friend of Eva's,' Celia says softly and leans forward to place her hand over mine. Her skin is cold and scratchy like parchment. I snatch my hand away and watch as she glances over to my mother to see if she notices. My mother doesn't appear to and instead sits down next to her, a bewildered expression on her face.

'Eva's?' she says as she screws her eyes up and stares hard at Celia, her eyes roaming over Celia's face. She scrutinises her features as she speaks. 'How did you know Eva was here? Have you been following her?'

I see Celia flinch at my mother's words.

'Following her? Don't be silly! Why on earth would I do that?' she replies with a forced conviviality that makes me want to vomit. 'Eva and I are close friends. Very close friends.'

'So why are you here?' my mother says quietly, confusion wrinkling her brow.

'Look, Celia,' I say, desperate to keep my tone light and non-threatening. 'I know you're trying to help here, but this is between me and my mother, so if you want to head back into town, perhaps I can meet up with you there later?'

'Is there something going on?' my mother asks, her voice laced with suspicion. 'I've already had Gareth here today. This all seems a bit odd if you ask me.'

I watch Celia's eyes widen at my mother's words. 'Gareth?' she shouts. Flecks of spittle fly out of her mouth and disperse in the air. My stomach churns as I see the look on her face. Celia spins around, taking in everything around her, scrutinising every little thing in the room. Her gaze rests on a photograph on the back wall. She narrows her eyes and looks at it for a long time before a darkness takes hold in her expression, twisting her features into something I don't care for.

'Well, well, well,' she murmurs quietly and although I have no idea what it is she has seen, I suddenly fear what she is about to say or do. I know Celia, you see. I know her all too well.

'Please, Celia,' I whisper softly, 'let me talk to my mother alone.'

She stares at me as I speak. I was hoping for a look of rejection, irritation perhaps, or even anger, but there is nothing. This is more unnerving than any of those sentiments. This is the calm before the storm.

'I'm here to help you, Eva, you know that. You can't manage on your own. You need me.'

A pain takes hold in my head: a thin streak of pressure against my temple that makes my eyes water. I see movement on the periphery of my vision and let out an uneven breath as my mother shifts forward, a troubled look in her eyes. She has her arms crossed and seems to have grown a couple of inches in the last few minutes.

'Look, lovey,' she says in an impatient tone that I fear will only exacerbate Celia's festering intent. 'You said out there that you knew Eva. I'd like to know exactly why you're here in my house.'

Celia acts as if my mother hasn't even spoken, and continues talking to me like we are the only two people in the room.

'Come with me, Eva. We can go back to how things were when we lived with Greta. They were good times, weren't they? I can protect you from all of this.' She turns and sweeps her hand around the room before leaning forward and clasping my hands in hers.

I attempt to move but she is stronger than she looks and her grip is like a vice around my wrists. My skin burns slightly as she increases the force, her fingers pressing against mine, making me dizzy with fear.

I have to find a way to get her to leave before this gets out of control, before she opens her mouth and a whole load of lies pour forth. Celia is the most fantastic liar. It's her one defining feature. Given enough time, I'm pretty sure she could even get my mother to believe her. She will convince her I'm a bad daughter. Rotten to the core. She will stop at nothing so she can have me all to herself. She did it when we were children: told others I was badly behaved, foul mouthed and not to be trusted. I lost more friends than I kept thanks to Celia.

'I really do appreciate what you're trying to do, Celia. I know I've not been the best friend just recently as I've had a lot on my plate but yes, you're right, we can go back to how things were. All I want is few moments with my mum to sort things out. Once I've done that, we can get together, you and I, and sort some plans out for our future. How does that sound?'

A twitch takes hold in my eye. I blink repeatedly to try to stop it. Nobody speaks. I stare into Celia's eyes to try to see beyond the darkness that is in there, to try to reason with her.

'Look, I've asked you a question and I'm still waiting for my answer,' my mother says. Her hands are on her hips and a crimson hue is creeping into her skin, accentuating her broken veins and rosacea. 'You can't just march in here and ignore me like this!'

But that's exactly what Celia does. It's as if nobody has even spoken. She continues to stare at me as I wait for her to say something – anything at all to break this horrible silence. At last she speaks, her eyebrows raised in mild shock as my words eventually sink in.

'Really? Do you mean that, Eva?'

I smile at her, relief flooding through me. I've got her. At last, I've managed to break through to her. 'Of course I mean it! Why would I say such a thing if I didn't mean it? Look, why don't you go and find us a café in town and when I'm done here we can—'

'You fucking little liar!' Her grip on my hand intensifies and her words bounce around the room, making me feel quite sick. Everything swims before my eyes. I press my legs into the edge off the chair to stop myself from falling forwards.

'Hey!' my mother cries, her voice deep and gravelly. 'Sort yourself out, young woman! I don't even know who the hell you are and yet you think you can come in here and—'

The sound of the slap reverberates around us. It rings in my ears, as Celia lets go of me and leaps up, bringing her hand into connect with the side of my mother's face. Trish staggers back, her fingers clasped to her cheek. Time stands still while I wait for something to happen. The after effect of the hit doesn't take long. Despite being a good twenty years older than her, my mother lurches forward and grabs a handful of Celia's hair, wrapping it tightly around her fist, strands of red clutched between her fingers as she pulls hard enough to make Celia yelp out in pain. It is the cry of a feral animal.

I sit frozen, unable to intervene, my body stiff with shock and panic. I should do something, anything to stop this, but I can't seem to think straight. Everything is happening so quickly and my mind is clogged up, full of cotton wool. Everything feels laboured, every movement a huge effort.

'Get out!' my mother screams as she drags Celia towards the door.

Celia's head is bent forwards, her face contorted with the pain.

She doesn't realise that she has set herself up against a woman who is accustomed to dealing with violence and more than able to defend herself. They don't get far, however. I watch as Celia brings her arm up and smashes it into my mother's face with such force that bile rises into my throat.

In a heartbeat, I am up out of the chair and hurtling towards them. Strands of Celia's hair are still knotted up in my mum's fist, wrapped around each individual finger, as she falls onto the floor, dragging Celia down with her.

'Get off her!' I scream, and attempt to pull Celia off my mother who is trapped underneath her entire body. The pair of them are deadweight as I try to roll Celia sideways to separate their inter-twined limbs. Long strands of hair come away in my mother's still tightly clenched fist as I drag her away from Celia. A bruise is already forming above her eye where she was punched but I don't have time to take in any more details as I feel my own hair being pulled so hard and tight, I am convinced it will come away from my scalp. Tears stream and snot runs as I am dragged across the living room and pushed down onto the sofa by a hand that has so much strength behind it, it feels as if it belongs to somebody twice Celia's size.

'Please!' I gasp through gritted teeth as a wave of pain passes over my skull. 'Just let me go, Celia, and we can talk about this. I promise we can sort everything out!'

She doesn't respond, and instead hoists me to my feet and drags me into the kitchen. Behind me, I can hear that my mother is rousing herself. I twist around to see her scrambling to her feet, her legs wobbly and weak. I try to mouth to her that she should run, but she clumsily follows us and even through my fear-addled brain, I can see this is a bad move. The worst move ever.

I hear the smooth swish of metal as a knife is dragged from its block and feel my stomach drop as something sharp is pressed into my back. A hard stone of terror sits there in my belly, solid and immobile. I can't breathe or swallow, and the room spins and sways. All I can concentrate on is staying upright and not making any sharp or sudden movements.

This whole thing is insane. I have got to do something, to talk her round or we are all done for. I knew she had issues and her mind often teetered on the brink of what we call normality but I had no idea Celia was this bad. The time she did this as a teenager was years ago, when she threatened another girl with a knife. We're adults now. She has a job, a home, everything to live for. Back then she was damaged, we both were, but we've moved on, or at least I have. Celia, it would appear, is still stuck in that negative rut of her life, the trauma of her childhood never leaving her.

'Please, Celia,' I squawk quietly, 'I'm your friend. I want to help you. Please put the knife down.'

I feel it being pressed into my back with even greater intensity and swallow down the vomit that rises. I'm wearing a thick sweater with a vest top underneath, a flimsy layer of protection against such a sharp weapon, but I hope it will stop the knife from going through to my skin. She is using just enough force to make sure I pay attention. She hasn't hurt me yet, but I know she is unhinged and could easily do it without a second thought.

'Shut up!' she spits into my ear as she drags the knife up and down my spine for effect.

'Get off her or I'll call the police.' My mother's voice is distorted as she wobbles her way into the kitchen behind us. She is holding the side of her face with one hand and in the other is a phone. She holds it aloft, brandishing it in front of us to show Celia that she means what she says.

'You do that and I'll drive this knife straight into her spine.' She wiggles the blade about and lets out a haunting giggle. 'If I lift it just a bit higher like this and push hard enough, it will go straight into her liver and if I get lucky, I'll maybe even hit her aorta and she'll bleed to death before anybody can get here to help her. Actually, even if they get here, she'll die anyway. Or I may miss her liver and go deep into her stomach or intestines. She might not die from the wound but she could develop peritonitis and then she'll take days to die. Your choice, Trish. You don't mind if I call you that, do you? Only with all the things I've heard about you over the years, I feel as if I know you really well.'

I'm going to faint. I have to use all my strength to keep my legs from buckling and giving way under me. I can hear my mother's deep gasp as she realises Celia has a knife pressed to my back. The sound of her breathing fills the room. I want to speak, to plead with Celia to think and act rationally but fear it's all too late. It's about damage limitation from here on in.

Despite feeling as if I am going to either throw up or pass out at any given moment, I have to draw on an inner strength I'm not even sure I have in order to get through this. I don't want to die. My only other option is talking her round, softening her up and persuading her to put the knife down.

I keep my tone neutral. I know she will pick up on a patronising inflection and will react badly. 'Celia, I'm your best friend. I know you're angry with me but this isn't the answer. You don't want to go to prison for hurting me, do you? Not after all the things we've been through. We're old muckers, you and I, aren't we?'

I can't see her face and have no idea if she is responding to me or if she's hell-bent on hurting me and my words are pointless. I have to try. I can't give up.

I feel her breath hot on my neck. She is so close. Could I try to give one huge push and escape, or would such a move be the trigger for something worse? I am too scared to exert any real strength, but my mother is here and she would help, or at least I hope she would. Her history doesn't paint her as the most compassionate of people. I feel at a loss and hope that Celia sees sense at some point. All I have are words that I can use to win her round and possibly the added strength from the lady who gave birth to me and hopefully feels enough of a bond to save me. And if she doesn't feel a bond or any sense of loyalty, I hope she has at least enough common decency to step in and help me if things turn particularly nasty.

'Stop talking or I'll slit your throat.' Celia's voice is husky. I barely recognise this woman. She is currently free-falling into madness. How am I going to reason with somebody who is this far gone? If I thought she was a virtual stranger before, she is now so far removed from me, she may as well be an alien from outer space. Sweet talking her could be a waste of time. But it's the only weapon I have, and my desire to live is strong. There is no way I will leave this world without a fight.

'This is all my fault.' My mother's voice comes out of nowhere. She sounds different: softer, sweeter than just a few minutes earlier. 'I've caused this so if you want to kill anyone, then kill me. I've got nothing left to live for, anyway.'

I hear Celia draw in a breath. I don't say or do anything.

'My son, Gareth, told me earlier today that he never wants to see me again, and after this, neither will she.' The phone has been put down and Trish is pointing at me with a shaking finger. Her mouth is trembling and she looks absolutely haggard, as if she is melting before my very eyes like hot candle wax.

'Your son?' For some bizarre reason, her words have struck a chord with Celia, brought her back to life and now she is speaking without the venom-laced tone she had adopted just a few minutes ago.

'Gareth is your son?' Celia's voice is a near shriek. I feel the knife wobble on my back. It scrapes across my spine, making me stiffen up with fear.

'Gareth, you say? Fucking Gareth?' She is panting hard. I have no idea what is going on but sweat prickles my armpits and the back of my neck, and saliva fills my mouth. There is something terribly wrong. There is some other connection going on that I know nothing about and I'm terrified by it. I have visions of her driving the knife deep into my back just because she has lost control. Or simply because she can.

'Yes,' my mother says softly. 'His name is Gareth. What of it?'

Celia tugs at my hair some more and turns my head round until I am staring into her eyes. Pools of pure hatred glare back at me, sending a ripple of terror over my skin. I don't have time to ask how she knows Gareth. She practically drools into my face as she speaks.

'Oh my. How's that for a coincidence, eh? You turn up here and so does your brother. Did you know you even *had* a brother?'

I try to reply but she pulls at my sweater, dragging me closer and pushing the knife even deeper into my back. I inhale sharply. I feel sure she must have pierced my clothes and drawn blood but am too petrified to move away. Her long, red hair hangs in my face as she leans in close to me, so close I can smell her stale breath.

'I've got a special secret, Eva. I'm going to tell you because you're my best ever friend.' She pulls her face away and giggles hysterically like a small child before leaning back in again, almost choking me with the warm, rotting air from her lungs. 'Did you know I've fucked your brother?'

I try to cover the horror I feel as she speaks. I don't want to give her any reason to hurt or maim me, or even worse. One slight movement, a facial tick, anything at all and I could be dead within seconds, my body split open by the knife she is holding. I would lie here on the cold floor like a piece of meat, my blood pumping out of me in great rhythmic pools until there was nothing left.

I run my tongue around my mouth and swallow. I need to work out whether or not she is lying. I won't ask. I can't. She is unravelling quickly and I cannot take any more risks. She would say anything to upset me and this is a way of doing just that. Celia thrives on keeping secrets. It's her forte, her only redeeming feature.

I tip my head around as far as her grasp will allow me, to try to catch my mother's eye. She is standing calmly, watching it all unfold. I hope to God she has some trick up her sleeve, some sort of plan that will save us from Celia's madness because if she doesn't, then we are both doomed.

'Yes, he came here earlier,' my mother says quietly. 'I'm a bad person, you see. He came to tell me that he never wants to see me again. I take it you know him?'

I watch as my mother's face softens. She is trying to gradually tone down Celia's anger. I hope she succeeds, I really do, as I have no clue as to what we should do next. I am all out of ideas. I have known Celia for many years and therein lies the problem. I know how difficult and controlling she can be. I also know all too well how volatile and unpredictable she is. I know exactly what she is capable of.

Celia nods. 'We've been staying at the same hotel.'

I listen attentively as she breathes hard. Her tone is less urgent, less angry. I could take a chance here, bring my elbow back into her body and knock the knife clean out of her hand. Then I could grab it and hold her still while my mother rings the police. But if I fail... I don't want to think about the consequences of what would happen if I didn't get it right first time and I'm not sure I have the strength to hold her down while the phone call is made. She would see through my phoney boldness and take back control, possibly using the knife to take her fury out on me for daring to overpower her.

'Right,' my mother says softly. 'As I said, he no longer wants anything to do with me, and poor Eva here, I let her down years go. It's what I'm good at – failing everyone – so if you want to use that knife on me, then go right ahead.'

Celia doesn't move. I can tell that she doesn't know how to respond. What Celia really likes, what she thrives on, is feeling powerful. Since we were kids, she has always done her best to be the superior one, claiming I need looking after, or telling people I am weak and vulnerable so they see her as my saviour, the person who stopped me from becoming some sort of society drop-out. It's not true. As the current situation shows, it's the other way around. Celia is deeply damaged, her mind still fixated on the past. I've got my issues and problems – I am the first to admit that – but I am not, and never have been, out of control. Celia is. She is very much out of control and it is me who has tried to stop her from carrying out many atrocious deeds. I am surprised she holds down such a decent job. She is a ticking time bomb and right now she is about to go off.

'Come on, lovey. Do your worst. Take it all out on me. I can tell by the look on your face and the tone of your voice that you're not keen on Gareth. What better way to get back at him than through me, eh? And if you're not prepared to do that, then put the knife down and leave poor Eva alone. You're supposed to be her friend, aren't you? If you're as good a friend as I think you are, then you'll know that she's already been through enough. Let her go.'

'Been through enough?' Celia screams, her voice shrill with unabated rage. 'What about what I've been through? What about my tragedies and fucking awful upbringing? When is somebody going to care about me? All my life, I've been cast aside and ignored while Little Miss High and Mighty here has been hailed as the golden one, the one who always says and does the right thing. Yes Greta, no Greta, three bags fucking full, Greta!' Foam gathers at the corner of Celia's mouth as she speaks.

I wince and close my eyes. A storm of memories pushes its way into my head. Celia screaming at Greta that she hated her, Greta trying to placate her, telling her she needed to stop it and be calm, that she should appreciate things and not be so angry all the time. That she should be more like me. I close my eyes to stop more tears from flowing. So much hurt and hatred and destruction. I know what is coming next. It's suddenly so obvious to me. She either wants to *be* me or kill me. There is no in between, no middle ground, no room for manoeuvre.

'I can see you've suffered enough for a hundred people, lovey. Doesn't give you the right to hurt other people though, does it? Put the knife down and we can start again. We can chat about what's going on here and nobody will get hurt or injured.'

I am beyond surprised at Trish's mediation skills. Is this what years of abuse does to a person? Arms them with strategies to get out of harmful situations? I desperately hope she can win Celia over but am riddled with doubt. How can you ever reason with a sick mind?

'You know nothing about my suffering,' Celia barks back. 'And as for your son... you managed to bring up a right charmer there, didn't you? Hopping in and out of bed with as many women as he can, treating them as commodities, toying with their feelings. Treating them like pieces of SHIT!'

My flesh crawls, goosebumps prickling me. Celia actually slept with Gareth? Christ almighty, he didn't waste much time, did he? A thousand questions gnaw away at me: did he see me with Celia at some point and do it to get back at me? Or was it the other way around? Celia is perverse enough to do something like that for sure, especially since she's taken on my traits. Does she actually think she is an extension of me? Dear God, what has she turned into?

I have total admiration for my mother's composed demeanour as Celia's words spew out of her. She is in full flow, anger and venom pouring forth and showing no sign of subsiding.

'And have you any idea of why *she* has come here to find you?' Celia jabs at my back with the knife. I remain as still as I can, too terrified to move in case the blade slips or she simply decides to drive it home into my flesh because her anger has gotten the better of her. I fear we are veering frighteningly close to that point but can't think of a way to drag her back from it.

'I'd like you to tell me why, Celia. I'm sorry my son has hurt you, I really am. He's had a tough time of it but that doesn't excuse what he has done. Eva and I haven't really had time to chat but I'd very much like to hear what you've got to say for sure. Shall we all go back into the living room and talk? It's more comfortable in there, don't you think?'

And with that, my mother turns and walks away, leaving me with Celia and her anger and that knife. I close my eyes and pray that for once, Celia sees reason. I am not a religious person but I pray for all I'm worth that these few seconds aren't my last.

I open them again and hold my breath.

28

CELIA

'Move!'

Celia pushes the knife further into Eva's spine, jabbing at her to go forwards, to follow the older woman back to where they came from. It's too damn small in this kitchen anyway. She needs more space to help her think. Her mind is cluttered and she can't seem to formulate her thoughts any more. It's like wading through treacle just putting everything in order in her mind. Fucking men and their pathetic primeval urges, blackening her good name. And then she has Eva to think about, and her family secrets. Why didn't Eva tell her she had a brother? This whole thing is so bloody confusing, Celia can't get her head around it all.

Something suddenly spikes into her brain, making her hot and unsteady. She needs to sit down. She pushes Eva onto the sofa and sits next to her, the knife placed at Eva's chest. Celia presses it further, feeling it split the fabric of Eva's sweater. It's a pity she has to do this at all. If Eva had been any kind of friend and kept her up to speed about what was going on in her life then none of this would be happening.

'You set me up!' The words feel thick in her mouth, as if her tongue is made of wool. 'All this time, you knew you had a brother and you got him to sleep with me to make me look like a fool!'

She watches Eva's eyes widen. She shakes her head and Celia has to use every ounce of self-restraint to not bring her hand up and slap her stupid little face. How dare she act as if she knows nothing about this whole thing? How dare she?

'Don't insult my intelligence, Eva! You've used me and hurt me from the very start: not keeping in touch, moving away from me, trying to ignore me! What do you think I am? Some sort of lapdog who will come running whenever you call me? I call the shots round here, okay? I am the one who looks after you. Not the other way around!'

'I'm sorry, Celia. I'm so, so sorry. I never meant to hurt you, but I swear I knew nothing about you and Gareth! You have to believe me. I would *never* do anything like that. You're my best friend.' Eva's face is pale, and her face is wet and streaked with mascara.

Celia stops at her words. She can't work out whether Eva means it or not. They are best friends, aren't they? Or at least they used to be. Everything suddenly feels muddled and out of balance like the world has moved off its axis and there has been some sort of time slip. She wants to believe her, she really does, but everything is so difficult to understand.

A voice punctures her thoughts, making her shiver. 'You don't mind if I sit here next to you, do you, my love?'

Celia turns her head to see Eva's mother perched on the sofa next to her. Celia can feel the heat radiating from her body. She stares at the pink slippers, noticing how ugly they are, and then raises her eyes to stare at this woman's face, thinking how dark her hair is and how ruddy her complexion is. The contrast is so stark she wants to laugh. Eva's mother looks ridiculous. Why can't older people just let age do its thing instead of trying to battle it by colouring their hair to conceal the grey? She is pathetic, this old bitch, pretending to be some sort of wise, old woman when they all know she is no more than a wizened old hag.

'That's it, dearie. Let's just have a chat, shall we?'

Celia watches her mouth move and tries to stay focused on what is happening around her. She gives the knife another little push and hears a whimper coming from Eva. This is going to be difficult. She has to remain calm and in control. They're trying to trick her again. She can feel it. One more thrust of the knife will show them who's in charge, then they might take notice of what she has to say.

'That's a beautiful bracelet you're wearing there. It looks just like Eva's. You're very alike you two, aren't you? Same hair, same sort of clothes. Where did you get it from? It's just so lovely.'

'Greta gave them to us.' Celia hears Eva's voice, brittle and childlike. She sounds so far away but she isn't, is she? She is here, next to her, speaking. Celia can even feel her hot breath on her neck as Eva carries on talking. 'She bought them for us when we lived with her in York. Do you remember that day, Celia? Trish is right. We're alike you and I, aren't we?'

Celia is finding it hard to breathe properly. Her lungs don't seem to be working and she feels dizzy as she tries to ignore the memory that is pushing its way into her brain.

'You broke mine,' Celia says quietly. 'You ripped all my charms off and I had to get it fixed years later.'

She feels tears build and swallows them down. She is sure that's what happened. Things are vague, the facts and timeline of that day hard to put in order, but her heart is telling her that something unpleasant took place on that visit and it wasn't her fault. It must have been Eva who broke it. Celia would never do such a terrible thing. She's a good girl. She isn't the horrible child her mother used to tell her she was. She always did her best and tried so hard to do the right thing. It's just that there were times when she would get so upset and angry and everything would go black, and then afterwards, she couldn't remember things too well. But she was a nice child. Always well behaved. Always a good girl.

Eva speaks again, her voice strained. 'I'm not sure that's exactly what happened but it was a lot of years ago and if I can—'

'Shut up!' Celia surprises herself by how loud her voice is and how it seems to fill the entire room. She almost giggles. The words just exploded right out of her. This is power. This is how it feels to be completely in control. And she likes it. It makes her feel alive. Fire is raging in her stomach, pushing through her veins.

She holds the handle tight and presses it a little bit more, feeling it lodge into something soft. There's a scream and an animalistic cry from somewhere close by. She ignores it. Nothing is going to distract her. She's the boss here. She knows it, they know it. She should have done this a long time ago to get Eva back on her side. Sometimes this is what people need to get them into line.

'A long time ago, I did an awful thing.'

Celia listens to the voice of the older lady, wondering where this is leading to. She doesn't have any time for sob stories. All she wants is the truth. All she really wants is Eva. Always has.

'I had a child and I let them take it away from me. I needed help, I know that now, but I was young – younger than you are, lovey – and I let it happen. What we need to remember is, it's never too late to ask for help. We can help you, my love. Me and Eva here, who is in pain and bleeding, we can help you. Even though you've hurt her, she will still help you, won't you, Eva?'

There is movement and a muffled sob coming from some-where close by. Celia breathes hard. More tricks? She can't be sure. What if she falls for it and they let her down? All her life people have let her down: her parents, teachers, social workers, every foster parent she has ever lived with. They all gave up on her and cast her aside, taking no notice of her feelings, never once asking her how she felt. Eva is all she has left. Celia doesn't think she could bear it if the only person she has left in the whole world lies to her. But then, if she doesn't believe Eva, what is the point of her life? Eva is all she's got, and if she no longer has her, then there is no reason for living.

'You're lying. You're lying!' Another gasp from next to her as she presses the blade further in again. A lovely tingling sensation settles in her belly as she feels more skin give way under her pressure.

'Come on, Celia. We can help you. Please put the knife down.' Trish's voice is quiet and gentle and echoes softly past her. Celia imagines it as a trail of wispy clouds, circling around the room, wrapping themselves over their bodies, soft as silk, binding them all together like a small, tight-knit family.

The smooth handle of the knife wobbles about in her grasp. It feels light, as if it's made of air. She could do it. She could just let go and it would simply float away from her and then she and Eva could leave. They could go back to York together, be the children they once were. Everything will be perfect.

And then she thinks of Gareth, sees his face close to hers, feels his hot breath on her naked body, thinks about his hands roaming over her flesh, and she wants to vomit.

Righting herself and sitting up straight, she tenses her jaw and closes her hand tightly around the knife, unable to believe that they almost had her there. She was so close to letting them win, so close to putting the knife down and forgiving them. And then she remembered that this whole thing is one big set-up. Eva, her mother and that bastard brother of hers; they are all in on it together. Toxic, that's what they are. One huge, rotting mound of toxic waste that needs disposing of.

And she is just the person to do it.

29

GARETH

Gareth clips his bag closed. He tosses the empty, miniature bottles of hotel shampoo and shower gel into the bin and glances around the room. Not much to check for. He travelled light and will return home the same way.

He glances at his watch and zips up his jacket, tugging at the collar to keep it upright. Plenty of time yet before his train leaves. He can check out of here and find somewhere in town to eat. He may even celebrate with an early beer. He reaches up and traces his hand over his face. Or maybe not. He's been drinking too much lately and needs to cut down. It's made him do things he's not proud of, things he would never have thought himself capable of. He can have a coffee and enjoy the buzz from the caffeine instead. As far as he knows, nobody has ever become aggressive and got into a fight after drinking too many cups of coffee.

He steps outside his room and stares around. Nobody there. Good. He doesn't fancy bumping into Celia. He's feeling pretty fragile and hasn't the stomach for any hassle today. All he wants to do is to get home.

Clutching the key, he heads downstairs to the reception area, hoping that there isn't a queue. The longer he hangs around this place, the greater the chances are of bumping into her. He slides his key across to the waiting receptionist, sees her taking in the scar and bruises on his face, and thanks her. He does actually mean it. Things feel different. *He* feels different, lighter and free, as if a huge weight has been lifted off him. Despite looking as if he has been ten rounds with a heavyweight, he feels better than he has in weeks.

He tightens the straps of his recently purchased backpack and strides outside. He feels a sudden compulsion to go up to the abbey. He hasn't been up there for years. Not since he was a kid. It'll do him good to blow off the cobwebs. His legs will probably give up on him after the run through town but he's determined to give it a go. He can use this as the turning point of his life: exercise more and drink less. Fewer takeaways and a healthier diet. Why not? He's determined to salvage something positive from this hideous mess. He couldn't have gone on as he was, with it eating away at him. This whole torrid escapade has helped clear his head, given him a firm footing again and got him back on track.

Taking a deep breath, Gareth feels the cold air dragging into his lungs and savours the sensation as it balloons in his chest, chilling his abdomen, cleansing him.

He sets off at a lick, enjoying the burn in his calves and thighs. It's a good feeling. It means he's alive. Sometimes you have to get kicked and feel the pain just to remind you that you're not actually dead.

He smiles, aware that he very possibly looks idiotic, but he doesn't stop. He isn't sure if it's because he has severed all ties with his mother or the fact that he let Eva know just how angry he was, how fucking outraged he felt by her behaviour. Either way, the whole thing has been cathartic and it wouldn't have happened if he hadn't knocked that old guy down in the street. Had it not been for that awful incident, he would still be in London chewing over this sorry mess and feeling as if he still wanted to kill Eva. Everything happens for a reason, doesn't it? That medic, her words: they all led him here, to this moment in time, and for that, he will always be grateful.

As soon as he gets back home, he'll contact the hospital and make sure the old man is on the mend. He should have done it before now but with everything that's happened, Gareth hasn't given the poor old guy a second thought. But he will do it. He has no idea which hospital they would have taken him to but he can soon find out. It shouldn't be too difficult with all the information and news that is bandied about on social media, and if he doesn't see anything on there then he will just ring all the hospitals in the area until he finds him. He owes the poor old man that much.

The sea is calm and the sky a long stretch of pale blue with a tiny scattering of cotton-wool clouds as he continues his walk into the main part of town. Life suddenly feels very good indeed. He will get some food, go and see the abbey and catch his train back home. Everything is great. Life is about as perfect as it can be.

30

TRISH

Trish does her best to stay calm even though her head feels as if a bomb has gone off in there and her chest is so tight, she can hardly breathe. What's wrong with this woman? She is completely insane and should be sectioned. For a second back there, Trish could have sworn her resolve was weakening but then out of the blue, she upped her game. She looked as if somebody had injected her with a shot of steroids and she had grown ten inches, her entire frame widening, her madness stretching as far as the eye can see.

She has no idea who this woman even is. She has no desire to know, either. Whether she is a friend of Eva's or Gareth's is neither here nor there. She just wants her gone, out of her house, and locked up somewhere secure.

She tries again to make her see sense, to plead with her to put the knife down. It's such a large blade, a hefty weapon with a serrated edge that flashes and glints with every movement, casting sinister shapes on the adjacent wall. If Trish leans back slightly, she can see Eva's pale face, see the tremble of her body, the red of her blood as it gathers and spreads out over her abdomen. Celia has it pushed into her chest just above her right breast and has jabbed her hard. Trish has no idea how far the blade has gone in but prays it's not too far. If it weren't such a lethal weapon, she would have made a lunge at her, grabbed it out of her hand and pinned her to the ground, but it's too big a risk. One second too slow and it would slice Eva open like she was a pat of butter.

'Celia,' Trish says as softly and evenly as she can, 'I'm begging you, please don't hurt her. You don't want to get into trouble now, do you? Imagine a lovely, clever woman like you in prison. That's not what you want, is it? They're awful places they are, full of nasty, mean people. They're not like you in there. You would hate it. All you need to do is put the knife down.'

'Down?' Celia shrieks.

Trish sucks in her breath and watches in slow motion as Celia swings around and points the blade under Trish's chin, tracing it down to the softest part of her throat and resting it there, the cold of the metal sending an icy chill across her skin.

She tries to look over to Eva to tell her to run, but she is locked into position, the sharpness of the knife keeping her in place, holding her hostage. She wants to scream to Eva to get out of here, to forget about Trish's current predicament and focus only on saving herself, but she can't seem to move. Even breathing is a struggle. Everything has slowed down. She can't think straight any more with that huge knife pushing at her neck.

She shivers and tries to keep still. Nearby, she can hear Eva sucking in her breath, a wheeze of pure terror coming out of her as she exhales. She is in shock. Her blood pressure will be dropping and she may even pass out. Trish has to act. She can't just sit here like a wet rag doing nothing. If she pushes forward, the blade will go straight into her neck. If she moves back, Celia could swing around and turn it on Eva, who isn't functioning properly. Her reflexes will be slow. There is no way Eva could fight Celia off, not when Celia is holding a weapon as sharp as this one. It's deadly, the sharpest knife in the house. Even Russ thought it dangerous. Were it not for the terror she feels at this moment in time, she would laugh out loud at the irony of it all.

Trish lifts her head slightly and stares into Celia's face. Aren't a person's eyes the windows to their soul? Maybe, just maybe, if she looks deep enough into them, she will find something in there, some dim and distant flicker of recognition, something she can reason with. Something that will save their lives.

Trish stares hard into Celia's wide eyes, into the blackness of her dilated pupils, searching for something – anything she can clutch onto and reason with. Her blood thickens, running like sand. There is nothing. Celia's eyes are empty. It's like looking into a bottomless pit. Trish's skin prickles and she finds herself saying a silent prayer. She hasn't prayed since she was a child at St Hilda's primary school yet the words come back to her like it was yesterday. She pleads with God to instil some sense into this woman, to make her put the knife down and let Eva leave here unharmed. Trish doesn't particularly care about herself; it's the young one she's concerned about. Eva's life matters. So many years ahead of her. She deserves a chance. She deserves to live.

She hears her daughter's voice and winces. She wants her to stay quiet, to not draw attention to herself. It feels as if every second is vital and as if every movement, every whisper of air that is in this room, could be the thing that tips Celia over the edge; the catalyst for bringing about their final few seconds.

'Celia, please listen to me,' Eva says breathlessly. 'I think you are a truly amazing person after what you've been through in your life, but please don't let this be the end of us. We're a team, you and I. We need each other, don't we?'

Every sound is accentuated as Trish waits, every thud of her heart, every breath that exits her body is heightened in the near silence of the room as she waits for Celia's reply.

The silence doesn't last long. A deep thudding echoes around them, piercing the sinister lull that has settled upon the room and sending Trish's blood pressure soaring.

Nobody says or does anything. Surely, they all heard it? Or is her mind playing up, making her think there's a way out of this, when in fact they are all done for?

She daren't breathe. Celia's eyes don't move. Her face is locked into a grimace as she grips the knife even tighter. If she were to force it a little bit further, Trish is sure her main artery would succumb under the pressure. She can feel every pulse, every throb in her aching body under the cold metal of the thin, pointed blade.

The air is still. No more banging. Whoever it was has gone. Their chance to escape, the person who could have helped them, has walked away. Suddenly, Trish is angry: angry at the predicament she is in, angry at this Celia lady who has burst into her home and done this terrible thing to them, but most of all, she is angry at herself for letting it all happen. She should have insisted Celia leave as soon as she walked in. She had bad vibes about her from the outset. She could tell by the way Eva looked at her when she saw her, the way her face crumpled when Celia marched in and sat down opposite her. And of course, she lied to Trish to get in the house. She is definitely no friend of Eva's. Whether or not she even knows Gareth is irrelevant. Anything that comes out of her mouth is absurd and meaningless. She is insane.

Trish exhales softly and tries to steady her breathing. She's weathered storms like this before, hasn't she? Russ never used a knife against her, though. His fists were his weapons. She feels the edge of the metal, sharp and cold against her skin and decides enough is enough. This pathetic creature is deranged enough to keep them here all day. Something has to give. She has to get things moving and end this situation. She has to save Eva.

Her breath billows out of her in a staccato rasp as she summons up all her strength, tenses her muscles and makes her move.

31

EVA

The actual events happen faster than my mind's ability to process them. The knock on the door could have been our chance, but we were all too terrified, too frozen and incapable of logical thought to do anything, so whoever it was, left. I heard their footsteps as they walked back up the path and I wanted to scream at them to come back, to help us, to call the police. But I didn't. I didn't do any of those things. I sat, unable to move, my heart thrashing around my chest, my blood soaring round my body.

And now this is happening. I don't know why she is doing it, but Trish has grabbed at Celia and is trying to wrestle the knife out of her hands. I should help her but my body is fixed into place, blind terror freezing me to the spot.

I watch as my mother tries to pull Celia's hands away from her throat. The blade is still perilously close to her skin and there is a tug of war as it seesaws one way then the other, rocking violently in Celia's hands.

I have to snap out of this. I need to move to break this up, or to call the police. My mind is so muddled and terrified I momentarily forget which number it is I need to call.

A whimper forces its way out of my throat as I stare at the sight before me. Celia has the strength of ten men. She has somehow managed to overpower my mother and is now leaning over her, the knife dangling over Trish's face.

Snap out of it! Move, body, fucking well move!

With an almighty roar, I spring up out of the chair and grab Celia's hair, feeling the softness of it under my palm as I tuck it tightly around my fingers and pull at it with all my might. Her head whips to one side and she lets out a howl of pain and anger. For a brief second, her eyes lock with mine. I go dizzy at the very sight of them. There is fire in there. Her entire body is ablaze with unrelenting hatred and madness. She is salivating like a rabid dog and her skin is almost translucent. A pulsing vein throbs at the side of her temple.

'You fucking bitch!' she spits wildly.

My legs almost give way under me as she swings her head back round to face my mother again, leaving me holding a handful of Celia's hair. A chunk of red strands dangle from my clenched fist. My mouth goes slack as I stare at the bald patch on her head where I have ripped her hair free. Spots of blood seep out of each and every tiny pore, covering the patch of scalp where her long silken hair should be. She seems impervious to it now. Adrenalin will be pumping through her system, masking the pain, fuelling her strength and anger, driving her on.

I lean towards her again, but she is too fast for me, whipping round with her free hand and hitting me across my face. I feel the blow but won't let her see how much she has hurt me. My cheek throbs and it feels as if my face is about to split in two, but I refuse to cave in. I scramble up on my knees and push her aside. It's like trying to shift solid stone. She stays put, her body immobile no matter how hard I push. There is a sudden snarl and I watch as Trish uses both her hands to shove her to one side. Celia falls on her back, the knife still clasped in her hands, the blade pointing skyward. She isn't there for long.

Within seconds, she is up again and running at me with the serrated edge pointing towards my face. An unearthly growl escapes from her mouth, her features twisted and crumpled into a tight grimace. I watch as the glinting blade aims its way to my neck. Celia is fast but Trish is faster. Grabbing her round her ankles, she drags Celia to the floor, the knife flipping out of her grasp and landing close to where she falls. I run to get it but again, she is nimble and has her fingers curled around it before I can get there, despite the fact she crashed to the floor with a clatter that would have felled a lesser person.

There is a deep throbbing sensation behind my eyes and I feel horribly cold. How much longer can we go on like this?

My head hurts as I crane my neck around to try to find the phone. I spot it on the floor next to where my mother is laid, trying to catch her breath. It's now or never. I will have to let Trish fight Celia off while I call 999.

Celia sees me move and already she has worked out what I'm going to do. With cat-like reflexes, she pounces, snatching up the phone with one hand while holding the knife up with her other.

Suddenly, I see red. A dark mist descends behind my eyes and I charge at her with my head down like a raging bull. The top of my skull crashes into her stomach and knocks her backwards. The phone flies out of her hand and lands with a crash on the marble fireplace. Small splinters of plastic fly out at divergent angles but I no longer care. I am beyond any type of rational thought.

I look down to see Trish getting up to her feet. Celia sees it too and gives a swift kick to the side of her head. There is a sickening crunch as Trish falls back onto the floor with a thump. My fury doesn't dissipate. If anything, it grows and multiplies, making me feel stronger than I have ever felt in my entire life. I can do this. If

I keep a clear head, I can overpower her and bring this thing to an end. She may be strong but I have the intelligence to outwit her. It's clear that Celia's sanity has long since evaporated into the ether, and as far as reasonable thoughts and brainpower is concerned, she is running on empty.

I let out an almighty howl and charge at her, my arms splayed out above my head, my mouth wide open, a burning rage licking at my brain.

My screaming has the desired effect, momentarily unnerving Celia, making her drop the knife at her feet. She leans down to pick it up and I seize my chance, barging into her. She falls back, her spine hitting the floor, closely followed by her head. It doesn't stop her but then having seen her in action, I knew it wouldn't. I continue to roar into her ear, spit from my mouth dripping onto her face. I will do anything to distract her. Anything at all.

We both grapple for the weapon, our fingers interlocking as we sweep the floor around our feet with desperate hands. We grab at it at the same time, Celia's fingers below mine on the handle. Immediately, I feel her pull at it, to try to wrench it out of my grasp but I am stronger than I look. I keep my hands wrapped tightly around it even though my arms are aching and my head feels fit to burst.

I have to beat her. This is absolute lunacy. She has lost all sense of direction and as far as I can see, there is no easy way out of this. There will be no winners, whatever the outcome.

I hear a moan coming from my mother who is slowly coming round. I daren't take my eyes away from Celia. I just hope Trish has the good sense and enough energy to clamber away, get another knife, and plunge it deep into Celia's back while Celia is fully focused on me.

Our fingers continue to slip about over the smooth handle, each of us frantic to keep possession of it.

I feel a sudden pain in the top of my head and air exits my lungs in a cold rush as Celia brings her free hand up and pushes her fingers into my eyes. The pain is excruciating, like fire has set in behind my eyeballs. I am sure that I'm going to throw up. Bile travels up my gullet, and I let out a scream, reeling back away from her, my fingers uncurling from the knife handle, my other hand covering my eyes as I rock back and forth in agony.

I crumple to the floor, sobs bursting out of me. Celia stands over my head and I imagine the warped smile on her face. She doesn't see Trish behind her, creeping up on her. Trish is weak and injured, but I watch with blurred vision, my eyes feeling as if a ton of grit has been thrown in them, as she sinks her teeth into Celia's ankle and bites down hard.

The shriek is intense, filling every corner of the room as Trish continues to bite at Celia's leg, her teeth grinding at the bone.

I try to see where the knife has landed but everything is hazy and distorted and there is still a terrible, crushing pain in my eyes. I bend down and feel about with my fingers, driven by anger and fear and terror. I need that knife. Our lives depend on it.

Continuing to grope about with limited vision, my fingers land upon something hard and I know immediately that it's Celia's foot. Her shrieks have stopped and an ominous silence now fills the room. I back away. I can hear a scuffle and a moan from my mother.

Then I hear it – the dreadful, unforgettable sound of metal being swished about in the air. And then a deep, gurgling rasping sound; somebody choking, trying to breathe.

Somebody dying.

I scramble around blindly, my freezing fingers trying to find a way out of here, a path to survival. Again, I land upon Celia's foot. I recoil quickly, falling back on my haunches. She is there above me – standing, watching me. I feel her tug at my hair, pulling my

head up towards her. There is a long, drawn-out scream as I leap
to my feet and spring at her, my nails clawing at anything I can
reach.

I have no idea where the knife is. My eyes are still in agony.
Celia has a distinct advantage over me, but I can't let that slow me
down. This is a fight for survival. And I very much want to survive.
I don't want to be the victim in this scenario. It simply wouldn't be
fair. Out of the two of us, I am the one who deserves to live, but of
course fairness doesn't always come into it, does it? Bad things
happen to good people every day of the week. Karma is a non-
existent ideology thought up by society to make us feel better
about some of the awful things that occur in everyday life to
decent, honest people.

Celia and I are locked together in an almighty struggle to
regain control of the knife. Our feet slip about on the floor and
our bodies twist and turn as we rotate this way and that in a bid to
fight one another off.

My leg slips sideways and my foot lands upon something hard,
something long and slim that scrapes on the floor as I rotate my
body away from Celia's vicelike grasp.

Almost colliding, we reach down at exactly the same time, our
heads barely touching, the heat from Celia's stale breath caressing
my face, making me retch. I swallow down the bile and take a
deep breath, holding it within my chest. We are poised, time
suspended as we both place our fingers on the handle of the knife.

32

GILLIAN

She knocked once and got no reply but now she has to do something. The final scream has sent ripples of shame over her skin. She should have barged in there earlier, gone with her initial instinct that something was terribly wrong and just walked right in. But she didn't. She took the coward's way out and left without doing anything.

Gillian dashes down the back path and peers over the garden fence to look at the house behind her. She should go back there and just march right in. But then, what if she puts herself in danger? She needs to be careful, and get some help. She shivers again at the memory of it: all that noise and that dreadful, dreadful scream...

Dropping the garden rake, Gillian rushes back into the house to find her phone. It was on the kitchen table last time she saw it. Jesus Christ, why did they not get a landline installed? She races around the kitchen, her fingers sweeping across every surface. It takes her a couple of minutes to locate it, tucked behind the curtains. Her hands are sweating, her fingers trembling. Every minute feels like an hour. She almost drops it as she shoves it in her pocket and rushes out into the hallway, stopping to grab her coat then putting it back on the hook again. She can't seem to think straight.

She pulls it back off once more and flings it over her shoulders before heading out the door. Something is wrong in that house. She can just feel it.

By the time Gillian races back to number forty-three, a shadow has already disappeared out of the back door wearing a heavy coat, their head hidden under a hat, their collar pulled up against the sharp, easterly breeze.

* * *

The shadow heaves a sigh of relief as they make it safely out of the house unnoticed and head over the road, standing staring out to sea like any of the other tourists milling about. Just another person taking in the sights, that's all they are. Just an innocent bystander waiting for the story to unfold.

* * *

Gillian knocks, then holding a pocket of cold air deep in her lungs, she turns the handle and walks in.

33

She watches as the crowd outside the house disperses. Anything for kicks. These people would stand here all day if they had to, just so they could catch a glimpse of a dead body. That's their link to pain and death – seeing it all from a safe distance. They know nothing about suffering these people. They have no idea.

She notices a young woman at the front who thinks she's in charge. Even with the breeze coming in from the sea, she's standing there wearing nothing more than some sort of cheap-looking, strappy top and jeans that have seen better days. How strange that these folk seem to have claimed this scenario as their own, as if everybody's lives belong to them.

The television van that turns up soon disperses the crowds, sending them scattering off in the hope of an interview. She smiles. Such shallow behaviour. So fickle and thoughtless.

She turns and heads away, thinking that the beach looks more inviting. Fewer people, less noise. A bit of solitude away from all of this.

It's bracing but bearable, being so close to the water. Plenty of dog walkers to hide her, to keep her away from any prying eyes.

She walks behind, keeping in line with them until she reaches the steps, at which point she departs, heading back up to the path.

She fights back tears. It's over. It's all over. Everything is behind her. She did what had to be done.

A strong breeze tugs at her, pushing her collar down. A strand of auburn hair tumbles over her face. She tucks it back into her coat and shoves her hand into her pockets, her head dipped down against the roaring wind.

She should get everything sorted, just in case the police come calling. She has no idea whether or not they would find her straight away, or if they would even link her to this scene, but she's not taking any chances. Her fingerprints will be everywhere. The sooner she gets moving, the better.

She hurries along the path and gently pushes her way through the crowds until she is over the swing bridge and heading towards the flat. Dipping her hand into the bag, she retrieves the key and scurries along the road with it at the ready. She only needs to collect a few things and she'll be on her way.

Letting herself in, she scrambles upstairs, her legs suddenly weak with exhaustion. She wanders around the bedroom, scooping up whatever she can find: jewellery, money, a handful of letters stuffed behind a vase. They all get pushed into her backpack. She has almost everything she needs in the bag anyway: her purse, ID, credit cards. Everything is there. All her worldly goods.

She takes a look around the room and sighs. She has no idea where she is heading to. Not that it matters. She has nobody left. They're all gone.

She heads back outside, locks up and posts the key through the letterbox, listening as it lands with a thin, metallic clank on the other side of the door. Her bag rustles as she breaks into a slight trot and heads for the train station further along the road.

Only as she emerges from the crowd does her plan nearly

come undone. She hears them coming after her, calling her, their voices stilling her blood. She begins to move faster, ignoring them, pretending she is focused on something else. She is busy, too busy to stop. She has to keep going. Why are they so keen to speak to her, anyway? What's wrong with them? She is nobody to them and yet they pursue her relentlessly. They are mistaken, anyway. She isn't who they think she is. They are chasing the wrong person.

She feels a hand reach out and grab at her arm, stopping her. Her head buzzes and irritation rips through her as she spins around to see two young women staring at her, their faces puckered with uncertainty.

'Celia? Wow, you are one fast walker! We've been calling you again. Did you not hear us?'

She stares at them and narrows her eyes, her voice hoarse and detached. 'I'm sorry? Do I know you?'

The girl colours up, her face flushing deep crimson at the abrupt response. The other one steps in, her eyes wide, confusion evident in her startled expression. 'Celia, it's us: Tyler and Lizzie. From the train, remember?'

She continues to stare at them, rummaging in her bag to prove she isn't who they think she is. With a flourish, she produces a purse and slides a card out of it, brandishing it in front of their timid, shocked faces.

It's a driving licence. There is a picture on it of a woman with long, red hair. She points at the name and taps at it with a certain amount of vehemence.

'Really sorry, ladies. I don't know who this Celia is that you're going on about but I'm not her. You must be mistaken.'

She slips the card back in its place and drops it into the bag.

'Eva?' One of the girls gasps. 'Isn't that the name of your friend? You told us your friend was called Eva!'

She walks away, her feet picking up pace with each consecutive step. She needs to leave these two behind. She has no idea who they think she is, but she definitely isn't this Celia person they speak of.

Her name is Eva. She is Eva, always has been and always will be.

She hears them shouting her back but ignores them. They mean nothing to her. She has never met them before in her life. They must be mistaken.

Her feet hurry along the pavement, her eyes lowered in concentration. She is Eva Tweedie. All the documentation in her bag says so. She has everything to prove it. She simply refuses to listen to anybody who says otherwise.

She pushes through the crowds, a purpose to her walk. Up ahead, she sees a familiar sight: a young man with a swarthy complexion and a crop of dark hair who stands head and shoulders above the rest of the people. He turns to one side to stare in a shop window. She stays behind at a safe distance, her heart pumping wildly, her body buzzing with excitement. She waits while he stares at the goods on display inside and then smiles as he moves on once more. She follows, mirroring his route, stepping on the ground he has walked on, the concrete feeling soft under her feet as near hysteria takes hold.

He turns into a side street, his footsteps echoing throughout the narrow road.

She smiles. It's devoid of people, everyone else taking the wider route, following the flow of tourists keen to visit the local shops and arcades.

They are all alone.

She opens her mouth and shouts to him, the sound of his name feeling erotic and tantalising as it rolls around her tongue. 'Gareth!'

She moistens her lips and smiles as the figure turns to look. A breath catches in her chest at the sight of him, at his bewildered expression. He looks different somehow.

'Sorry?' the figure says as he stops and stares at her. The distance between them closes as she moves forward.

'Gareth,' she says, 'it's me. Remember me?'

He shakes his head and takes a step back away from her. 'Sorry. I'm not Gareth. I think you must be getting me mixed up with somebody else.'

She stares at him. More tricks. That's all this is. More tricks to confuse her. She examines his face, watching as he widens his eyes and smiles.

'I'm definitely not Gareth. That's my wife down there on the beach with my young son. I'm Malcolm, Mac to my friends. Sorry to disappoint you.'

She shakes her head and takes another step closer to him. It's Gareth. It has to be. Why does everybody lie to her? They think she's an idiot. She isn't. This man is Gareth. She knows it. He is lying. They are all fucking liars.

He turns away from her and she listens to the smooth click of his heels on the concrete as the distance between them grows. Celia creeps up behind him, excitement and pent-up energy driving her on, her body alight with it.

She steps in his shadow, so near to him, so fucking close she can almost smell him. Slipping her hand into her pocket, she coils her fingers around the cold, smooth handle of the knife. She grasps it tightly before pulling it out, her hands hot with excitement. The blade shimmers in the dim light of the narrow street as she lifts it up to stare at the blade, so beautifully formed and exquisitely sharp, it takes her breath away. She brings it up above her head, steps forward and lets out an ear-splitting, unearthly scream.

ACKNOWLEDGMENTS

A huge thank you to my new publishers, Boldwood Books, for taking on *Finding Eva* and revamping it to *The Toxic Friend*. It goes without saying that as always, Emily Ruston is a superstar and the best editor a girl could ever wish for.

Many of the character names in this book were derived from my hobby of genealogy after discovering that some of my family lived in Whitby in the late 1700s to the early 1800s. The buildings in which they lived still stand and since I live only an hour away, Whitby is one of my favourite haunts. It holds a special appeal to me and my family, and setting *The Toxic Friend* there felt like the right thing to do.

It's been said many times that if you think writing a book is difficult, wait until you try selling it. This is so true so again, I am truly thankful to Boldwood Books and their superb marketing team, and also to bloggers who give their time freely to read and promote books, including mine.

It goes without saying that I'm grateful to my family and friends for their ongoing support, but I'm going to say it anyway. Thanks guys. You're the best!

I'm always available for chats on social media if you fancy getting in touch. I can be found hunched over my laptop, consuming cake and coffee if you ever want to join me.

Facebook.com/thewriterjude

Twitter.com/thewriterjude

Instagram.com/jabakerauthor

MORE FROM J. A. BAKER

We hope you enjoyed reading *The Toxic Friend*. If you did, please leave a review.

If you'd like to gift a copy, this book is also available as an ebook, hardback, large print, digital audio download and audiobook CD.

Sign up to J. A. Baker's mailing list for news, competitions and updates on future books.

https://bit.ly/JABakerNews

Explore more twisty psychological thrillers from J. A. Baker…

ABOUT THE AUTHOR

J. A. Baker is a successful writer of numerous psychological thrillers. Born and brought up in Middlesbrough, she still lives in the North East, which inspires the settings for her books.

Follow J. A. Baker on social media:

- facebook.com/thewriterjude
- twitter.com/thewriterjude
- instagram.com/jabakerauthor
- tiktok.com/@jabaker41

THE

Murder

LIST

**THE MURDER LIST IS A NEWSLETTER
DEDICATED TO ALL THINGS CRIME AND
THRILLER FICTION!**

**SIGN UP TO MAKE SURE YOU'RE ON OUR
HIT LIST FOR GRIPPING PAGE-TURNERS
AND HEARTSTOPPING READS.**

SIGN UP TO OUR
NEWSLETTER

BIT.LY/THEMURDERLISTNEWS

Boldwood

Boldwood Books is an award-winning fiction publishing company seeking out the best stories from around the world.

Find out more at www.boldwoodbooks.com

Join our reader community for brilliant books, competitions and offers!

Follow us

@BoldwoodBooks

@BookandTonic

Sign up to our weekly deals newsletter

https://bit.ly/BoldwoodBNewsletter

Printed in Great Britain
by Amazon

33184392R00169